AF488803

SPINSTER

SUZANNE G. ROGERS

IDUNN COURT PUBLISHING

CONTENTS

Spinster, Copyright © Suzanne G. Rogers, 2017

All Rights Reserved. Except as permitted under the U.S. Copyright Act of 1976, no part of this publication may be reproduced, distributed, or transmitted in any form or by any means, or stored in a database or retrieval system, without prior written permission of the publisher.

Idunn Court Publishing
7 Ramshorn Court
Savannah, GA 31411

First print edition, April 2017
First published in ebook format, January 2017
The characters and events in this book are fictitious. Any similarity to real persons, living or dead, is coincidental and not intended by the author.

❀ Created with Vellum

Dedicated to Robert

JILTED

High Wycombe, Buckinghamshire
Summer Solstice, 1891

"Sterling returned home to Bramble Manor late yesterday afternoon, but he wasn't alone. He—" Eudora Yates winced. "Oh, Clare, my brother brought his wife!"

Clare stared at the young woman, uncomprehending. "His *what?*"

"Lottie and Sterling were married on the ship from India."

As the news sank in, her knees grew wobbly and she was obliged to sink down on a needlepoint-covered tuffet. The walls of the cozy parlor seemed to close in on her, and she felt dizzy.

"I-I hadn't had a letter from him in weeks," she managed.

"Now you know why."

Clare fumbled for some way to make sense of an event which had just utterly and completely ruined her life. She glanced up at Dora, who was pacing as if she were a caged, spectacularly plumed bird.

"Why didn't Sterling come with you? Isn't he planning to explain himself to me properly?"

Dora shook her head. "He implored me to come in his stead. I rather imagine Lottie forbade him from seeing you. In fact, I'm sure of it."

"I can't believe this." Clare's lips were so numb she could barely form the words.

"It goes without saying, Papa and Mama are furious with him." Dora crossed over to sit on the chair nearest the tuffet. "I'm really very sorry."

Clare's vision swam and she suddenly felt cold. "And the ring of engagement?"

Dora swallowed and averted her eyes. "It's a family heirloom, so Sterling pleads for its return."

Although Clare had been stunned until now, her temper flared at last. "Does he indeed?" She shot to her feet, tugged the opal ring off her finger, and pressed it into Dora's gloved hand. "Anything else?"

"Yes." Another wince crossed the girl's features. "Sterling requests the return of his letters." A lift at the end of the sentence made it sound like a question.

"Ha!" Clare's spine straightened. "Upon that point, he must remain unsatisfied. I reserve the right to burn them myself."

She moved to the window, half expecting to see black storm clouds rolling across the sky. Instead, the midsummer morning sunshine was unaccountably cheerful.

"I told him not to ask, but he insisted." Dora stood and joined her at the window. "As I said, Mama and Papa are put out with Sterling for being a jilt. Furthermore, they aren't happy he married a nobody."

Clare's shoulders moved up and down in the semblance of a shrug. "The Ladd family is hardly prominent. Perhaps Lord and Lady Yates should be relieved at Sterling's narrow escape."

"Don't be silly. After all, your father was a prominent barrister before he retired." She sighed. "Unfortunately, jilting you so publicly reflects poorly on Sterling, and casts our entire family in a bad light."

Clare gave the young woman a sharp glance. "I wouldn't be too concerned about it. By the time you're ready to make your debut next spring, society will have moved on to some other scandal. Your reputation will be untainted by your brother's minor misstep, but mine is another matter."

She made no attempt to keep the ice from her tone, and Dora had the grace to blush.

"I suppose you think me selfish to worry about how this affects me, and you're right. But now that Sterling has chosen to misbehave, my chances of marrying well diminish accordingly."

Clare's lips tightened. "Quite so. Once you've come of age, you've only a few short years in which to catch a husband. After all, if a girl can't marry before she's considered on the shelf, she becomes a horrible embarrassment."

"Exactly." As the implication of her reply sank in, Dora's blush deepened and she began to babble. "I didn't...er...Sterling's wife, Lottie, is insufferable and I can't help but hate her. You and Sterling were engaged for so long, I've come to think of you as a member of our family. Mama and Papa feel the same way."

A sense of decency surfaced—albeit grudgingly. "Don't hate your sister-in-law. None of this is her fault."

"Isn't it? Lottie drew Sterling in."

Clare looked at her askance. "How could you know that?"

Dora's color rose. "I'm really not supposed to say anything but she's..." the girl leaned forward to whisper "...she's to have a baby before the end of the year."

At that, Clare nearly fainted. "Merciful heavens."

"I'm so sorry." Dora's face crumpled as she gave Clare a hug. "You deserve better than this."

She fled the house. Once Clare was alone, it took several long, slow breaths for her to quiet the trembling in her hands.

Then, she went to break the bad news to her mother. Less than three months shy of her twenty-fifth birthday, the eldest Ladd daughter had become a hopeless and permanent spinster.

LADD HOUSE and its grounds were modest, and very few corners afforded Clare privacy or refuge. Nowhere in the residence could she escape her family's sidelong glances of pity or fail to catch whispered conversations regarding her utter humiliation, Sterling's betrayal, and her resulting tragedy. Had she been free to seek another husband a year and a half ago, she might have been able to make a good match still. Now, however, few gentlemen would be interested in marriage to a woman so easily discarded.

Clare spent most of her waking moments sitting on the swing hanging from the oak in the back yard. As she stared off into space, the housekeeper, her mother, or her sister would approach her with a message, speaking in solemn tones suitable to a woman in mourning.

"Lady Yates has come to call, Miss Ladd."

"I'm not at home, Bess."

"The vicar is here to speak with you, dearest."

"I'm not at home, Mama."

"The church circle has come to condole with you, Clare. Won't you come visit with them awhile?"

Her sister, at least, warranted a wan smile. "I'm not at home to anyone, Nell."

After five days passed, her diminished status finally sank in. As Sterling's wife, she would have lifted the social standing of the Ladds and improved her eighteen-year-old sister's chances to make a socially prominent match. Instead, her very public rejection by the son of a baron had brought embarrassment and shame to her family. Worse, she was now an old maid. She used to poke fun at the notion when she was a child, never dreaming of any possible circumstance the label would apply to her. In her mind, girls who became spinsters were always plain or dull in some catastrophic way, or perhaps were possessed of such a shrewish nature as to drive men off. Now she realized spinsters were sometimes youthful, pretty ladies who'd trusted a promise to their detriment and without recourse.

In the end, however, she was forced to admit she'd contributed to her pitiable situation. The Yates had sent Sterling off for six months to check on their Indian plantation. He'd been willing to marry her before he left, but she'd put him off until his return. Obviously, he'd found another woman in her stead, and Clare was on the shelf. The worst had happened, and she must accept it.

As a result, however, her residency in High Wycombe was no longer palatable.

~

AT THE DINNER table that evening, Clare decided to broach the topic of her future to her family.

"You've been walking on eggshells around me since I was jilted, and I feel dreadful for causing you such discomfort."

"Nonsense." Her father's voice was gruff. "You've held up remarkably well, all things considered."

Her sister's response was far more dramatic. "If it had been me, I would have taken to my bed for weeks."

Lady Ladd gave Clare a sympathetic glance. "We've just been worried about you, dearest."

"I know, and I love you for it. But you needn't worry about me any longer." Clare cleared her throat. "On Monday, I'm going away."

"I concur." Sir Andrew glanced up from his cucumber soup.

"A holiday might be just the thing to take your mind off your troubles."

"Yes, indeed, that's a wonderful idea." Lady Ladd seemed relieved. "Perhaps a few days in London will pick up your spirits?"

"If you're going to Brighton, do take me along." Nell's expression was hopeful. "I'd love to go sea bathing."

"I'm not going on holiday." Clare paused to let a sudden rush of emotion relax its grip on her throat. "Grandmama left me her cottage just outside of Stroud and a reasonable income. I'm going there to begin a new life on my own."

Her pronouncement was met with a long moment of shocked silence.

"No." Her father finally erupted in protest. "Are you out of your senses? It's not proper for you to live alone and unchaperoned."

"Unchaperoned?" Clare's laugh sounded bitter, even to her own ears. "Papa, we must face the fact I'm no longer a debutante whose reputation must be carefully guarded. Forgive me for speaking plainly, but I'm on the shelf. Your eldest daughter is a spinster."

"Why should that be?" Nell frowned. "You've always been admired everywhere you go. There's no reason you can't find a husband still."

"Thank you for the compliment, Nell, but ladies who are unmarried by my age are generally considered old maids. Since Grandmama thoughtfully provided me with the wherewithal to be independent, I mean to take advantage of it. I'm moving into Robbins Nest."

"You can't be serious." Sir Andrew turned to his wife with a plaintive look. "Say something to discourage her from this ridiculous notion! It's obvious she doesn't give a fig for my opinion."

"That's not true, Papa." Clare lowered her gaze to the white linen tablecloth. "Please don't make this any more difficult than it already is. After everything that's happened, I can't bear your disapproval."

Lady Ladd sighed. "I don't wish to be disagreeable, Andrew, but Clare is right."

Her husband gaped. "What?"

"The Yates are our closest neighbors, and a socially prominent family. She won't be able to avoid them if she stays in High Wycombe. To preserve her dignity and to spare her feelings, I think it's best if she moves to a town where no one knows her."

Sir Andrew swelled up with indignation, but Clare's eyes prickled with moisture. "Thank you for being honest, Mama. I respect you all the more for it."

Her mother frowned. "One need only put themselves in your shoes to understand how you must feel—especially since Sterling and his wife are to welcome a child before too long."

"Just so." Mention of the baby struck Clare like a blow, and she reached for her water glass with a trembling hand. A long drink restored her composure somewhat, but the ache in her chest remained.

Nell pouted. "Clare's been wronged, yet she must leave her home and family? It's unfair."

It *was* terribly unfair, but Clare felt as if she must put up a good front for her family's sake.

"It's not so very bad. Thanks to Grandmama, I'm far more fortunate than most girls in my position." She forced a smile to her lips. "Once I'm settled in Stroud, I'll make all manner of new friends and be exceedingly happy. You can come visit me."

"You haven't been there in a long while, have you?" Nell wrinkled her nose. "You mightn't like it."

"I liked it quite well whenever I visited Grandmama, and I doubt if the town has changed much since then."

A muscle worked in Sir Andrew's jaw. "I'm not happy about this. I'm not happy at all."

"Come now, Papa. I may be too old to marry, but I'm too young to lay down and die. Rather than moping about feeling sorry for myself, I intend to make the best of a difficult situation."

Sir Andrew regarded her for a few moments before giving her a curt nod. "If you wish to try living on your own, I won't stand in your way—despite my misgivings." He shot his wife a level glance. "But if I get any inkling of trouble—anything at all —you're coming straight back here, understand?"

"Yes, Papa."

He sighed. "It's not the life I would have wished for you, but I do admire your backbone. Sterling Yates will never understand what he's lost."

"He's no longer my concern." Her tone was deliberately light. "If anyone should inquire about me, say I've gone off on an adventure."

"You make it sound exciting," Nell said.

"And so it is, in a way." Truth be told, the prospect of leaving High Wycombe terrified Clare, but she would never admit as much to her family. "I'm to run my own household and tend to my own garden. Truly, I'm looking forward to it."

Her mother gave her a worried glance. "Mama's house has been vacant for nearly ten years now. I'm not sure it's still in good repair."

Sir Andrew cleared his throat. "I'll go with Clare, just to make sure."

"No, Papa. I'm a grown woman, and I'd like to be treated as such. I'll deal with whatever problems I find, I can assure you. Now that the worst has happened, things can only look up."

Clare spoke with far more conviction that she felt, but what choice did she have? If she revealed any doubt whatso- ever, her father would insist on accompanying her to Stroud.

Should the stubborn man spot the slightest flaw at Robbins Nest, he might refuse to let her stay. No, it was prudent to feign the utmost confidence in her venture, to set his mind at ease.

Her sister spread butter on a roll. "Clare, are you taking the gowns you had made for your trousseau?"

"No, I thought I might store them in the attic for now. Why?"

She shrugged. "I was wondering if I might have them."

Lady Ladd gasped. "Nell! That's terribly insensitive."

Clare's sister blinked in surprise. "I'm just trying to be practical."

A SERVANT LOADED several trunks onto the trap, where her father stood ready to drive her to the train station. Lady Ladd and Nell assembled to say good-bye, and the servants left their duties long enough to wish her safe travels.

The cook held up a small, covered hamper made of woven wood slats. "This is a picnic lunch for the train, Miss Clare. I'll put it on the gig for you."

"Thank you, Mrs. Morrell. I'll miss you…and your cooking."

"Not to worry. I put a copy of Mrs. Beeton's *Book of House-hold Management* at the bottom of the basket. It'll come in handy."

"I'm terribly grateful." Clare turned to her mother. "I'll miss you, Mama."

"And I'm going to miss you more than I can say." Lady Ladd produced a postcard from her pocket. "Drop this in the nearest pillar box as soon as you get to Stroud. We need to know you arrived safely."

"Of course." Clare slipped the postcard into her own pocket. "And I'll write you my news as soon as I have any." Her glance flickered toward Sir Andrew, who was standing near the trap. "I hope I haven't caused trouble between you and Papa. I know you have a difference of opinion on my leaving."

"Don't give it another thought." Lady Ladd patted her cheek. "It's nothing we can't weather."

As Clare exchanged an embrace with her sister, Nell's lower lip began to tremble. "Must you really go?"

"Don't cry! This is for the best." Clare stepped back. "You're eighteen, now, so you must turn your attention to suitors. It won't do you any good to have an unmarried sister hanging about. Gentlemen might begin to wonder if there was something wrong with both of us."

"Perhaps so, but there's nothing wrong with you." Nell hung her head with a pout. "And I don't care about marriage—not to anyone around here, at any rate."

"You ought to care—very much. I've had spinsterhood thrust upon me and intend to make the best of it. Nevertheless, I would wish otherwise for my younger sister. Besides which, once as I'm settled, you can come for a long visit. Perhaps there are eligible young gentlemen in Stroud in want of a wife exactly like you."

Nell stepped back and drew her sleeve across her eyes. "Invite me as soon as may be."

"I shall, I promise."

After Clare climbed into the lightweight open vehicle, her father picked up the reins and urged the horse forward. Sir Andrew made little attempt to make conversation, other than remarking on the fine weather. As the train station came into view, however, he gave her a sidelong glance.

"You're certain you haven't any misgivings, Alice?"

Clare smiled at her father's use of her middle name, which he preferred to use when they were alone.

"I've never been more certain of anything in my whole life. Please don't worry about me, Papa. I spent a great deal of time visiting Grandmama as a child and I'm not wholly unfamiliar with the neighborhood. I imagine I'll be welcomed with open arms."

He scowled. "I don't feel right about this. I'm going to escort you to Robbins Nest myself and stay there until you're settled in. Can you wait until tomorrow to leave?"

"No, we discussed this already! If I'm to look after myself the rest of my life, I must be as independent as possible."

"You've a good head on your shoulders." A muscle worked in his jaw. "I'll never forgive Sterling Yates for jilting you as long as I live."

Although Clare wouldn't forgive her former fiancé either, she sought to ease her father's pain.

"To be honest, Papa, I'm glad to be rid of him and consider my narrow escape a fortunate one."

"You were always more clever than Sterling, but I was willing to overlook that due to his social standing and your regard for him."

"Perhaps we should be grateful things have worked out as they have."

"If that's to be my only consolation, so be it." He leaned over to press a kiss on her forehead. "You'll always be my little Alice."

Sir Andrew waited on the platform while Clare boarded the train and found a seat next to a window. Her throat tightened when the train began to roll forward and she waved good-bye to her father for the last time. Although he lifted his hand in response, his shoulders drooped and he had the appearance of a man forlorn. Moments later, however, he was out of view and she was completely on her own.

Her heart suddenly began to race and her chest felt tight. To avert complete and utter panic, she reached for the bone needles in her carryall and began to knit a scarf from a ball of cherry red wool. As she worked, she tried to focus on the benefits of living alone. She could decide when to arise and when to retire. The food on her table would be only that which pleased her. Similarly, her manner of dress need only be suitable to the activities of the day, not to what would catch a man's eye. She could even leave off her corset if she wished, with no one the wiser. Would her solitude grate after a time? More than likely, but for now she was looking forward to a lengthy period of peace and quiet. Furthermore, since few people in Stroud knew her, she would enjoy privacy.

Clare's hands slowed their frantic movements. She took a deep breath, sat back in her seat, and closed her eyes. For good or for ill, she'd taken a fork in the road. For all the uncertainly involved, at least her path was of her own choosing. Unfortunately, if anything in Stroud went amiss, her father would yank her home before she could say "curiouser and curiouser."

ROBBINS NEST

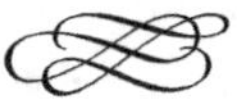

$\mathcal{W}$hen Clare arrived at Stroud, she hailed a cab outside the railway station and gave the driver the address to Robbins Nest.

He helped her into the carriage. "I'll load your trunks and we'll be off straightaway."

"Actually, before we leave town, I need to purchase some food and supplies."

"You can purchase what you need at the Emporium, I warrant."

Once her trunks were secure, the driver climbed into the cab and urged the horse forward.

"Are you here on a visit, miss?"

"No, I'm moving into my late grandmother's house. She left me her cottage and some fond memories of the neighborhood."

Stroud was a charming town, brimming with historic gray Cotswold stone buildings ranging from medieval to Elizabethan architecture. The driver drove Clare to the Emporium and waited curbside while she bought enough basic foodstuffs, paraffin lamp oil, soap, and candles to get her through a few days. She also stepped into the bakery across the street to purchase a small loaf of bread. On the way back to the cab, she dropped her mother's addressed postcard in a pillar box, for collection by the postal service. As soon as possible, she'd write a lengthy letter to her family, telling them about Robbins Nest. Hopefully, she'd be able to give a positive account of its condition.

Her grandmother's former residence was located in a sparsely settled section of countryside within walking distance of Stroud. The roughly triangular parcel of land, consisting of about four acres, was situated at the corner of two roads, with a narrow stream forming the diagonal boundary on the far side. Some of the property was pasture, but a quarter acre was devoted to a garden. Her grandmother had been an avid gardener and used to spend hours outdoors pruning rose bushes and tending to vegetables. Clare hoped to revive the neglected plot. After nine years the effort might prove to be challenging, of course, but she was in no mood to entertain discouraging thoughts.

When Robbins Nest was less than a quarter mile off, Clare noticed a handsome residence had been built on the far side of the stream, a short way up a slight rise.

"There've been some changes since I was here last. What can you tell me about that Tutor house?"

"That's Phoenix Downs, miss. Mr. Meriweather Holcroft lives there, he docs. Built the place about seven years ago."

"Is Mrs. Holcroft a pleasant sort of person?"

"Mr. Holcroft is unmarried."

Clare was disappointed. It would have been nice to have befriended a female neighbor. Before she could ask any more questions about Mr. Holcroft, however, the cab cleared a gentle curve and she caught her first glimpse of Robbins Nest. As she regarded her new home, her high hopes flattened. After nearly a decade of neglect, the property had become an eyesore. The yard was overgrown and unkempt, and she shuddered to think what the garden looked like. Her grandmother should have sold the residence when she'd come to live at Ladd House, but the headstrong woman had continued to insist she would get well enough to return.

After the cab stopped in front of the unassuming, two-story structure, the driver gave Clare an incredulous glance.

"This is the address, but you're not going to live in an abandoned cottage all by yourself, are you? Maybe I should drive you to one of the inns in town while you sort it out."

For a long moment, Clare's resolve nearly wilted. Despite all her words about independence and running her own household, nobody would force her to stay here or look at her askance for declining to do so. On the other hand, she was not the sort of person to shrink from a challenge. How could she decide anything without first giving the place a chance?

She squared her shoulders and lifted her chin. "It's not abandoned any longer. I'll make it work somehow."

"All right, then." The man still seemed unconvinced, but he set the brake. "Just remember, it's a three mile walk to town if you need anything."

"I'm a good walker, fortunately."

She climbed down from the cab and hastened along the path to the front door, where a weathered brass plate to one side of the entrance was inscribed with *Robbins Nest*. The driver followed closely behind with her lunch basket and box of supplies from the Emporium. More fearlessly than she felt, she turned the key in the lock, opened the door, and stepped inside the cottage. The vestibule was small and dark, and she suppressed a cringe. If a spider should happen to fall on her head, she would not be able to avoid screaming. Nevertheless, she feigned confidence.

"If you could put those supplies in the kitchen and stack everything else next to the staircase, I'd be most grateful."

The driver shook his head and sighed. "If you're sure."

"I am."

While the man was unloading her things, Clare wandered through the ground level of the stifling hot residence, pulling back yellowed curtains and throwing open filthy windows. Dust coated every surface and cobwebs filled the corners. To the left of the vestibule was a parlor, and the room on the right was a sitting room with a small library and writing desk. The rest of the cottage consisted of a decent-sized kitchen, pantry, and dining room, with all the bedrooms upstairs. Next to the kitchen was also an indoor privy. Although the privy was only an earth closet, her grandmother had been quite proud of it.

As Clare stood in the kitchen with a view to the garden, her worst fears were realized. Overgrown, dried-up masses of weeds were growing where once beautiful, well-tended rose bushes and vegetables had been. Her enthusiasm plummeted, but she chose not to think about it at that moment. She couldn't go back to High Wycombe. With a thin veneer of optimism, she returned to the vestibule just as the driver carried in the last trunk.

"That's it, miss."

Her eyes watered from floating dust motes as she counted out coins into the man's weathered hand.

He touched the brim of his herringbone cap with gnarled fingers. "Much obliged. The name's Gus, if you ever need to hire a cab. You can book me through the only livery stable in town. It's only a short distance from the train station."

"Thank you, Gus. I'm Miss Ladd."

The man glanced around the vestibule, grimaced, and shook his head. "Welcome to Stroud."

He closed the door behind him. Moments later, the sound of horse's hooves faded, and she was alone. Although her grandmother's furniture and possessions surrounded her, the house felt empty and devoid of charm without the elderly woman's presence. Worse, the cottage was so grimy that Clare didn't know what to address first. If her father had accompanied her, he'd never have let her stay—and she might not have argued the matter. She draped a handkerchief on a staircase tread, sat down on it, and buried her face in her hands.

Even as tears stung her eyelids, however, she refused to give in completely to despair. If she thought about everything to be done, she would remain paralyzed and unable to cope. The household tasks would have to be prioritized, starting with cleaning the kitchen and the room she was to sleep in that night. Although it seemed overwhelming, the deplorable state of the cottage was probably providential. Her grandmother used to say, "idle hands are the devil's workshop." If she stayed busy, she'd have little opportunity for self-pity.

Clare removed her gloves, jacket, and hat so she could tour the rest of the property. Hoping the now-open windows would improve the air in her absence, she left the cottage to inspect the two-story outbuilding. The structure, which served as a modest carriage house and stable, seemed to be in fairly good condition. A wide horse stall filled half the space, and an area large enough for a gig occupied the other half. Her grandmother had owned a rig but had sold it when she declined in health and left Stroud to live with her family. The many shelves and bins on the walls were filled with gardening tools of various kinds, and an old sidesaddle hung from a hook overhead. Behind the carriage house was the outhouse erected when the cottage was originally built.

The exterior staircase of the carriage house led to the spartan living quarters overhead, which were meant for the help. The sight of cobwebs and scores of dead insects littering the floorboards made her shudder. When she accidentally trod upon the crunchy remains of a cockroach, she shrieked, picked up her skirts and fled. Not much frightened her as a rule, but she couldn't abide bugs—dead or otherwise.

Once she returned to the cottage, she went upstairs to view

the bedrooms. The wardrobe in her grandmother's former room still contained the dresses and hats the elderly woman had donned to work in the garden. Clare touched the worn muslin with a lump in her throat. No doubt her irascible grandmother would have been delighted to know she'd moved in to Robbins Nest—and probably more than a trifle apologetic about the condition of the premises.

Very little differentiated the bedrooms other than view, so Clare chose the room overlooking the garden for her own. When she leaned out the dormer window to take a breath of clean, fresh air, she noticed the upper level and roof of Phoenix Downs was visible to the right. The pretty Tudor-style house wasn't particularly imposing, but she found it aesthetically pleasing. Would Mr. Holcroft think to welcome her to the neighborhood?

Sadly, her view of the stream running between their properties was blocked by tall grass and overgrown bushes. She cocked her head to listen, but couldn't hear the water, either. Either the sound was muffled by the growth, or the water level was down due to lack of rain. From the brown patches in the grass, it seemed as if summer in the Cotswolds had been dry.

When Clare gazed down at the rose garden, she grimaced at its condition. Nevertheless, she was cheered by a few splashes of color where several hardy blooms had survived their long neglect. Admittedly, scant else about Robbins Nest had pleased her. The fragrance of roses would go a long way to lift her spirits and freshen the stale air, so she decided her first task would be to bring some blooms indoors.

Clare changed from her traveling suit into one of her grandmother's shapeless gardening gowns and went down to the kitchen to assemble a few vases. When she tried to pump water into the sink, however, she realized the device was dry and would have to be primed to work properly. She lifted a bucket from a shelf in the pantry, left the house, and crossed over to the pump located between the stable and the garden. To her dismay, that pump was dry, too. With a sigh of resignation, she carried the bucket through tall grass to fetch water from the stream, praying she didn't tread upon any adders in the process.

When she arrived, she was greeted by the sight of an eight-foot-wide stream bed with only a minor amount of water at the bottom. Dumbfounded, she climbed down into the ditch and spied a stacked-stone dam upstream, not thirty feet away. Apparently, Mr. Holcroft had built a dam to divert water onto his property, allowing only a trickle of water to continue downstream. Because the water flowed underneath the bridge in the road and into a larger waterway beyond, hers was the only property affected by the obstruction.

Fury swept over Clare at the sheer audacity of what the neighbor had done. How dare he imagine the water was entirely his for the taking, just because her grandmother was no longer in residence? She made her way up the muddy stream bed and pried a few rocks from the dam with her fingers. Her anger was such that she didn't stop her efforts until a thin sheet of water began spilling down the wall and into the parched ditch at her feet. After she filled her bucket from the breach, she examined her handiwork with grim satisfaction. Although she'd made a good start, if she could find the proper tool, she'd remove the wretched dam entirely.

MERIWEATHER HOLCROFT LET his horse pace himself for the last leg of the journey from Gloucester. Although the rider was saddle-sore and dusty from the long journey, that was nothing when compared to his frustration. He'd dressed in his finest clothes and had wasted an entire day on a fool's errand. He leaned forward to pat Gawain's neck. Well, at least he'd spent time with his horse.

The mount picked up speed when he passed the cottage known as Robbins Nest, evidently sensing he wasn't far from home. Meri's eyes slid past the abandoned property at first... until he noticed the windows were open and a thin wisp of smoke was rising from a chimney. As his horse turned left at the next lane, Meri observed the door of the outbuilding in the back was ajar. He frowned with puzzlement. The place had been vacant since before he built Phoenix Downs, so who would move in now? The cottage had to be nearly uninhabitable by civilized standards, so he assumed the occupant must not be terribly civilized. How annoying to have such a lowly neighbor! On the other hand, perhaps something would finally be done about the neglected grounds.

Outside his own residence, he handed Gawain off to a stable boy. "Be sure to brush him down well and let him eat all the oats he wishes."

"Yes, sir."

"Wait a moment." Meri retrieved a small, wrapped package from a saddlebag. "Carry on."

After he entered his Tudor-style house, a man in his mid-forties approached. "Welcome home, lad. Was your journey successful?"

"Thank you, Franklin." Meri gave the fellow his bowler hat. Franklin's left hand was encased in a black glove, of which only the thumb moved, but he managed the item with aplomb nevertheless. "Most of the better paintings were spoken for, I'm afraid."

"That's unfortunate."

"Yes, indeed." Meri waved his parcel, which wrapped in heavy brown paper and string. "I did manage to acquire a rather handsome profile."

He pulled the end of the string until it came undone. When the paper came away, the framed artwork was revealed—the silhouette of a young woman with a beautiful face.

"A very handsome lass, she is." Franklin smiled his approval. "Where would you like to hang her?"

"I can't quite decide. I'll have to think where would be best."

Meri brought the profile into his sparsely furnished study, left it on his desk, and crossed to the bar set up on the butler's cart in the corner. After he sank into a brown leather chair with his glass of whiskey, he pressed fingers into his temples to quiet the throbbing.

Franklin appeared in the doorway, waving a folded newspaper in the air. "You were off before breakfast this morning, so you didn't have the opportunity to read this."

"Was there something particular you wished to bring to my attention?"

"Indeed." The older man laid the folded newspaper on the desk and tapped a large notice. "There's an auction and estate sale in Kingscote on Saturday. An elderly viscount named Greeley passed away, with only distant cousins as heirs. Everything is to be liquidated."

"An aristocrat?" Meri's interest was piqued. "Might be a great opportunity there. Good work, Franklin."

"Thank you." The man gazed at the profile. "She's indeed a lovely lady, but I'd rather see her counterpart here at Phoenix Downs…in the flesh, as it were."

Meri lifted an eyebrow. "The subject of my bachelorhood is not allowed."

Franklin shrugged. "So you've said."

Meri cast about for a topic to change the conversation. "Did you know someone has taken Robbins Nest?"

"Really? I can't think why, unless it's to raze it."

"Neither can I. In fact, I'm not altogether convinced he's even entitled to occupy the place. Will you send a message to Sergeant White to stop by here tomorrow morning, first thing? I'll ask him to look into the situation."

"I'll compose a note right away." He paused. "Would you care for some tea?"

"Not just yet. I've a raging headache." He drained his whiskey and stood. "I'm going to walk over toward the stream, to see if I can catch a glimpse of this new neighbor."

Franklin produced a pair of spectacles. "Hadn't you better take these? You left them behind this morning."

Meri waved him off. "I've no need for spectacles."

"Don't you realize your headaches are from eyestrain?"

The assertion earned Franklin a level glance. "Must you always be so cocksure of everything?"

"Only when it involves the truth."

With a shake of his head, Meri stepped around the older man on his way out the door.

CROWBAR IN HAND, Clare stripped off her shoes and stockings, climbed into the stream bed and began to pry rocks loose. As a little more water slid down the wall, the newly moistened soil beneath her feet became muddy. She slipped, falling nearly flat on her face in the brown gooey sediment. Her hair came down from its pins, and when she tried to push it back from her eyes, she realized her hands were coated with mud. After cleansing them as best as she could in the water spilling over the dam, she returned to loosening stones.

A man appeared on the far side of the dam, waving his arms to get her attention. "You there, stop that!"

She tried to glare at him but had to squint against the bright late afternoon sun slanting down to one side. "Are you responsible for this monstrosity, sir?"

"I am, and what the devil do you think you're doing? You've no right to destroy my dam!"

"I've every right under common law. As you're likely well

aware, under the riparian principal, all landowners whose properties adjoin a body of water have the right to make use of it as it flows over the land." She pointed her crowbar at the wall of stone. "This obstruction has infringed on my rights and must be removed!"

He made a sound of disgust. "I put in a great deal of work on this dam and pond, and you're ruining them. Besides which, the property you're standing on is vacant. Nobody's lived there for at least ten years."

Clare's chin lifted. "Mrs. Robbins was my grandmother and the owner of Robbins Nest. She passed away in January and left it to me."

"I'm sorry for your loss, but the dam stays. Your grandmother could have objected to it at any time, but she failed to do so. It's not as if it's a secret."

"Since she's been in ill health and living with her family in High Wycombe, she couldn't possibly have known about it. Besides which, if you're arguing adverse possession of the stream, you won't prevail. My grandmother left almost ten years ago, and the statute of limitations for a claim of adverse possession is twelve."

"We'll see about that, madame. I'll be speaking to my attorney directly."

"Go right ahead. He'll tell you nothing different!"

As she fumed, the man turned on his heel and strode off. Because of the peculiar angle of the sun's rays, she hadn't managed to have a terribly good look at his face. Nevertheless, she'd taken full notice of his arrogant voice and overbearing posture. The bully was used to getting what he wanted, evidently, despite the facts. How dare he defend his actions in building the dam instead of apologizing and promising to remove it!

Her gaze fell to the muddy ditch at her feet and she clucked her tongue. Enough of the dam had been removed to create an infinitesimal waterfall, but not enough to restore anything like a robust flow. When she grasped the crowbar to remove more stones, however, she gasped with pain. Her efforts had abraded the skin on her palms and she had the beginnings of blisters.

As gingerly as possible, she tucked the length of metal under her arm, picked up her shoes and stockings with a thumb and forefinger, and tip-toed across the grass toward the cottage. Removing her mud-stained dress in the kitchen and leaving it hanging to dry became a laborious chore which left her raw hands stinging. Why hadn't she thought to wear gloves?

Upstairs, Clare slid into a wrapper and went into her grandmother's room to locate another gardening frock. She slipped a frayed and faded paisley-patterned garment over her head and peered at her reflection in the wardrobe's spotted mirrored door. Clad in a shapeless gown, with a mud-smeared face and damp hair in horrible disarray, not even her mother would recognize her. Worse, she looked every bit the discarded, batty spinster.

This was her future.

Deep inside, something broke. The tears Clare had held back since learning of Sterling's marriage burst forth at last, and she sank to her knees on the worn oriental rug. She'd been unwilling to come completely undone in front of her family, but now that she was alone, she could admit exactly how much she felt sorry for herself. Because of Sterling, her life had been utterly ruined, she had no status at all, and she was an embarrassment to her family. On a more emotional level, spinsterhood meant she would never feel a man's arms around her or savor his kisses. The sweet, soft coos of babies would never lift her spirits, and no child would ever call her Mama. All these things had been within her grasp before, but no longer, and the loss was simply too much to bear. Shuddering sobs wracked her body and waves of grief sapped her strength until she felt wrung out.

Finally, the waning daylight combined with the hunger in her belly to rouse her from her pathetic state. God hadn't seen fit to take her as she lay in a heap, so she supposed she would have to get on with things. She returned to the kitchen to prime the pump. Thereafter, she washed the mud from her face and arms, cleaned and smoothed her fingernails, and combed her hair. In the pantry, she found a jar of soothing salve, applied it to her blisters, and pulled on a pair of old cotton gloves to protect her hands from further injury. Thus fortified, she managed to build a fire in the oven with bits of kindling and thereafter boiled water for tea. For supper, she toasted cheese and bread. The meal was scarcely a banquet, but she had scant appetite anyway.

Once she'd sated her hunger, she went around the house making sure all the doors and windows were fastened before retiring upstairs. While twilight was still lingering outside, she changed the sheets, pillow, and bedspread on the bed for the fresh ones she'd brought with her—things from her bottom drawer. Dust from the old bedspread made her sneeze, and the seams of her grandmother's pillowcase fell apart as she removed it from the pillow. She'd have to tear the fabric into strips to use as cleaning rags.

That done, Clare readied herself to sleep. Although she wouldn't have ordinarily retired so early, the day had been physically and emotionally wrenching and she longed to sink into oblivion for a few short hours. Furthermore, the muscles in her arms and back were shaking and strained from her effort to tear down Mr. Holcroft's dam.

As she lay in bed, she began to reflect on her destructive behavior with regret. The more she thought about it, her lack of restraint had been so out of character that she could scarcely believe her actions. It seemed as if rage and frustration against her fate had temporarily transformed her into a demonically possessed shrew. Next time she felt the need to destroy something, she'd don a pair of work gloves and chop wood instead. At least she could use the wood for cooking afterward.

Due to exhaustion, both body and soul, Clare managed to drift off to sleep. Unfortunately, every creak in the cottage jerked her awake in a wide-eyed panic. Never in her life had she slept alone in a house without even a cat for company, and she was dismayed to discover just how much it affected her. She knew that the likelihood of intruders breaking in was exceedingly low, but logic and common sense were lost on her nerves. She brought the poker to bed with her, and sometime in the wee hours of the night, she finally fell into a deeper sleep that lasted until morning.

STROUD

A muffled noise made Meri's eyes snap open, almost as if the butler had struck the dinner gong next to his ear. For a few moments he tried to go back to sleep, but something wouldn't let him. He turned onto his stomach and slid off the raised four-poster bed until his bare toes touched the cold wooden floor. The nanny had tried to insist on a portable bed step, but he'd refused. Bed steps were for babies, and he was nearly ten. Nevertheless, getting down from the bed was harder in the dark.

Meri went through the door to the adjoining room. "Miss Lapin, may I have a glass of water?"

When he found the nanny's bed was empty, he continued out into the hallway. There, the distinct smell of smoke assailed his nostrils. To his increasing alarm, the haze grew thicker the closer he came to his parents' bedchamber. Even though his eyes were stinging, he opened the door to their room and was greeted by a horrific sight...

Meri woke up with a gasp, seemingly unable to breathe. He fumbled for the matches on his bedside table and lit a candle. As his racing heart slowed and his panic eased, he was forced to admit it had just been a horrible nightmare. Again.

His timepiece told him the hour was too early for sane

people to rise—but admittedly he hadn't exactly been in his right mind for years. After lighting a lantern, he pulled on a pair of trousers and fled the suffocating interior of the house. Cool, pre-dawn darkness soothed his fevered skin as he hastened across the lawn to the pond. Once he reached the edge, he put the lantern down, shed his clothes, and lowered himself into the water. Despite the fact summer was in full throat, the stream-fed pond was wickedly cold. He shrank into himself for several minutes until he was more accustomed to the temperature, and then swam to the center. As he floated on his back and stared up at the stars, he finally felt at peace.

When the first fingers of dawn began to tug the dark horizon aside, Meri emerged onto the grass, and shook moisture from his hair. Would he be able to. return to the house before any of the servants caught sight of his dishabille? While he was pulling on his trousers, a lantern bobbling toward him answered his question. A middle-aged man appeared, haphazardly dressed, with a towel over his arm.

Meri sighed. "Sorry if I disturbed you, old boy."

"Not at all. I was up reading."

"Liar."

Franklin put down the lantern and used his one good hand to drape the towel over Meri's shoulders. "This is the first nightmare you've had in a long while."

"I'd rather hoped they'd stopped plaguing me altogether." Meri stood and began to dry himself off with the towel. "It was that aggravating woman, trying to destroy my dam."

"Was she good looking?"

"Are you mad? I could scarcely tell what she looked like under the mud."

"What about her figure?"

"Stop it." Meri pulled on his clothes. "She's a crazed she-devil."

"You weren't wearing your spectacles." Franklin retrieved

the gold-rimmed eyewear from his jacket pocket and held them out. "Like now."

He scowled and slid the hated things onto his nose. "Happy?"

"At present."

Meri drew in a deep breath and blew it out slowly. "Thank you for coming to check on me, Franklin, but I'm all right." He scooped up the lantern. "Go back to bed."

"Sleep is too much like death these days, lad." Franklin rested his one good hand on Meri's shoulder. "I want to see you settled before I pass away."

"You're not going anywhere." A shaft of fear suddenly pierced his chest. "Wait a minute…are you feeling unwell? I'll send for a doctor immediately."

"No, no, that won't be necessary." Franklin chuckled. "My presence is the only leverage I have, so I refuse to die until you're wed. And I warn you, I come from a long-lived family."

"You know marriage is impossible for me."

"I know nothing of the sort, lad. It's been over two decades since the accident." Franklin gave him a meaningful glance. "You must form your own family now instead of acquiring the remnants thereof by auction."

"Gah!" Meri scowled. "You're more horribly disagreeable than usual this morning."

Annoyed beyond measure, he thrust the lantern into Franklin's hand and strode off. The fellow was becoming more officious by the day and his attitude was insupportable. Once Meri was halfway to the house, however, his footsteps slowed. Despite Franklin's frequent chiding, he harbored a great deal of grudging affection for the man. In addition, he was literally the last living link to his parents.

He turned on his heel, returned to Franklin's side, and reached for the lantern.

"Come along."

The man grinned. "Miss me already?"

"Cheeky monkey. We can't have you stepping in a gopher hole in the dark and breaking your ankle."

"You haven't any gophers at Phoenix Downs."

"There's always the first."

THE DISTANT SOUND of a cock crowing, coupled with the gray light spilling from the edges of the curtains, roused Clare to consciousness. When she stirred, the soreness in her muscles made her wish she hadn't woken up at all. Unable to go back to sleep, she lay in bed and thought about the confrontation that had transpired the day before. Another wave of embarrassment prompted her to pull the covers over her head.

If her goal in moving to Stroud was to fit into the neighborhood, she'd made a poor start. Her actions in trying to destroy the dam, although not wholly without legal justification, had been ill-considered. She could have easily filled her pail with water by traipsing upstream, and thereafter written Mr. Holcroft to complain. Now that she was thinking more clearly, she realized she'd made an utter fool of herself...with the blisters to prove it. She sat up and pulled off her cotton gloves to reveal her tender and raw skin underneath. The salve had helped, fortunately, but she didn't relish the work day ahead. Furthermore, she didn't look forward to repairing her relationship with her neighbor.

What should she do now? The sensible thing to do would be to swallow her pride and pay a visit to Phoenix Downs that very afternoon. It wasn't strictly proper for her to call on a man, particularly unaccompanied, but perhaps this was an exceptional case. She could introduce herself to Mr. Holcroft, apologize for her unforgivable outburst, and then politely ask him to remove the dam. His reaction would help her decide if legal action was necessary. Even if he proved unreasonable, she would have made an effort to demonstrate good will.

Clare slid from her bed, went to the window, and drew back the frayed curtains. The vase of roses on the dresser had filled the room with a pleasing floral fragrance, at least, and the bright splash of crimson lifted her spirits. As she opened the window and leaned out onto the sill, she felt almost optimistic again. She might be a spinster, but nobody could know for certain what the future would bring. It was possible some handsome gentleman in Stroud would catch her eye and she might find happiness, wasn't it? On the other hand, she'd always been overly fond of Jane Austen novels.

She donned her grandmother's gardening dress, which was also perfect for cleaning, and went downstairs to make breakfast. As she drank tea and chewed toast, she contemplated what to do with her morning. Dusting, the removal of cobwebs, and sweeping the floor would take her days. What better place to start than with the kitchen?

The pantry yielded a basket of cleaning rags and a broom. Before Clare could begin, however, an insistent knock at the front door disturbed the silence. She opened the door to discover a uniformed constable waiting on the other side.

She blinked in surprise. "Good morning, officer. May I help you?"

"Good morning, miss." The portly, middle-aged man touched his hat. "I'm Sergeant White."

"I'm Miss Clare Ladd."

"I understand you're related to Mrs. Robbins?"

"Indeed, I am." Clare was increasingly bewildered. "I'm her granddaughter. She passed away six months ago and left me this cottage."

"My condolences on your grandmother's passing." He cleared his throat. "Your neighbor, Mr. Meriweather Holcroft, has lodged a complaint against you for the destruction of a dam on his property. He's asked me to investigate."

Her mouth opened in shock. "Mr. Holcroft has made a complaint against me? It's *I* who should make a complaint against him! He built an obstruction across the stream running between our properties, effectively depriving me of my riparian rights."

"Riparian rights, eh?" The man's eyebrows rose. "So you admit to destroying the dam?"

Clare tossed her head. "The dam is still there, Sergeant, although perhaps a trifle shorter in spots than before. If Mr. Holcroft doesn't agree to remove the obstruction in an expeditious manner, I'll seek legal counsel and pursue the matter in court."

"I see." He gave her a reproachful glance. "Until you have a favorable ruling from a judge, Miss Ladd, I'm advising you to stay away from Mr. Holcroft's dam. If you don't, I'll have to charge you with criminal mischief."

Her throbbing palms prompted a completely truthful reply. "I wouldn't dream of touching it, I assure you."

The constable lifted his hat. "Welcome to the neighborhood, lass. I knew Mrs. Robbins, and I must say you're just as feisty as she was."

After Sergeant White left, Clare's anger and resentment grew. How dare Mr. Holcroft send a constable to threaten her with arrest! The man was an arrogant tyrant, and any notion she'd had of apologizing fled the realm of possibility. She'd sooner be struck by lightning than ever visit Phoenix Downs.

Clare drew a deep breath into her lungs and tried to compose herself. At least now she could spend her entire day cleaning and would make a good start on what needed to be done. And on her next visit to town she would visit a lawyer about filing a lawsuit.

~

AFTER SPENDING several days fighting dirt and dust, Clare sorely needed a bath before walking into town to run errands. She located an old copper slipper tub in the kitchen pantry and dragged it next to the stove. After she'd heated up enough water to fill the tub halfway, she stepped inside and groaned with pleasure. She washed her hair with egg yolk and scrubbed her skin until it was pink. Once she blotted water from her face with a towel draped on the side of the tub, she sat back and sighed. It was a strange but welcome sensation to linger in the bath for as long as she wished. At home, Nell was always banging on the bathroom door, urging her to hurry.

She'd risen early that morning to write a long-overdue letter to her mother but had been frustrated in the attempt. Plenty of stationery and pens were stored in her grandmother's writing desk, but the bottle of black ink had long since dried up and the stub of sealing wax was a brittle memory. Not only must she purchase new writing materials at the stationery shop in town, but she'd also have to visit the post office to send her mother a telegram. Otherwise, her father would arrive at her doorstep before long to make sure she was still alive. In addition, she would be visiting Mr. Brown, who'd handled her grandmother's legal affairs over the years. Finally, Clare's meager supply of food was dwindling and another shopping expedition at the Emporium was a necessity.

Unfortunately, the walk into town and back would take a frustratingly long two hours, which was a huge part of her day. If anything significant was to be done about the garden in the future, she would have to hire a cook/housekeeper and purchase a horse. Although she could afford the servant, the horse was beyond her means unless she sold the brooch Sterling had given her. Ironically, she'd planned to wear the jewelry on her wedding day. Now, however, it was a loathsome symbol of her spinster-hood and she couldn't bear to look at it. A jeweler in town might give her a fair price and she could rid herself of the last remnant of her former fiancé at the same time. In a way, she'd be trading Sterling in for a horse. Something for nothing, in other words.

M r. D andridge examined the brooch through a loupe. "This is a beautiful *trembleuse* piece, with exceptionally high-quality diamonds. Are you sure you wish to part with it?"

"Quite sure…if we can agree on a fair price."

The man sucked in his cheeks and held the brooch up to the light for another few moments before voicing his offer.

Clare knew better than to settle for the first figure he named. "Thank you, but I think I should ask for a second opinion." She reached for the brooch. "Perhaps the jeweler down the street might find it's worth a trifle more?"

Mr. Dandridge recoiled slightly. "Let's not be hasty. Let me have another look."

After another lengthy examination of the piece, he increased his offer substantially. Clare pretended to consider the matter before nodding her acceptance.

"Done." She feigned a sigh. "I probably should have taken the brooch to a London jeweler, but I've no other business to take me to town this time of year."

Her statement was bluster, of course, since she could count the occasions she'd been to London on the fingers of one hand and had no plans to travel there in the future. Nevertheless, she didn't want to seem provincial.

Mr. Dandridge drew up a bill of sale for her to sign. Afterward, he counted out her money, which she tucked away into her reticule.

"It's been a pleasure, sir."

"Likewise. If you have any other such distinctive jewels to sell, please don't hesitate to bring them in."

Although Clare nodded out of politeness, she knew she'd likely not set foot in the shop again. Unless she acquired another former fiancé, she'd never have another significant piece of jewelry to sell.

~

MERI PEERED AT HIS SOLICITOR, aghast. "Mr. Brown, are you absolutely sure that horrible woman is in the right?"

The lawyer's silver hair shone in the morning sunshine filtering in through the lattice-work window.

"I'm afraid so. If she sues, she'll prevail."

"Can't you think of any remedy which would allow me to keep the dam and avoid legal entanglements of a public nature?"

"You could negotiate a monetary settlement in exchange for an easement."

He frowned. "I wouldn't want to give her the satisfaction!"

"In the alternative, you could purchase Robbins Nest outright. Once it's yours, you can do anything you like with it."

Meri nodded. "That last possibility would suit me quite well, actually. Write a letter detailing an equitable purchase offer and have a messenger deliver it immediately. If the woman is agreeable to the terms, perhaps I can put all this unpleasantness behind me forthwith."

"All right. The parcel of land is about four acres, I believe, and the cottage isn't worth anything at all. We'll base our offer on what you paid per acre for Phoenix Downs, plus five percent. Will that do?"

He gritted his teeth. "Yes, although it pains me to enrich her unjustly."

"I understand, but I urge you to put your personal feelings aside if you wish to preserve your dam." The older man donned his spectacles and drew a blank piece of stationery toward him. "In the interest of full disclosure, I should tell you I handled Mrs. Robbins' legal affairs over the duration of her residency here. I was exceedingly fond of her."

"I don't imagine that will influence you in this matter, will it?"

"Not at all. In fact, although Miss Ladd and I corresponded about the disposition of her grandmother's will, I've never met the young lady in person."

"An enviable position, I assure you. I take it her grandmother was amiable?"

"Amiable, witty, and warm. Mrs. Eleanor Robbins was also an exquisite beauty back in the day. She was Miss Caldicott back then." Mr. Brown chuckled, and the lines around his eyes softened. "Many hearts were broken when she became engaged to Frederick Robbins, including mine." He paused. "Did Miss Ladd inherit her grandmother's looks, perchance?"

"The woman was so disheveled I rather thought she was unbalanced." He shook her head. "I didn't find anything attractive about her in the least."

Mr. Brown bent over his letter. "Pity."

Meri peered at him. "What do you mean?"

"I didn't mention a third possibility." The solicitor peered at him over the rims of his spectacles. "You could marry Miss Ladd."

He winked, but Meri was in no mood to laugh.

"In this particular case, Mr. Brown, marriage would be an awfully extreme way to acquire property. I'd sooner marry my horse."

WHEN CLARE REACHED STROUD, she put in an order at the newspaper publisher's office for a subscription, and then visited the post office to purchase stamps and send a telegram to her mother. The cheerful postmistress gave her the form to fill out and introduced herself as Mrs. Kitt. A couple of ladies entered the establishment to conduct a transaction, so Clare stepped aside to fill out the telegram. The ladies left after mailing a parcel, and she returned to the counter with the telegram form.

"I hope I've filled it out properly? I've actually never had an occasion to send a telegram before."

The woman glanced over the form, then nodded. "Yes, this is all the information I need. Be assured, I'll send your message straightaway, Miss Ladd."

"I'd appreciate it very much. While I'm here, might I ask for the postman to put Robbins Nest on his rounds? Since I'm newly arrived in Stroud, my family and I will likely exchange a great deal of correspondence."

The woman's nutmeg and white curls danced as she nodded. "I'll tell Mr. Ingram about you and ask him to stop by tomorrow. Are you related to Mrs. Robbins by any chance?"

Clare was pleased Mrs. Kitt remembered her grandmother. "I'm her eldest granddaughter, actually. I inherited her cottage."

"Welcome to Stroud, dear." The woman gave her an appraising glance. "Are you all by yourself then?"

"Yes, but now that you mention it, I need to hire an experienced cook and housekeeper. Do you know anyone looking for such a position?"

Mrs. Kitt gestured toward a bulletin board on the wall. "You're welcome to put up an advertisement. Everyone in Stroud comes through here sooner or later."

The postmistress furnished her with a scrap piece of paper so she could write down her requirements. Afterward, Clare stuck it to the bulletin board with a pin, alongside solicitations for governesses and notices of pianos for sale. Although she scanned each card, she didn't see anyone offering to sell a horse.

Mrs. Kitt cocked her head. "Looking for something in particular?"

"A reasonably priced saddle horse."

The postmistress's expression grew thoughtful. "Hmm…Mr. Pflug's mare just foaled, but it'll be a while before the colt will be old enough to ride. Maybe you could purchase a horse at Lord Greeley's estate auction on Friday?" The postmistress took a handbill from a stack at the end of the counter and gave it to her. "A man from the auction house left these the other day, hoping to drum up interest."

Clare perused the handbill. "Is Kingscote far from here?"

"It's only about eight miles. Perhaps you could hire a cab?"

"I imagine so."

Didn't Gus say she could reach him through the livery stable? As she folded the handbill and tucked it into her carryall alongside the stamps, an audible gurgle came from her midsection.

Mrs. Kitt chuckled. "You must be hungry."

Clare winced with embarrassment. "I'm afraid so. I didn't eat a very good breakfast this morning."

The older woman nodded. "When my stomach has the grumbles, a meat pasty from the bakery sets me right for hours."

"That's a good suggestion. Thank you, Mrs. Kitt. You've been a great help."

Despite Clare's gnawing hunger, she had a few more errands to run. At the stationery shop, she purchased sealing wax and a bottle of ink, and then stopped in at the Emporium. A shiny new Whippet safety bicycle was on display in the window, and she spent several minutes admiring it. She might have considered the purchase and braved societal disapproval, but the cost of the bicycle was higher than that of a horse. Furthermore, she'd have to acquire a proper riding costume, such as the loose pantaloons and shortened skirts available inside the shop. If her mother knew she were even considering such a thing, she would be scandalized, and her father might even have an apoplectic fit. Nell, on the other hand, would beg to go for a ride.

With a sigh of regret, Clare turned away from temptation and filled her basket with sensible gardening gloves, a jar of preserves, cheese, and a jar of cucumber relish. She also put in a large order for fresh produce, bacon, butter, beef, and a variety of other staples to be brought to Robbins Nest on the next scheduled delivery day.

After her shopping was done, she was hungrier than ever. As she debated whether or not to visit Mr. Brown first, or the bakery, a sharp cramping in her middle made the decision for her. If she didn't have something to eat soon, she might keel over in the street. What an unfortunate way to make a spectacle of herself in a brand-new town!

HUMPTY DUMPTY

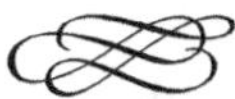

Clare hastened along the pavement, her mouthwatering in anticipation of food. She was so intent on her destination that she nearly barreled headlong into a tall, bespectacled man in casual clothes who'd just emerged from an office building. The fellow grabbed her arms to prevent her from stumbling.

"I beg your pardon." He released her from his strong grip. "I wasn't looking where I was going at all, I'm afraid."

"It's far more my fault than yours." She recovered her composure enough to give him a tentative smile. "I hope you're unhurt?"

"The only injury is to my hat."

He retrieved his bowler from where it had fallen on the pavement. As he brushed dirt off the felt, she couldn't help but notice how ridiculously good-looking the fellow was, especially for a working man. His eyes appeared to be hazel behind his spectacles, but she couldn't be completely sure. What was undeniable, however, was the breadth of his shoulders, the way his muscular arms and chest filled out his sack jacket, and his powerful bearing of masculinity.

"You did me a service, actually, by startling me out of my doldrums." He sketched a bow and returned the hat to his head. "So, thank you."

"You're welcome."

A black stallion tied to a post at the curb snorted and swished his tail. Clare glanced over at the glossy steed. "Is this your horse?"

He nodded. "That's Gawain."

"He's extraordinary."

She moved over to scratch the magnificent animal behind his ears with her gloved hand, and the tail swished harder.

"You've made a friend for life." The man chuckled. "You enjoy horses?"

"Very much. My family kept only work horses, but our neighbor, the baron, had an extensive stable. He kindly allowed my sister and me to ride any time we wished."

"How fortunate. You had the use of his horses without the expense."

"That's it, exactly." She stroked Gawain's neck one last time before dropping her hand to her side. "Well, I hope your day improves."

"I believe it already has."

"What a gallant thing to say." A smile curved her lips. "The horse and his master are well matched, it seems."

Still smiling, she continued on her way. Moments later, when the black stallion and his rider rode off down the street, Clare felt slightly giddy. Gawain's owner wasn't handsome in the same refined way Sterling was, but his tall athletic frame and well-developed muscles set him in a superior category. The spectacles he wore were almost incongruent to his features but made him seem more approachable somehow. In addition, he radiated a powerful masculinity that made her toes curl. If Sterling had possessed half his magnetic energy, she would have agreed to marry him before he left for India, just to share his bed. The scandalous thought made her laugh out loud, causing an elderly woman passing by to look at her askance.

At the bakery, Clare ate a warm and wholesome meat pasty and purchased a second to take home. She sat at a small table set aside for customers and consumed her small repast along with a refreshing glass of iced raspberryade. While there, she read over the auction handbill in more detail. Every bit of portable property on the estate was to be sold, from the horses in the stables to the rugs in the drawing room. She'd never attended an auction before, and a thrill of anticipation went down her spine.

Her tummy and mind were both full when she left the bakery. Stroud had been her home for only a scant few days, and she felt as if she were beginning to settle in. Yes, she'd picked a fight with her neighbor, the outcome of which had yet to be resolved. But she'd also made strides both in cleaning up Robbins Nest and matriculating around town. Indeed, she would have so much good news to relate in her first letter to her family, she'd have no room to disclose any of the bad.

She fished Mr. Brown's address from her carryall and set off toward the man's office. To her mild surprise, she realized she'd passed by the place earlier without realizing it. An older man— the solicitor himself, she presumed—was writing as she walked through the door, but he put down his pen and stood to greet her.

"Good afternoon, miss. May I help you?"

"You're Mr. Brown? My name is Miss Ladd. You used to advise my grandmother, Mrs. Robbins."

His bushy white eyebrows rose. "Indeed, I did. Welcome to Stroud."

"Thank you. I'd like you to represent me in a dispute with my neighbor, Mr. Holcroft. You see..." She trailed off when he held up a quelling hand.

"I'm afraid Mr. Holcroft has already engaged my services in the matter, so I can't help you."

Clare managed to keep her countenance, but she was exceedingly vexed with herself. If only she could have ignored her hunger, she might have reached Mr. Brown's office soon enough to engage him first.

"What a shame." Her shoulders drooped. "Could you refer me to another attorney, preferably one within walking distance from here?"

"I'm the only one in town, unfortunately."

Since Mr. Brown was advising her neighbor, Clare didn't want to leave the man with the impression she was a defenseless lady, wholly without resources.

"I'll have to enlist the services of my father, then. You may have heard of Sir Andrew Ladd?"

The older man nodded. "I daresay few attorneys have not heard of the inestimable Sir Andrew, and I look forward to negotiating with him. You see, my client has asked me to prepare a proposal for you."

"A proposal?"

"Mr. Holcroft is prepared to offer you a handsome sum for your property." He gestured to the papers on his desk. "I'll have the offer delivered to Robbins Nest as soon as possible. Perhaps you could have your father review it on your behalf?"

Clare frowned. "Thank you, but I'm not inclined to sell, Mr. Brown. I suggest you advise your client to remove his dam before I file suit."

She turned on her heel and left the office, annoyed beyond measure. So her neighbor thought to rid himself of her by acquiring Robbins Nest? Such arrogance was not to be borne.

CLARE REACHED THE LIVERY STABLE, but no attendants were outside to speak with her. To her pleasant surprise, however, she recognized the handsome black stallion tethered next to a trough of water. Would Gawain's owner be long in joining him? As she stroked the horse's neck, the man himself emerged from the building, his shirtsleeves rolled up over his elbows.

"Why, hello again." He gave her a slow smile that warmed her from head to toe. "Can I help you?"

She answered his smile with one of her own. "Good afternoon. Do you work here?"

"You could say that." He stuck a thumb at the stables behind him. "I own the establishment."

For the first time, Clare noticed the sign affixed to the side of the building. "Holcroft Stables?"

"Yes. I'm Meriweather Holcroft."

Her smile froze and her feelings of pleasure flew away like a flock of starlings. This was the arrogant neighbor who wished to buy Robbins Nest? Obviously, he hadn't recognized her either, but once he did, no doubt he'd refuse to let her hire one of his cabs. If she could speak with his employee, however, she might still have a chance.

"I-I'm looking for Gus. I wish to go to Kingscote Saturday morning, and I'd like to hire his cab."

The man turned businesslike. "I can make those arrangements for you. You must be attending the Greeley estate auction?"

"Yes. I want to acquire a horse, if possible."

"Might I ask your name and address?"

"Um…" She bit her lower lip. "If you could tell me where to find Gus, I'll speak directly with him."

A puzzled expression crossed Mr. Holcroft's face. "He's usually waiting for customers outside the train station, but I saw him drive past a few minutes ago with a fare. I imagine he won't return this way again for at least a half hour."

"I see."

Clare's heart sank. Since Mr. Holcroft owned the only livery stable in town, clearly she had no way to get to the auction.

Furthermore, she had no wish to spend a moment more in her neighbor's company.

"Thank you, sir, but I'm terribly pressed for time. Excuse me."

Disappointed, she hastened down the street without looking back. If she couldn't purchase a horse at Lord Greeley's estate sale, she'd have to obtain one elsewhere—perhaps by putting an advertisement in the local paper. Frustrated, she kicked an overgrown weed next to the road. Mr. Holcroft's idiotic dam was beginning to feel like an impenetrable wall between her and happiness, and she'd inadvertently taken on the role of Humpty Dumpty. Worse, why did her neighbor have to be so handsome?

Lady Yates beckoned Dora into her sitting room and bade her take a seat. "I can't help but notice how unhappy you've been lately, dearest."

The young woman rolled her eyes. "How could I not be?" She sighed. "Everywhere Lottie and I visit, nobody is at home, and nobody returns our calls. I've tried to help her fit in, but it seems as if our family is being shunned."

Her mother sighed. "The situation isn't entirely her fault. Clare was very well liked in High Wycombe, and it's going to be difficult for Lottie to overcome the role of usurper."

Dora's shoulders moved up and down in a helpless shrug. "What are we to do, Mama? Should whispers and hard feelings follow me to London next spring, my debut will be ruined. I daresay Sterling's status as a jilt won't be readily swept under the rug by then."

"Your father and I are not insensible to your dilemma." Lady Yates frowned. "It would have been best if Clare could have introduced Lottie to our mutual friends and thereby amelio-rated their resentment."

Dora scoffed. "I doubt Clare would have made such an offer, and I wouldn't have considered asking her. You realize Sterling put her in a disadvantaged position, don't you? By anyone's reckoning, she's on the shelf."

"That's why I sent for you. Why don't you invite Nell to be your companion when we go to town next Season? I could even sponsor her presentation at St. James's."

Dora's face lit up. "I'd adore it, but how will that help Clare?"

"It won't directly, but she'll be happy to know her sister will have the best possible chance to make a good marriage. More importantly, Nell's presence will hush up any whispers regarding Sterling."

"What do you mean?"

"If Nell Ladd is your companion, people will naturally assume any injury to her elder sister is of a minor nature."

Dora's lips parted. "But I genuinely like Nell! I wouldn't want to think we're using her for my own ends."

"Nell won't mind in the least, under the circumstances. Furthermore, if she makes a good match, she might be able to introduce Clare to an older gentleman in want of a wife."

"That's true." Dora jumped to her feet and gave her mother a kiss on both cheeks. "Thank you, Mama!"

"You're welcome. But tell no one of our conversation just yet —not even your brother."

"I won't say anything until you give the word, but why?"

"We're in a bit of an awkward—" Lady Yates broke off and her gaze settled on the doorway. "Is someone standing in the hallway?"

Dora hastened over, but when she looked up and down the corridor outside, it was unoccupied. "No one's here, Mama."

"It must have been my eyes, playing tricks on me." Lady Yates rubbed them. "To answer your question, I particularly don't want Lottie to know of our plans until she and Sterling return from their jaunt to Bath. She may feel as if it's disloyal of us to take Clare's sister under our wing."

"All right, Mama, I'll keep it to myself. But to be honest, I don't care what she thinks."

A FRESHLY BAKED loaf of bread sat cooling on a wire rack, mocking Clare with its Quasimodo-like ugliness. She'd let the dough rise too long, and the sides had sagged over the top of the pan. Worse, the loaf had sunk in the middle and appeared undercooked when compared to the crisp edges. The thing was probably edible, but it certainly didn't appear particularly appetizing. No doubt her skills would improve with practice, but she might starve to death before then. Her order at the Emporium had included raisins, so maybe she could use the misshapen loaf to make bread and butter pudding.

Clare leafed through Mrs. Morrell's copy of *Mrs. Beeton's Book of Household Management* and tried to find a very simple dish to make for dinner, along with something sweet for teatime. If she picked a few sun-ripened berries from her garden, perhaps she could make a cake with fruit topping. She hastened into the pantry to check on her supply of sugar and was disappointed to discover she had only a quarter cup left. Cake and pudding would have to wait for her delivery of groceries, then, which was scheduled for tomorrow morning. With a growl of frustration, she grabbed a large glass bowl and went out to pick berries anyway. The fruit could be eaten alone, at least.

She left the cottage through the kitchen door and made her way to the garden. Unlike the rose bushes, the blackberry, blueberry, and raspberry bushes were alone in thriving from neglect. The fruit was huge, with a dull sheen that looked like wax. As she released fat, juicy berries from their stalks, her mouth watered, and her fingers became stained.

A deep male voice called out. "Hullo! Is anyone home? I've brought a delivery from the Emporium."

Clare brightened. The delivery meant sugar, and sugar meant cake. "Yes, I'm here!"

Bowl in hand, she hastened through the remnants of the garden. As she approached the cottage, however, her footsteps slowed and her smile disappeared. Mr. Holcroft was standing next to the kitchen door with his arms around an open wooden box filled with groceries.

He stared at her with widened eyes. "Are *you* Miss Clare Ladd?"

"I am." She lowered the bowl of berries onto an arbor-covered, weathered stone bench. "Why are you delivering my groceries, Mr. Holcroft?"

"The Emporium contracts with my company to make their deliveries. I usually don't do them personally, but this time I volunteered. I was on my way home, you see, and wanted to meet you."

"Well, now you have." She moved over to the back door and opened it so he could pass through. "If you'll put the box on the counter, I'd appreciate it."

"As you wish."

She followed him inside, moving the rack of cooling bread to one side to make room. Mr. Holcroft dropped the crate on the counter, none too gently. As he turned to leave, Clare decided an attempt to diffuse the hostilities a trifle would be wiser than allowing them to fester.

"Wait a moment." She took a deep breath. "I regret attempting to destroy your dam. I should have made my objections known in some other and more construction fashion."

His eyebrows rose. "Does that mean you're going to drop the matter?"

"Of course not. You'd no right to divert the stream."

If she expected him to argue, she was surprised.

"I'm aware of that now." He folded his arms over his chest. "I'd just spoken with my solicitor when you barreled into me earlier today. Mr. Brown is writing up a purchase offer for Robbins Nest as we speak. I'm prepared to be generous."

"I don't want to sell. This was my grandmother's home and now it's mine."

"Are you joking?" The man glanced out the window, toward the ruined garden. "You'd be far better off to accept my offer and buy some other property in livable condition. This place is an eyesore and an embarrassment to the neighborhood. I can scarcely ride past without averting my eyes."

Stung, Clare gestured toward the open kitchen door. "Good day to you, sir."

He strode from the cottage and disappeared from view. Almost as soon as he was out of sight, she began to sob from frustration and despair. He was right. The property *was* rundown and a blight, and she wasn't making much headway in improving it. Her plan to acquire a horse had been stymied, and it was anyone's guess when she might have a response to her advertisement for a servant. Despite her attempts at cooking for herself, she wasn't eating properly, and her gowns were loosening with each passing day. Furthermore, whenever she thought about her family, a dull ache of homesickness settled in her chest. Despite the overly cheerful letter she planned to write to her mother, Clare was horribly discouraged. Mr. Holcroft had asked just now if she were joking. Well, perhaps *she* was the joke. Certainly, Sterling had thought so.

As she scrubbed berry juice from her fingers at the sink, a sound at the doorway startled her. To her horror, her neighbor had returned with a second box of groceries and was witnessing her mortification. She turned her face away and grabbed a corner of her apron to dry her hands...and her tears.

"Sorry to disturb you." He cleared his throat. "This is the last part of your order."

"Thank you. Just put it next to the other one." Her voice was shaking but she couldn't help it.

"Are you all right?"

"Perfectly. The dust made my eyes water."

After she blotted the moisture away with her apron, she glanced over her shoulder to make sure Mr. Holcroft was gone. Unfortunately, he was leaning against a counter, studying her. Clare's lips tightened. Couldn't he leave her in peace?

"I settled the bill for my groceries ahead of time at the Emporium, if that's what you're after."

"I know." He studied his shoes. "My remarks about Robbins Nest were ungentlemanly and uncalled for."

Her shoulders moved up and down in a shrug. "You said nothing about the property I didn't already know."

His gaze met hers. "Nevertheless, I apologize."

Emotion tightened its grip on her throat once more. "I can assure you, Robbins Nest didn't always look this way and I find myself somewhat overwhelmed...and disheartened." A tear escaped and dribbled down her cheek. "The cottage was not in as good a condition as I'd hoped, but I mean to improve it as soon as I can hire some help."

He made no reply. To fill the awkward silence, she moved over to one of the grocery boxes and began to unpack the contents.

"Thank you for your apology, Mr. Holcroft, but I'm fine now." Another tear traced its way from the corner of her eye to her chin, but she brushed it away impatiently. "If you'll excuse me, I have work to do."

Her neighbor glanced over at the box of kindling in the corner and frowned. "Is this all the firewood you have at hand?"

"Certainly not. There's a rack of firewood outside."

Since her arrival, she'd collected twigs and fallen branches to use in the stove in lieu of regular firewood. The rack outside was completely bare, in fact, but she was loathe to admit anything to Mr. Holcroft. Unfortunately, he was more observant than she'd anticipated.

"I seem to recall the rack was empty."

"Perhaps so, but please don't concern yourself about it."

Without another word, her unwanted visitor doffed his bowler hat, slid out of his jacket, and headed toward the outbuilding. Dumbfounded, Clare dashed from the cottage and ran after him.

"What do you think you're doing, sir?"

"I'm fetching an ax to chop a quantity of wood. I noticed a fallen tree alongside the stream that would provide an excellent supply."

She couldn't resist a mild reproof. "The former stream, you mean."

Mr. Holcroft chuckled and shook his head as he disappeared into the carriage house. Moments later, he emerged, ax in hand.

Clare frowned. "This is genuinely admirable, but I'm sure you have work to do elsewhere."

"My time is my own."

Indeed, as he strolled off with the ax resting on one broad shoulder, he acted as if he had all the time in the world. Clare scowled at his back. Undoubtedly, Mr. Holcroft was imagining himself as the future owner of Robbins Nest and wanted to get a feel for the place.

She filled a bucket with water and brought it to Gawain, who was hitched to a dog cart in the drive. As the horse bent to drink, she stroked his mane.

"Your master is a very strange man."

Gawain snorted into the water, spraying Clare's skirt in the process. She sighed, retrieved her bowl of berries from the garden bench, and set about making blueberry cake. As she mixed the ingredients, she peeked out the window several times to monitor her visitor's progress. She couldn't see him from her vantage point, but she could hear the report of the ax as it struck wood. On several occasions, the chopping sound ceased, and a shirtless Mr. Holcroft would appear with his arms full of wood. His sculpted musculature—enhanced by a sheen of perspiration—gleamed in the sunlight. The man's physique was magnificent, but Clare forced her attention elsewhere lest she be caught staring. No doubt he knew full well the effect he had on women and didn't need the neighborhood spinster fawning over him.

An irrepressible giggle escaped her lips. If anyone had suggested a few weeks ago she'd be stealing glimpses of a half-naked man in her back yard, she would have laughed herself sick. Of course, if anyone had suggested Sterling would throw her over for someone else, she wouldn't have believed that either.

MRS. GALLAGHER

His work done, Meri returned the ax to the outbuilding and made his way to the trough pump to wash up. He hung his shirt from the fence and removed his spectacles before sticking his head in the flow of water. As he rinsed perspiration from his neck and arms, Miss Ladd left the cottage to bring him a towel.

He nodded. "Thank you."

While he dried himself off, she glanced over her shoulder at the large quantity of firewood he'd stacked next to the kitchen door.

"That will see me through all winter, I imagine. I'm quite obliged to you."

"I daresay you won't be in residence long enough to deplete it."

Her eyes narrowed. "An erroneous conclusion, if I ever heard one." Clare edged back. "Excuse me while I'll fetch your hat and jacket. I don't want to detain you."

She whirled around and as Meri watched her walk away, he wished he hadn't spoken out of turn. No good could come from antagonizing the woman. He dried his hair with the towel more thoroughly, noticing the monogram embroidered at the bottom —CYS. *Clare* he could account for, but what did the initials Y and S signify? The middle initial of a lady's monogram ought to represent her surname, and the last letter of the monogram should represent a lady's middle name, unless she were married. In that case, it would be her husband's Christian name in the third position and his surname in the middle. Perhaps the towel wasn't Miss Ladd's?

After draping the damp rectangle over the nearby rail, he donned his shirt and spectacles and glanced over at Gawain. He was pleased to see a bucket of water had been placed where the horse could reach it. Miss Ladd was a shrew, perhaps, but apparently not heartless. He patted the creature's flank before retrieving the water pail and setting it down next to the pump.

Clare emerged from the cottage, carrying his jacket, hat, and a small, covered basket.

"I baked blueberry cake while you were cutting firewood." She thrust his clothes at him without ceremony. "I thought you might like to have something to eat after your exertions. After all, it's almost tea time."

"Thank you." He donned his hat and shrugged into his jacket. "Blueberries are one of my favorite fruits."

"Good. I hope the cake turned out well." She gave him the basket and a curt nod before turning back toward the cottage.

"Er…Miss Ladd? Don't forget your towel." He retrieved it from the pump handle and held it out. "And…I'll make sure you have transportation to the estate sale on Saturday. A cab will call for you at nine."

She seemed wary as she took the towel. "That's decent of you, Mr. Holcroft."

Meri waited until she disappeared into her cottage before returning to the dog cart. Before he set off for Phoenix Downs, he took a moment to peek inside the basket. Nestled inside a white linen napkin was a large warm chunk of a thinly sliced cake dotted with berries. His mouth began to water from the delectable fragrance and he suddenly realized how hungry he was. Before he'd even left the driveway, he'd eaten two pieces, and on the way home, he ate one more. Knowing how partial Franklin was to sweets, Meri saved the last two slices for him.

When he walked into his house a few minutes later, he found Franklin training a bonsai tree in the solarium. Meri dropped the basket onto the table, rang for tea, and sank into a chair. His afternoon's exertions had finally caught up with him.

"You look worse for wear, I must say." Franklin peered at his face. "A bit tan as well."

"Hopefully the skin on my back isn't lobster red." Meri related the day's news and gave Miss Ladd's basket a little nudge. "That's for you."

Franklin chewed the cake with obvious pleasure. "Mmm… splendid." He smiled. "You cut Miss Ladd's firewood and she made you cake. I'd say it's time to apply for a special license."

Not amused in the least, Meri rolled his eyes toward the domed, stained-glass ceiling.

"The lady is threatening to sue me, and I'm attempting to purchase her property. There's no love lost between us."

"Other than that, what were your impressions?"

"Before I knew who she was, I liked her looks and manners well enough." Meri shrugged. "Later on, once I realized she was my neighbor, my opinion diminished. When she was crying, for example, her nose and eyes became red and swollen and her skin grew all blotchy." He grimaced. "At that point, I decided her appearance left a great deal to be desired."

Franklin laughed. "You can't deceive me. A fellow doesn't cut firewood for a young lady for over an hour without an ulterior motive."

"Ah. Clearly, you've found me out. To be perfectly honest, I felt remorseful for making her cry."

"Yes, perhaps that's all there was to it." Franklin paused. "Then again, you removed your shirt while you were working."

Blood rushed to Meri's cheeks and he felt obliged to defend himself. "What if I did? Good shirts are hard to come by and I didn't want to rip the fabric."

The older man chortled. "The male peacock displays his feathers to the peahen, in the hope of attracting her admiration."

"Nonsense."

Tea arrived just then, and Meri wished he could avail himself of something stronger. He rose, crossed over to a trolley containing bottle of whiskey and splashed a small amount into his tea cup.

"Besides which, Miss Ladd was in the cottage while I was working and didn't spare me a glance."

"How would you know that unless you'd been watching for her?" Franklin chuckled. "Vanity, thy name is Mr. Holcroft."

"And all this time I thought my name was Meriweather."

Franklin peered at the linen napkin he'd removed from the basket. "This is embroidered with the initials CYS. Clare I can make out for myself, but what name do the initials S and Y represent?"

Although he'd wondered the same thing, Meri feigned disinterest. "I don't know, but that's not the relevant inquiry." He frowned. "Miss Ladd seems extraordinarily attached to her property. How can I get her to part with it?"

"The easiest way to settle the matter would be to marry her."

Meri flicked his eyes toward the ceiling and made a sound of disgust. "Have you been conferring with my solicitor? Mr. Brown said nearly the same thing."

"No, but I've often been told I have incisive wit."

"Who tells you that?"

"My reflection does, every morning in the mirror."

"You're incorrigible." Meri shook his head. "At any rate, Miss

Ladd would sooner hit me with an ax than accept my offer of marriage. And I'd sooner be hit with an ax than to make one."

"That's rather harsh."

"Perhaps."

Meri returned to the table and reached for one of the ginger biscuits furnished with the tea. After the blueberry cake he'd eaten, the treat tasted bland. As he put the biscuit aside, he felt Franklin's eyes on him.

"Don't worry, old boy. I do intend to know Miss Ladd better."

"Aha!"

"It's nothing like that. If she thinks me less a monster, perhaps she'll accept my offer."

"Of marriage?"

"My *purchase* offer." Meri shot him a withering glance. "Didn't you mention there was a particular lady you'd admired from afar? If you're so interested in marriage, why don't you pursue her?"

The older man's expression grew sober. "I would if it weren't for my infirmity. Not too many women want to tie themselves to a cripple."

His reply held no trace of self-pity or accusation. Nevertheless, the taste of ginger turned bitter on Meri's tongue and he felt as if he'd been hit between the eyes. The room was so quiet, he could hear the soft ticking of his pocket watch.

"I'm sorry, Franklin. My remark was terribly insensitive."

"No offense taken."

The man turned back to his bonsai tree and adjusted a wire with a pair of needle-nosed pliers. Consumed with remorse, Meri studied him for a long moment.

"You've all but given up your life for me, old boy, and I'm truly grateful."

Franklin's answering smile seemed sad. "Things don't always

go according to plan, I suppose." He shrugged. "You understand that better than I."

Meri refilled his cup with tea, but he merely stared into the steaming liquid instead of drinking it. Out of the corner of his eye, he could see Franklin fiddling with the tiny tree. The man wished to see him settled, so for Meri to deny him that simple request seemed incredibly selfish. Yet to do otherwise was—regrettably—too much to ask.

SEATED ALONE at her kitchen table, Clare ate a thick slice of blueberry cake as slowly as possible, reveling in the bursting flavor of the berries. Because of her disastrous experience baking bread, she'd followed the recipe meticulously, and had been rewarded with a moist and delicious treat. Although she probably should have asked Mr. Holcroft to join her for tea, she couldn't imagine what pleasantries they could have exchanged. Furthermore, she hadn't wanted him to think the cake was anything other than a gesture of gratitude for the firewood. So she'd packed up a generous portion for him to take home instead. No doubt he'd thrown it into a ditch on the way back to Phoenix Downs, but she'd at least made an effort to be civil to the arrogant man.

Once the last crumb had disappeared from her plate, she set a huge pot of water on the stove to boil for laundry. As she was gathering together things to be washed, a knock came at the front door. A bicycle messenger had arrived, carrying an envelope from Mr. Brown. Clare brought the missive into the sitting room, broke the seal, and read the letter. True to his word, Mr. Holcroft had made an offer to purchase her blighted property. She tossed the letter on the writing desk and sank into a chair.

First and foremost—and perhaps against all reason and logic—she didn't want to leave Robbins Nest. Second, she had nowhere else to go. Yes, she could slink back to High Wycombe with her tail between her legs, but to what end? Except for her family, nothing awaited her there except to embrace the role of spinster.

She picked up the offer again and skimmed its terms. The amount was probably more than the property was worth, especially in its current condition. If she accepted, she could use the proceeds to buy Nell the sort of wardrobe likely to attract a wealthy husband. What she didn't spend on her sister, she could use to travel the continent. If so, she would have to acquire a dog to accompany her. Wasn't it *de rigueur* for lonely spinsters to sightsee in Paris or Milan with a poodle on the end of a leash?

A surge of melancholy pulled down the corners of her mouth. To Meriweather Holcroft, the purchase of Robbins Nest was merely an expedient means to rid himself of a pesky problem and a distasteful neighbor. To her, however, revitalizing the grounds, the house, and the garden would give purpose to her life in a way no amount of money could address. Although helping Nell would be wonderful, she also yearned to enjoy her grandmother's property. A free-flowing stream was part of what had made Robbins Nest so charming. Was it so terrible to want it restored?

With a sigh, she tucked Mr. Brown's missive in the desk drawer. Mr. Holcroft may have been in a hurry to make his offer, but she was in no rush to respond. Since the purchase offer didn't specify time was of the essence, she could take several days or weeks to consider the matter fully. Should Mr. Holcroft choose to withdraw the offer before she notified him one way or the other, so be it.

Clare returned to the kitchen to finish preparing her laundry. As she tossed the towel she'd lent Mr. Holcroft into the boiling water along with a myriad of old curtains, sheets, and other linens, she realized the towel sported what would have been her monogram, CYS. Furthermore, the napkin she'd used to line the basket of cake had been monogrammed, too. She shrugged. Most men never paid any attention to things like that, did they?

After she stirred the soiled towels and linens in the pot along with a generous quantity of soap and soda, she left off stirring and set up a drying rack. Tonight, she'd begin the laborious process of picking gold-threaded monograms out of her remaining linens, and thereby avoid any future embarrassment.

ALL NIGHT LONG, Clare dreamed about food. The minced ham omelet she'd made for dinner was edible—although it had stuck to the pan—but she would have greatly preferred some sort of savory meat and vegetable pie. When morning came around, she drowsed in bed, imagining she was home again with the delicious smells of breakfast wafting up the stairs from the kitchen. She even pictured Mrs. Morrell singing Irish folk tunes as she went about preparing all manner of wonderful dishes... except that Mrs. Morrell never sang, and especially not in Gaelic.

The sound of pots and pans rattling made Clare's eyes pop open, and panic ensued at the realization that someone was actually in the cottage. She quickly donned her wrapper, grabbed a poker, and crept downstairs, peeking around the doorjamb until she had a view of the intruder in her kitchen. The woman wore a mob cap, had donned the very apron Clare had worn the day before, and was in the midst of rolling out what appeared to be crust for a pie. The intruder could not have been any less threatening if she'd been Father Christmas, so Clare relaxed her defensive stance, lowered the poker, and cleared her throat.

"Excuse me, but who are you?"

The woman jumped. "Merciful heavens, Miss Ladd, but ye startled me." A smile spread across her features, making her cheeks resemble two mounds of whipped cream. "There ye are, all grown up! I think I was expecting to see a wee lass." She wiped her hands on her apron and bobbed into a curtsy. "I'm yer new cook and housekeeper, Iverna Gallagher. I used to work for Mrs. Robbins before she left Stroud ten years ago. Don't ye remember me at all?"

A dim memory surfaced of the young woman who'd served her grandmother.

Clare nodded. "Yes, I do remember you now." Her eyebrows drew together. "But why are you here?"

"I saw yer notice, of course!" Mrs. Gallagher reached into her pocket to produce the advertisement Clare had left at the post office. "It was the answer to my prayers, I must say. After Mrs. Robbins let me go, I was obliged to take work as a kitchen maid. After years of commanding my own kitchen, it's been hard on me to go lower. At any rate, I handed in my notice this morning and came here so you could try me out. If ye don't take me on, I'll be on my way to London, so I will."

Still, Clare was bewildered. "How did you get into the house? I double-checked all the doors and windows before I retired last night."

The woman chuckled as she gestured toward a weathered key sitting on the counter. "Mrs. Robbins always left an extra key hanging behind the stable door."

Clare's eyes widened in dismay and Mrs. Gallagher laughed.

"Don't ye fret about it. Nobody could have found it unless they knew exactly where to look."

The whole situation was rather unorthodox, but whatever was baking in the oven smelled appetizing, and slices of bacon were sizzling in a pan. Furthermore, the ironing board had been set up in the corner, ready for the copious amounts of laundry hanging from the drying rack. If Mrs. Gallagher was prepared to take over those chores, Clare would be free to weed the garden or do whatever else struck her fancy. A warm sensation suffused her, almost as if she were a child enfolded in her mother's arms.

"Thank you, Mrs. Gallagher. I'm grateful to have you here."

"I can't tell ye how glad I am to be at Robbins Nest again, lass. 'Tis like coming home."

Clare noticed a large worn carpetbag sitting next to the door. "You'll be moving into the room over the carriage house, I imagine?" She grimaced. "I'm afraid it needs a great deal of cleaning."

"Not to worry, Miss Ladd. I'm up to the task."

"I've no doubt you are." Clare suddenly remembered she was still clad in her wrapper. "Er…I'll just get dressed then."

"Yer breakfast will be waiting for ye when ye come down."

As Clare ascended the stairs, she heard Mrs. Gallagher break into song. It was obvious the woman loved her work, and from the delectable sights and smells in the kitchen, Clare couldn't be happier. Yesterday, she'd been at a low ebb, but today had dawned brighter. Things might just be looking up after all.

MRS. GALLAGHER WAS ARRANGING SCRAMBLED eggs, crisp bacon, fruited muffins, porridge, and tea on the sideboard when Clare entered the dining room. Especially when compared to the crusts of toast she'd been preparing for herself, the breakfast was a luxurious feast.

The woman glanced up. "Good morning again, Miss Ladd. I couldn't remember what ye fancied, so I made a bit o' this and a bit o' that. We can discuss menus and such when ye have the time."

Clare surveyed the food. "This is perfect. I wouldn't have asked for anything different."

Mrs. Gallagher beamed. "We're off to a good start, then." She gestured toward the table, where three letters waited next to Clare's place setting. "Mr. Ingram came by with the post and took the letter ye left for him. And I ironed the newspaper for ye. There'll be nary a smudge on yer fingertips now."

"Thank you, Mrs. Gallagher."

The woman bustled from the room, humming under her breath. The table had been set with a white linen tablecloth and napkin, and a vase of fresh roses in the center lent fragrance and color. As Clare was seated, she couldn't suppress a smile. Under her parents' roof she would have taken such niceties for granted, but no longer. She wanted to hum like Mrs. Gallagher but occupied herself with the post and her breakfast instead.

Her mother had written to say how empty the house was without her. Also, her father was moping a bit in her absence. More generally, however, her departure had created a stir in the community, and a resulting resentment toward Sterling and Lottie Yates had set in. A sigh escaped Clare's lips as she put the letter aside. Mama would receive her missive soon, and perhaps her cheery news would help calm the waters. She disliked being the subject of gossip under the best of circumstances, but in no case did she enjoy being seen as pitiable. Her happiness—though largely invented at the end of her pen—would go a long way toward ameliorating the controversy. And if word of her supposedly felicitous situation should reach Sterling's ears, so much the better.

The next letter was from Nell, to say the Yates had invited her to go to London next Season as Dora's companion. As she read her sister's sentiments, Clare's feelings were mixed. Neither she nor Nell had ever had any pretensions toward having a London Season, which was ordinarily the purview of the wealthiest families. Nevertheless, accompanying Dora as her companion would afford Nell the opportunity to meet many members of society and potentially catch a gentleman's eye.

Despite that, Clare suspected the Yates were attempting to whitewash Sterling's reputation by showering Nell with their generosity. Since she would never dream of casting a wet blanket over her sister's excitement, she vowed to respond to the letter with enthusiasm—however sorely she was tempted to do otherwise.

She was taken aback when she read the third letter, from Dora Yates. Sterling had confided that marriage to Lottie had not been at all as he'd imagined. His bride had already asked for an increase in her allowance and a carriage of her own. Furthermore, she was demanding to be presented at Court next spring, along with Dora. Worse, a doctor had come to examine Lottie, and had discovered she was not now and had never been with child. Sterling was bitterly disappointed.

Clare rolled her eyes. Lottie wouldn't be the first woman to deceive a man into marriage by claiming to be *enceinte*, but she had difficulty feeling any sympathy for Sterling whatsoever. Nevertheless, how quickly events had turned to make her glad she was unmarried still! Instead of feeling a vague sense of shame at her spinsterhood, she should wear it as a badge of honor. Furthermore, although Robbins Nest was in disrepair, it could be mended—unlike a marriage built on deception.

The simple, uncomplicated act of pulling weeds suddenly seemed even more appealing now.

PERSISTENT

When Mr. Brown arrived at Phoenix Downs mid-morning, Meri had the man shown into his study. Once he learned what the attorney had come to say, however, he wished he could have had him shown out forthwith.

"I spoke with Miss Ladd not a half hour after you left yesterday. If you fail to remove the dam, she intends to pursue her legal remedies in court. Unfortunately, her father is one of the best barristers in the country—or was, until he retired."

Meri gripped the arms of his chair. "She can't file suit if she's considering my offer, can she?"

The attorney shrugged. "Certainly she can. Once she receives a favorable ruling, you'll have to remove the dam without delay."

A sound of frustration erupted from Meri's throat. "Increase my offer ten percent if she agrees to sell within thirty days."

"Fair enough." Mr. Brown stood. "We'll have to put it in writing, but I'll stop by Robbins Nest and inform Miss Ladd to expect the new offer shortly."

After the attorney took his leave, Meri continued to scowl at the empty chair the man had vacated. He wanted to purchase Robbins Nest to save his pond, but the entire situation had become far more complicated than before. Despite all his protestations and posturing to the contrary, he was forced to admit he found Clare Ladd rather attractive. Perhaps even devastatingly so. He could have avoided acknowledging the truth to himself if it hadn't been for that intriguing moment in her kitchen when she was feigning bravery. In the past, all the women he'd known had always sought to play on his heart-strings, hoping to accrue an advantage of some sort. Clare, on the other hand had sought to hide her pain—a concept with which he was intimately familiar. Yes, he'd begun to like her... but it mattered little. Whichever way things played out, no romantic relationship between them was possible—ever.

WHEN CLARE first brought a short stool and a basket out to the garden, she had the same feeling of overwhelming dismay she'd had when she first entered the cottage. Despite that, she reminded herself that a decade of neglect couldn't possibly be fully addressed by one person in a day, and at least she had something productive to do. She donned her gardening gloves, sat down next to a bed of rose bushes, and began pulling out weeds. After a relatively short while, her basket was full, and a scant few feet of soil were clear.

Clare sighed. "Well, it's a start."

She dumped the contents of the basket in the beginnings of a compost pile around the back of the old outhouse and returned to the garden. Just as she tossed another huge handful of weeds into the basket, Mrs. Gallagher appeared.

"Mr. Brown is here to see ye."

Clare stripped off her gloves, dropped them into the basket, and followed the housekeeper back into the cottage. She couldn't imagine what had brought the solicitor to Robbins Nest, unless perhaps he mistakenly believed she was eager to accept Mr. Holcroft's offer. When she entered the parlor, Mr. Brown stood.

"Good morning, Miss Ladd."

"Good morning. If you're here for my answer, you may tell Mr. Holcroft I don't intend to sell Robbins Nest."

"Actually, Mr. Holcroft has authorized me to increase his offer ten percent, so long as you vacate the premises in one month's time."

She shook her head in exasperation. "I can't fault the man for single-minded persistence and determination."

Mr. Brown removed his spectacles so he could wipe them with a handkerchief. "I believe you and he are well-matched in that regard."

Clare let the annoying observation pass. "I don't want his money, sir. I just want to enjoy Robbins Nest in its original condition, which includes the stream." She frowned. "Mr. Holcroft's new offer is merely a tactic to delay the inevitable."

The attorney gave her an abbreviated smile. "Nevertheless, I'll have the offer sent to you in an expeditious fashion."

Clare frowned harder. "Despite that, I still intend to file suit at the soonest possible opportunity."

He clucked his tongue. "Think what you're doing, Miss Ladd. Mr. Holcroft is offering you a rather substantial sum for a property in distressed condition. If you were my client, I'd advise you to delay the lawsuit until you make up your mind."

"Money doesn't mean as much to me as Robbins Nest."

The older man shrugged. "Can you not think of any way to spend such a tidy sum? You could purchase a pristine cottage alongside a stream, or perhaps assist a member of your family."

Visions of beautiful gowns for Nell swam before her eyes. Suddenly indecisive, Clare bit her lower lip. Mr. Brown seemed to sense her doubt and pressed his advantage.

"My client begs you not to file suit until you receive the increased offer, and your father has had the opportunity to look it over."

She gave Mr. Brown a polite smile. "I promise to consider it carefully and let you know my decision as soon as I've reached it."

After the solicitor left, Clare returned to the garden. She'd already told her neighbor she wasn't interested in selling her property, so why would he throw more money at a fool's gambit? Obviously, he must be counting on her to be swayed in his favor by his generosity, as well as his supposed altruism. Mr. Holcroft had spent over an hour at Robbins Nest yesterday, chopping wood in the hot sun, undoubtedly hoping to dazzle her with his physique. Unfortunately for him, she was not particularly romantic any longer.

As she pulled a chunk of grass from the flower bed and tossed it into the basket, a sigh escaped her lips. Although she hated to admit it, the notion of a financial windfall *was* tempting, particularly in light of Nell's invitation from the Yates. It would be within Clare's power to refurbish her sister's wardrobe, making her as attractive as any aristocrat's daughter.

The daydream brought a smile to Clare's face for only a brief while. However appealing it might be to support Nell next Season, she had her own future to plan. If she sold Robbins Nest and spent most of the proceeds on her sister, she'd have nothing left for herself. No, her grandmother had not provided her with a home just to have her sell it at the first opportunity. Her resolve stiffened, Clare tended her garden with renewed enthusiasm. Mr. Holcroft would just have to live with disappointment.

∼

AFTER LUNCH, Clare went into the parlor to answer her letters. In her response to Dora, she expressed the sincere hope Sterling's marriage would thrive. Skirting an outright falsehood, she mentioned a newly formed acquaintance with an extraordinarily handsome neighbor. Since she named no one, and said nothing of consequence regarding their supposed relationship, the chance she would be exposed in her guile was slim. Dora would likely mention something about her possible *amour* to Sterling, so he wouldn't think she was pining away for him. Once the envelopes were addressed and sealed, she left them on the vestibule table for the postman.

The afternoon heat made working in the garden less than tempting, so she brought an armful of monogrammed hand towels into the sunny parlor, along with a needle and a pair of tweezers to pick out the embroidery. Although the task was tedious, she was glad for the opportunity to salvage the towels for future use. Once all her towels were monogram-free, she would work on the sheets.

The sound of an approaching carriage caught her attention, particularly when it turned into her drive. Mystified, she put down her work, peeked through the curtains, and gasped in dismay.

"Oh, bother!"

She wheeled around and rushed toward the kitchen, where her housekeeper was preparing a pan of biscuits for the oven.

"Mrs. Gallagher, I've a visitor and I need to tidy myself. Will you show Mr. Holcroft into the parlor and say I'll be with him directly?"

Without waiting for a response, Clare fled upstairs and into her room. As quickly as possible, she washed her face and re-tied the sash on her gown. The broad-brimmed straw hat she'd worn to work in the garden had made her formerly sleek hair resemble weeds, so she unpinned the mass, brushed her tresses smooth, and then twisted them up again. Her dress was too plain for visitors, but unfortunately she didn't have time to change it.

As she was pinching her cheeks to bring out the color in her face, she froze. Why was she attempting to make herself presentable for Mr. Holcroft? It wouldn't matter to him if she walked downstairs wearing clogs and a burlap sack. He was likely delivering the new offer and had no wish to speak with her at all. Feeling exceedingly foolish, she stopped fussing with her appearance and descended the stairs.

When she entered the parlor, Mr. Holcroft was sitting on the sofa with her lunch basket on his lap. His coarsely woven shirt was rolled up to the elbows, revealing thick well-muscled fore-arms covered with downy fair hair. He also wore workman's trousers and weathered boots—as if he were about to spend the day in a field. Clare fervently wished his rugged presence didn't affect her so.

"Good afternoon, Mr. Holcroft. I'm sorry to keep you waiting."

He rose. "Good afternoon, Miss Ladd. I'm returning your basket, with my compliments regarding the cake."

"Thank you." She blinked. "You could have given the basket to my housekeeper."

A half-smile played on his lips. "Yes, but there's something inside I wanted you to see." He extended the basket to her. "Don't drop it."

The basket was considerably heavier than yesterday, and something was stirring inside. When she heard a whine, she gasped and opened the lid. Out popped a tiny black and tan puppy with a fat pink ribbon tied around its neck. Her visitor forgotten for a moment, Clare lifted the wiggling creature out of the basket.

"She's adorable!"

As she cuddled the puppy, Mr. Holcroft took the basket and set it aside. "Do you like her?"

"Very much so. What's her name?"

Her neighbor's smile broadened. "She hasn't got a name yet. I was hoping the task would fall to you, if you wish to keep her."

Clare peered at him. "You brought me a dog?" She felt a wet, rasping sensation on her chin as the creature bestowed affection. "Why?"

"She needs a home." He shrugged. "A stray beagle who lives in back of the stables had a small litter of puppies eight weeks ago, but this is the only one that lived."

Mr. Holcroft's thoughtfulness was laced with ulterior motives, Clare knew, but she couldn't resist the pup.

"I'll call her Dinah." She stroked the creature's fur even as she gave her neighbor a reproachful glance. "Thank you for the puppy, but please don't assume your gesture will sway me in your favor."

"Mr. Brown told you about my newest proposal?"

"Indeed, he did, but I've not yet seen it in writing."

"I brought it with me, but the puppy has nothing to do with influencing your decision. I merely thought she would provide you with a bit more security."

His expression was so sincere, Clare felt contrite. "If I misjudged you, I apologize."

"I don't blame you, really. Under the circumstances, it's natural you would feel suspicious." He reached for his hat. "You should probably let Dinah outside regularly. She's not housebroken."

Clare grimaced. "Good point."

"Before I go…" Mr. Holcroft produced an envelope from his pocket, along with a folded linen square. "The new offer and your napkin. I'll just put them over here with your other things."

He draped the envelope and napkin on top of the towel she'd been working on just before he arrived. Although she managed to keep her countenance, inwardly she was dismayed. Surely he'd noticed the pile of embroidery thread she'd picked out already, but she owed him no explanation.

His eyes crinkled at the edges. "Good afternoon, Miss Ladd."

"Er…thank you for the puppy, Mr. Holcroft. She's terribly sweet, and I regret giving any offense by impugning your motives."

"Don't be so hasty. My motives were pure as to your decision on the offer, but I *did* wish to encourage your good opinion of me."

He winked and let himself out the door. Clare made a sound of exasperation as she kissed Dinah on the nose.

"My adversary just made it difficult to dislike him. What am I to do now?"

The puppy gave an anxious whine and wagged her nail.

"Right you are. Outside we go."

Clare carried the dog down the hall and into the kitchen, where Mrs. Gallagher clasped her hands in delight.

"What a wee precious pup! Did Mr. Holcroft bring it?"

"Indeed he did."

"Mr. Holcroft's a thoughtful neighbor, so he is."

Mrs. Gallagher hastened to check on her biscuits and Clare stepped outside to let Dinah relieve herself properly. As the pint-sized creature sprinkled the bushes, Clare glanced toward Phoenix Downs and shook her head. The charming Mr. Meriweather Holcroft was growing on her by the day.

She sighed. "He's not even trying to play fair."

~

"You're making this too easy." Franklin moved his queen on the chessboard. "Check."

Meri groaned. "Sorry, old boy. My concentration is off tonight." He moved a white pawn to block the black queen.

Franklin's gaze was piercing. "Didn't Miss Ladd like the puppy?"

"Yes, very much."

The older man scanned the board before moving his rook. "Did she reject your offer?"

"No. Not yet, anyway." Meri sighed. "I wish I knew more about her. Do you remember that monogram we discussed before? She appears to be in the midst of removing the embroidery from her towels."

"Hmm." The older man frowned. "One might imagine an engagement to a Mr. S.Y. was broken."

"Possibly. It might be a coincidence, but when I entered Robbins Nest, I noticed a letter waiting for the post, addressed to The Honorable Miss Eudora Yates in High Wycombe." Meri moved a bishop into position. "Check."

Franklin's brow furrowed as he studied the board. "And the significance of that would be…?"

"The surname beginning with Y caught my particular attention."

One of Franklin's eyebrows rose. "How perspicacious of you."

"If that's a polite way of saying I was prying, you're probably right."

"I seem to recall there's a baron by the name of Lord Edwin Yates. Do you suppose Miss Ladd was writing to His Lordship's daughter?"

"It's possible. One might conclude, therefore, Miss Yates is the sister of Miss Ladd's former fiancé." He paused. "If so, who was the injured party in the affair?"

Franklin cocked his head. "Might I inquire why the topic of Miss Ladd's matrimonial status has captured your interest so fully?" He moved his king out of danger.

"My influence might be more persuasive if I become better

acquainted with her." Meri pretended to ponder his next move. "That's all there is to it."

"If you say so."

Meri moved his king and then sat back in his chair. "Even if I were intrigued by the woman—which I'm not—the situation is quite hopeless. I can never take a bride."

"Do you think Miss Ladd wishes to form a friendship with you?"

"I doubt it, but I'm no Gypsy fortune teller."

"Come now. A man observant enough to notice monograms on linens and addresses on letters is observant enough to discern a woman's feelings."

Meri's thoughts drifted back to his first encounter with Miss Ladd. Although his conversations with her had been brief, he might have characterized their interactions as...flirtatious. A smile crept onto his lips, but he marshaled his countenance before Franklin noticed.

"I'd judged her to be amenable, but that's before I knew about her broken engagement." He made a dismissive gesture with his hand. "She still has esteem for Mr. Yates, undoubtedly."

"In my opinion, a lady who goes to the trouble of removing a man's initials from her towels possesses no lingering sentiment toward him. If you wish to pursue her, you might consider removing the largest obstacle in your path."

"I can't pursue her, Franklin."

"You could, if you decided she was worth taking into your confidence. In the meantime, you should remove the dam."

"I need my pond, Franklin. Desperately."

The man nodded. "When you need Miss Ladd more desperately than you need your pond, you'll know how to act." Franklin moved his queen. "Checkmate."

SOLD

For Clare, the day of the auction dawned with a feeling of excited anticipation. To give the impression she meant business at an event where there would certainly be a preponderance of gentlemen, she donned a sober gray suit. Although the suit itself was severely tailored and lacked much in the way of ornamentation, the white lace jabot and cuffs on her blouse gave her ensemble a feminine appeal. She tucked her brooch money into a reticule, pinned a dainty hat on her hair, and spent a few moments fussing with a few loose strands. Her reflection pleased her—until she remembered her birthday was less than ten weeks away. Who would give a jot how she looked then?

Clare took a deep breath and blew it out slowly. "Your birthday is only another day in the year, and you'll be just as on the shelf then as you are now." She forced a smile to her lips. "There, that's better. Be of good cheer, go forth, and spend money."

A tap on her bedroom door startled her from her reverie. "Yer ride is here, Miss Ladd."

She called out, "I'll be right down."

Clare scooped up Dinah, who was batting a ball of yarn to and fro, and brought her down to the kitchen to pass the day with Mrs. Gallagher.

"You should probably let Dinah out every few hours or she'll stain the floors." She frowned. "I hope she doesn't cry for me while I'm gone."

Mrs. Gallagher chuckled. "Don't ye fret about that sweet doggy. She and I will get along just fine while yer out."

After Clare patted Dinah on the head one last time, she hastened out the front door. She'd expected to see Gus waiting alongside his cab, but she discovered Mr. Holcroft leaning against a glossy ebony Phaeton instead. The man wore a sack suit of tweed with a bowler hat and looked casually attractive.

Her lips parted with surprise. "What are you doing here, sir?"

Her neighbor doffed his hat and bowed. "Gus couldn't be spared from his duties at the train station, so I came in his stead." He stuck his thumb toward the carriage. "I hope you don't mind riding in this old thing. The stable didn't have any uglier cabs to spare." He winked.

The showy Phaeton's wheels were painted a fiery red, and the leather bonnet had been raised against the ravages of the sun. Gawain completed the rig, his mane and coat glowing from the prodigious use of a brush.

"I requested a carriage for hire, sir." She edged backward. "I don't think it's necessarily proper or wise for me to ride in your private rig."

His eyebrows drew together. "Perhaps I've gone about this all wrong. Miss Ladd, I was planning to attend the auction and I'd be honored if you would join me."

She studied him. "Let me make this clear so we can have no misunderstanding. Nothing you do or say will induce me to sell Robbins Nest. Although I'm genuinely grateful for your kindnesses, I won't be swayed by puppies or firewood."

Inexplicably, he smiled—as if she'd just said the exactly right thing. "Splendid."

"What?"

"Your plain-spoken manner is exactly why I enjoy your company. I can't abide young ladies who hide their true feelings behind fluttering fans and ubiquitous blushes." He extended a gloved hand to help her into the carriage. "Let's enjoy the day together as friends and neighbors and we won't discuss business at all."

Her gaze fell to his outstretched fingertips. Two alternatives lay before her—a daring and somewhat scandalous adventure or a prim and utterly proper refusal.

She grinned and put her hand in his. "Let's get started, shall we?"

As GAWAIN SET off for Kingscote at a fast trot, Meri felt unaccountably buoyant. A rational man should have been annoyed by Miss Ladd's continued rebuff of his purchase offer. Instead, however, he was thrilled she'd chosen to accompany him for the day, regardless. When he glanced over at her, he couldn't suppress a smile.

"Well, Miss Ladd, we've quite a drive ahead of us. What shall talk about?"

She shrugged. "Of shoes and ships and sealing wax, perhaps?"

He laughed. "Of cabbages and kings."

Her dimples deepened. "And why the sea is boiling hot."

"And whether pigs have wings."

She nodded. "I see you're familiar with *The Walrus and The Carpenter*. My father was quite fond of Carroll's first novel, *Alice's Adventures in Wonderland.* My middle name, Alice, was inspired by the book. In fact, Papa calls me Alice when we're alone."

"How charming. You're close to your father, then?"

"Very, although he can be rather severe upon occasion. And you?"

"I'm not sure." Meri frowned. "That is to say, I probably was, but I can't remember him well. He was taken from me at an early age."

"That's terrible. And your Mama?"

"She was taken, too. They died in a…common accident."

"How perfectly dreadful!"

He frowned. "This conversation is far from cheerful! You spoke before about restoring the charm of Robbins Nest. What did you mean, exactly?"

For the duration of the drive to Kingscote, Meri conversed with Miss Ladd about her plans for her cottage and its grounds. They talked about chicken coops, raising sheep, and the garden, including planting vegetables suitable for harvest this fall. Although he enjoyed their discourse, in the back of his mind he wondered why he'd mentioned his parents at all. The subject was one he ordinarily refused to broach, much less disclose to a near stranger in such an off-handed manner. The only person who knew the facts of the situation was Franklin, and Meri had forbidden the man from ever mentioning it.

When they arrived at the imposing Greeley estate, the driveway and courtyard were choked with carriages. The manor was a quietly splendid seventeenth century home marked by a picturesque series of dormer windows, ivy creepers, and impressive stonework in mellow tan. The estate conjured visions of monied aristocrats hosting lavish parties for hundreds of their acquaintances. Auction employees were directing overflow traffic to park on the gently sloping grounds, and young lads ran to and fro with little shovels and buckets to pick up after the horses. Meri drove across the lawn and parked next to an enormous landau.

Clare's head turned as she surveyed the sea of carriages. "The auction is to be well-attended, apparently, and by people with means."

"I've been to a fair few of these things and they usually are."

She grimaced at the grass, which was torn up from carriage wheels. "The traffic is certainly not benefiting the sod overmuch."

"No. The groundskeeper is likely drowning his distress with a bottle of Scotch."

Meri tipped one of the young boys to bring Gawain a pail of water.

"And can you tell us where to find the stables?"

He pointed. "On the far side of the house. Just follow the white gravel path."

The boy hastened off to fetch the water, and Meri helped Clare step down from the gig. She lifted her skirts up several inches once she reached the lawn and took a few cautious steps.

Meri laughed. "As this rate, we won't get to the house until nightfall." He stood next to her. "Put your arm around my neck."

Her eyes widened. "Pardon me?"

"I'm going to carry you to the pavement."

"Are you mad?" She recoiled. "I don't see any other ladies being carried around like a sack of potatoes!"

"If there were more ladies here, I can assure you they would insist." He picked up her arm and draped it around his neck. "Here we go."

Without giving Clare the opportunity to protest further, Meri scooped her up into his arms and strode toward the house. She let out a little squeak at first, but then she merely held on to him. Although the lady was tall, he was quite confident of his ability to carry her wherever and whenever necessary. His muscles reflected a daily engagement in physical work, be it chopping wood, riding horses, or tossing bales of hay. Franklin often despaired of such behavior as ungentlemanly, but Meri didn't care. His towering, athletic frame was built for brute force and he didn't mind who knew it. Out of the corner of his eye, he noticed dapper, well-heeled gentlemen watching his progress with smiles on their faces.

Clare whispered, "People are laughing at us."

"It's envy. Not one of them would pass up the chance to carry you in his arms, but not one of the scoundrels could manage it."

She laughed. "In one fell swoop, you've complimented us both. Well done, sir."

When he was clear of the lawn, he set her down on the clean alabaster gravel in front of the Greeley manor.

"I'm your humble servant, Miss Ladd."

"You're neither humble nor my servant." Her tone was dry as she smoothed her skirt. "But thank you for your gallantry."

Pleased with himself, he chuckled. "Before we have a look around the house and stables, we should show our letters of credit to the cashier and register for the auction."

She grew pale. "Must I have a letter of credit?"

"Yes, if you wish to buy something. The auctioneer requires letters of credit, mainly to keep out the riffraff."

"I-I only brought money. Won't that do?"

"You may settle your purchases with money, but you'll still need to register. If you like, I'll register for the both of us and you may use my number."

"I confess, I'm rather embarrassed to say I'd no idea about the protocol. I've never attended an auction before." She gave him a rueful glance. "Why don't you go on in to register, and I'll meet you at the stables?"

He frowned. "I ought not leave you unattended."

"I'm an independent woman, Mr. Holcroft. If you'll respect that, we'll get along far better."

"As you wish." He sketched a little bow. "I won't be long."

~

As Clare watched Mr. Holcroft climb the steps to the manor and disappear inside, she felt a lingering thrill of attraction. The man cut a dashing figure, and she could attest to the fact he needed no padding in his jacket shoulders to appear manly. Despite her racing pulse, breathlessness, and elevated mood, however, she'd been foolhardy to accompany him today. There was no future for the two of them, so what was the point of encouraging a flirtation? Her attention should be focused on acquiring a horse, and not on her handsome escort.

She strolled across the grounds, pausing in front of the carriage house to admire several fine vehicles parked outside. A large SOLD sign was propped up in the driver's seat of a gorgeous barouche. The sign puzzled her greatly since she thought the auction itself hadn't yet begun. As she passed a dog cart, she overheard a gentleman haggling over the price with one of the auction company representatives, and she finally understood not every item for sale was being formally bid upon. That made sense, actually, because if every gold candle snuffer, ebony shoehorn, or bed warmer in the great estate were to be sold at auction, the event would stretch on for weeks.

Clare moved toward a feminine sky blue and silver filigreed Phaeton. As she ran a gloved fingertip over the glossy finish, a pretty dark-haired girl of perhaps seventeen years of age rushed past, climbed into the carriage, and plopped down on the blue leather seat.

"I hope you're not planning to buy this carriage." She giggled and flicked her fingers, as if shooing her away. "I want it rather desperately."

The young woman's lack of manners was annoying, but Clare made allowances for her youth.

"I don't blame you in the least. It's quite lovely."

The girl smoothed her pink silk skirt with hands encased in rose-colored kidskin gloves.

"My husband mightn't approve of the extravagance, but I deserve my own carriage, don't you suppose? I'll have to have a whole new wardrobe to match!"

"If you want the Phaeton that much, I'm certain your husband will buy it for you." Clare's response was polite, but she had no wish to linger in the young woman's company. "Excuse me."

She walked on, inwardly shaking her head. The young woman was about her sister's age, far less mature, and yet already a matron? When Clare was that young, she could barely decide what dress to wear, much less choose an appropriate husband. Of course, since she and Sterling had been expected to marry, she'd never given the topic of husbands much thought.

When she passed a display of saddles hung with SOLD tags, Clare began to wish she'd arrived at the estate sale sooner. Was she already too late to acquire a horse?

Clare headed inside the extensive stables, which were neatly kept and commensurate in size with the august manor. The appearance of a honey-colored filly pleased her very well, and she could imagine riding the pretty creature through Stroud to good effect.

A masculine voice intruded into her reverie, sending ripples of pleasure down her spine.

"There you are. It seems we're destined to meet over beautiful horses."

She gave Mr. Holcroft a smile. "Did your letter of credit pass muster, sir?"

"It more than satisfied the auctioneer's requirements." He produced a small booklet from his pocket. "He gave me a list of auction items, and I noticed all manner of portable property available to purchase inside the house. When we're done here, we can walk through the place. Perhaps you might find a bauble or two for yourself?"

"I look forward to it." Clare wrinkled her nose. "I confess, it feels strange to be buying up a man's life this way."

"Yes, but it's a necessary evil. As I understand it, Lord Greeley's distant heirs weren't acquainted with him at all and would prefer to receive money." He shrugged. "The late viscount would surely be delighted to know the sum and total of his life will be put to good use by so many other people."

"That's a practical way to look at it, I suppose." She glanced at the mare. "I tend to be more sentimental about possessions."

"Some people can't afford to be sentimental about possessions."

To Clare's puzzlement, his tone was oddly dispassionate. "What do you mean?"

"Oh, nothing." With a twinkle in his eye, he leaned closer. "Do you intend to breed, Miss Ladd?"

Clare's eyes widened. "Excuse me?"

He jerked his head toward the horse. "The mare."

She hoped her glance was suitably reproving. "You're making an attempt at vulgar humor."

"An attempt?" He pouted. "I rather thought I hit the mark square on."

His mischievous manner was ingratiating, and she laughed despite herself. "You *are* wicked. No, I merely need a horse for transportation."

"In that case, you might be best served by a gelding. Mares can be intractable when in season, which occurs roughly every three weeks from spring to fall."

She looked at him askance. "I never had a moment's trouble with the baron's mares."

"No doubt the baron's groom selected a horse for you. He would have known which ones were between cycles."

"I hadn't thought of that." Clare frowned. "Perhaps so."

"Let's search for a horse which would better suit your purposes."

He ushered her down the straw-laden passageway, flanked on either side by spacious stalls. She'd begun to give up hope of finding a gelding when Mr. Holcroft paused.

"Here we are."

The horse was a lovely, sleek sable with a white star on his forehead. Clare was captivated but reminded herself to act prudently.

"He's handsome, but I should watch him walk and cantor before I decide."

"Very sensible." He beckoned to a stable boy, who came running. "Has this gelding been sold, do you know?"

"I don't think so, sir."

"We should like to see him exercised before we make an offer."

"Of course. If you'll wait for me at the paddock, I'll be happy to oblige."

"Thank you." Mr. Holcroft gave the lad a coin and offered Clare his arm. "Shall we?"

Once she was free of the stable, she sucked fresh air into her lungs. "Ah...that's much better. I'd forgotten how fragrant horses can be."

He gave her a sidelong glance. "Speaking of which, can you take care of a horse by yourself?"

"I'll likely hire a man eventually, to help with the grounds and garden. He'll just have to be willing to muck out stalls in the bargain." She frowned. "In the meantime, I suppose I'll do it."

"Not really?"

One corner of her mouth quirked up. "After I tried to destroy your dam, you can't possibly be surprised to learn I'm capable of unladylike behavior?"

"I'd never accuse you of that."

"You may be too gallant to say so, but we both know better."

They made their way to the horse ring several yards off, where Mr. Holcroft regarded her with an admiring gaze.

"Have you any idea how unusual you are? Not many well brought up ladies are willing to shovel horse dung."

"Perhaps not in a literal sense." Her thoughts slid to Sterling and his new wife. "If one is trapped in an unhappy marriage, however, I suppose shoveling horse dung becomes a way of life."

He laughed. "Either you're a philosopher or you've had a narrow escape."

Nothing would induce her to disclose her broken engagement.

"John Milton wrote, 'Was I deceived or did a cloud turn forth her silver lining on the night?'" She shrugged. "Every tragedy may actually be a blessing in disguise."

"No." A muscle worked in his jaw. "Some tragedies are senseless no matter how you look at them."

Too late, she was reminded of the accident which had taken his parents.

"You're right, of course, sir. I've been fortunate in that regard, so I imagine I'm talking nonsense."

Although he shook his head and murmured, "Not at all," she was grieved when a shutter came down over his face. The bereft look in his eyes had touched Clare's heart, and she wished she hadn't spoiled things. Up until that moment, the day had been coming along so beautifully.

Once the stable boy led the sable gelding into the ring, Clare watched as the horse was put through his paces. When she was satisfied, she beckoned the lad over.

"Has the horse been trained for a harness?"

"Aye. His name is Nero."

"All right. Thank you."

"Put a hold on the beast, lad." Mr. Holcroft held out another coin. "The lady and I must have ten minutes to discuss his purchase."

A clerk came running over, waving his arms. "Sorry, but that horse has just been sold!"

Clare's shoulders drooped. "Oh, no."

The stable boy's expression was sheepish. "Beg pardon, sir. I didn't know." He led the horse off.

Mr. Holcroft pocketed the coin as he regarded Clare. "I'm awfully sorry."

"So am I. He was perfect."

"Would you like me to negotiate with the buyer on your behalf? The clerk might be willing to give me his name."

Clare shook her head. "I'll only end up spending more than I intended." She sighed. "It seems as if I came here for nothing."

"You never know. Perhaps you'll find something inside the house that will make the journey worth it."

Determined not to put any further damper on the day, she smiled. "I'm sure you're right."

MRS. YATES

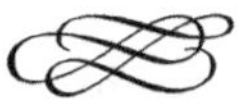

Clare and Mr. Holcroft left the stables and crossed the courtyard in front of the carriage house. As she passed the blue and silver Phaeton, she noticed a SOLD tag propped up on the seat. Presumably, the young woman in pink had prevailed upon her husband after all. Clare pushed a surge of envy aside and tried to decide how best to provide for her own transportation. Suddenly, she knew exactly what to do.

"Never mind the horse. I'm going to buy a bicycle instead."

To her surprise, Mr. Holcroft smiled. "I've been toying with the notion myself."

"You have?" She shrugged. "I suppose it's not scandalous for a man to ride a bicycle."

"Since I make a living with horses, it's a bit scandalous for me."

"Oh, you know what I mean."

"I do." He gestured toward a sitting area, where an enterprising costermonger was selling bottles of ice-cold lemonade from his pushcart. "Let's talk about it over a drink."

"That would be lovely."

Mr. Holcroft bought two bottles and gave one to Clare.

"Thank you." She sipped her drink with pleasure. "Papa has nothing good to say about ladies with bicycles, but I think he's too old-fashioned about it. A lady ought to be able to get around by herself, don't you think?"

He nodded. "I believe attitudes are slowly changing where independent women are concerned. I can only speak for myself, of course, but I admire a lady who says what she thinks. It shows an appealing sort of indomitable spirit."

"I daresay I evince too much spirit at times, but I can't afford not to stand on my own two feet." She laughed. "I hope I can learn to ride a bicycle without falling off and splitting my skull open."

"I imagine you're more than up to the challenge." He tasted his lemonade. "This is good. Maybe not quite as delicious as the cake you made the other day."

"That was the first thing I baked that came out well, to be perfectly honest."

"May I also be perfectly honest? I'd like us to be friends."

She shook her head. "We can't be both adversaries and friends."

"Adversary." He seemed to savor the word. "When I use a word, it means just what I choose it to mean—neither more nor less. And I say adversary and friend are the same thing in our case."

His charm was utterly ingratiating, and she was beginning to feel helpless to resist it. Nevertheless, she felt obligated to protest.

"You can't do that! You can't quote Humpty Dumpty from *Through the Looking Glass* at me. It's simply not fair."

"Why not? You're Alice, aren't you?"

"Nobody but my father addresses me that way."

"With your permission, I should like to call you Alice."

"Mr. Holcroft, we must maintain—"

"My Christian name is Meriweather, but please call me Meri."

A familiar voice rent the air, about twenty feet distant. "Alice?"

Her spine straightened and her eyes widened in panic. What was Sterling doing here? Meri frowned as he glanced over at the man and then back at Clare.

"Is anything amiss? I can send him away if you like."

His murmur was meant for her ears only, but she had no time to explain. She shook her head slightly and stood to greet her former fiancé. Unfortunately, a second shock awaited her. Sterling had a beaming young woman in a pink gown at his side. Instinctively, Clare reached out for Meri, who closed the gap between them smoothly. As she clutched his sleeve, he covered her hand with his. In that moment, she'd never been so glad to have a friend.

Sterling had a strained expression on his face as he spoke. "Alice—Miss Ladd, I should say—I'm quite surprised to see you here. I'd like to introduce my wife, Lottie."

The girl's brown eyes narrowed and her smile faded. "*You're* Miss Ladd?" She leveled a glance at her husband. "I was told her name was Clare."

From Lottie's cold manner, Clare concluded she had learned the identity of Sterling's former fiancée and was not at all pleased to make her acquaintance. Truth be told, Clare wasn't pleased to meet her either, but she had enough wherewithal to hide her antipathy.

"My name *is* Clare, but a very few people call me Alice." She glanced at her neighbor. "Mr. and Mrs. Sterling Yates, may I present Mr. Meriweather Holcroft of Stroud."

Meri shifted his weight. "Yates, did you say?"

"Yes." Clare tried to breathe through the tightness constricting her chest. "The Yates have recently returned from India."

"Actually, this is my first time in England." Lottie smirked at Sterling. "My husband just bought me a beautiful carriage and an adorable gelding so I can see the sights in style. We're on our way to spend the night in Bath before returning to High Wycombe."

"How fortunate for you." Clare flashed Meri an overly bright smile. "We should probably head inside the house, shouldn't we?"

He took the hint. "Yes, indeed. Let me take care of our debris."

Meri picked up the empty bottles of lemonade with one hand and returned them to the costermonger. His actions brought the cart to Lottie's attention.

"Oh, Sterling, I'm so very hot! Buy me a lemonade, please? I thought I left all the heat behind in India. Nobody told me England could be warm, too."

The plaintive whining made Clare cringe. Worse, it made Lottie seem even younger than before. Sterling had broken his engagement to her so he could marry a girl scarcely out of the schoolroom? Although her feelings for her former fiancé were not tender, she couldn't help but take umbrage at having been thrown over for a much younger woman. Sterling might as well have tossed a handful of salt on her wounds.

Meri gave Sterling and Lottie a curt nod. "Enjoy the auction."

He whisked Clare away. Numb, she said nothing as they mounted the steps to the house. Meri was obliged to show the number written on his auction brochure to an attendant before they were admitted. Once they'd joined the throngs of people in the entrance hall, she was horrified to discover tears were threatening.

Clare gave him a supplicating glance. "Is there somewhere we can be alone? I must have a few minutes to compose myself."

Meri beckoned to one of the young runners and palmed him

a coin. "My sister is feeling a little faint. Is there any place we could sit in peace for a short while?"

The lad screwed up his face a moment as he pondered the question. "Er…the butler's pantry. Follow me."

THE BARE PANTRY was lit by a window at the far end. After Meri ushered Clare inside, he closed the door and turned the key for privacy.

Feeling awkward and unsure of himself, he cleared his throat. "Take all the time you need, Alice."

She turned to give him a wan smile, revealing the moisture coursing down her face. "Thank you."

Meri produced a handkerchief. "I'm supposing Mr. Sterling Yates is the S.Y. memorialized on your monogram?"

"You noticed that?"

"I did."

She blotted away moisture. "Sterling and I have known each other our entire lives, and our families always assumed we'd be married one day. I kept putting things off, but we became engaged just before my grandmama died. Then, when he was away on business, he married someone else without so much as a letter to me about it."

Meri grimaced. "Forgive me for being blunt, but I think you're better off. The man has very little in the way of shoulders and even less taste as far as women are concerned."

His quip made the corners of her lips turn up a trifle. "You're quite right on both accounts, but I'm shocked to discover he married a girl so very young." She averted her eyes. "Worse, he left me a spinster."

The absurdity of her statement made Meri's jaw drop. "I've never seen anyone who seemed less spinsterish than you do."

"I'll be five and twenty in September, so indeed I'm an old maid."

"Is that the rule then?" He looked at her askance. "I'm older than you by nearly five years and unmarried still, so what does that make me?"

"You're an unmarried *man*, so that makes you a desirable commodity whatever your age." She took a deep breath and let it out slowly. "I do believe I took my anger at Sterling out on your dam."

"So that was it." Meri thought back to the afternoon when he'd first seen her, wild-eyed and wielding a crowbar. Now that he realized she'd been distraught, he was far more sympathetic. "And do you still care for him?"

"Not romantically." She smiled through her tears. "I'd sooner be an old maid than be married to him now."

"He's not worthy of you." He took the handkerchief and blotted any lingering moisture.

"Thank you, Meri. You've made all this exceedingly bearable."

"It's my pleasure."

His gaze fell to her lips, but he quickly stepped back lest he be tempted to kiss them. The last thing he wanted was to be accused of taking advantage of her emotional state, particularly when he had nothing honorable to offer in return.

He cleared his throat. "Well...having met Mr. and Mrs. Despicable, I think we should leave them to themselves."

"Mr. and Mrs. Despicable?" Her giggle became a laugh. "You really are dreadfully wicked."

"I'm wicked, am I?"

"In a manner of speaking." She gave him a sidelong glance. "As Humpty Dumpty said, when I use a word it means just what I choose it to mean—neither more nor less. In this case, the word wicked means..." she thought a moment "...*estimable*."

He grinned. "That suits me quite well."

~

WHEN CLARE REGAINED HER EQUANIMITY, she and Meri rejoined the throngs of buyers, who were negotiating with auction company representatives for the portable property inside the manor. As she passed an elegant grandfather clock, she noticed a SOLD tag dangling from one of its decorative finials.

"I feel as if we're part of a swarm of locusts, eating everything in sight." She glanced at Meri. "Where shall we fly first?"

"All the important artwork is displayed in the ballroom."

"Artwork?" Her eyebrows rose. "You're an aesthete, then?"

"I wouldn't say that, but purchasing portraits is rather a hobby of mine."

"All right. The ballroom is just down the hall. We passed it on the way here."

When they entered the large, elaborately decorated space, Clare noticed rows of chairs arranged in front of a dais, rather like a theater.

"So this is where the auction will be held?"

"Yes." Meri gestured toward the small raised platform up front. "That dais is for the auctioneer, so he can describe and display whatever item is up for bid."

Various oil paintings, portraits, and sculptures dotted the periphery. Some of the paintings were too substantial for an easel and were propped against walls instead.

Clare frowned. "Why are these items up for auction but not, for example, the grandfather clock in the hall?"

"Artwork and other antiquities are more difficult to value. The auctioneers can only arrive at the best possible price when bidders compete against one another. Whatever isn't sold today will undoubtedly be shipped to a London auction house."

A particular piece of artwork caught her eye. "Excuse me a moment, will you? I'd like to see something more closely."

She hastened over to a charming oil painting, which

appeared to have been inspired by John Tenniel's illustration of Alice at the tea party with the March Hare and the Mad Hatter. When Meri joined her, she gave him an apologetic smile.

"Forgive me for dashing off." She nodded at the painting. "Isn't it clever?"

His eyebrows rose. "It seems you and Lord Greeley had common tastes." He opened his auction booklet. "This oil painting, entitled *Alice*, is the work of William Learned. Would you like to buy it? Bidding starts at only twenty-five pounds."

She gasped at the princely sum. "No, I couldn't possibly spend that much."

Disappointed, she stepped back. Almost immediately, she heard Lottie exclaim, "Oh, Sterling, look!"

A swish of pink skirts brushed past and Clare gritted her teeth in annoyance. Lottie blocked everyone's view as she stood in front of the painting, clearly entranced. Sterling approached, auction booklet in hand.

"Sorry. My wife's enthusiasm sometimes overrides her manners."

Clare couldn't restrain herself from making a mild jab. "It's the impetuousness of youth. I imagine she'll grow out of it eventually, with the proper guidance."

Although Meri chuckled, Lottie ignored the exchange.

"Sterling, I simply must have this painting. *Alice's Adventures in Wonderland* is my most favorite book and this would be perfect for a nursery."

A ripple of pain crossed Sterling's countenance. "Let's not get ahead of ourselves. Are you absolutely sure you want to stay for the auction, dearest? Wouldn't you rather go on to Bath?"

"No." Lottie trained her large brown eyes toward her husband and pouted. "I won't ever be happy again unless the painting is mine."

Clare glanced at Meri. "I think I'll walk around the house to see what other treasures I might discover." She lowered her voice. "It's grown a bit crowded in here."

"So it has." He chuckled and turned over his auction booklet to show her a number. "Memorize this and give it to the clerk each time you buy something. He'll put your purchases in a bundle for us to take later."

She nodded. "All right."

"And be back here shortly after the bell has rung if you wish to watch the auction itself. I'll be sitting in one of the chairs up front."

"Save a seat for me." Without thinking too much about what she was doing, she rose on her tiptoes and pressed a kiss onto his cheek. "See you later."

As she hastened off, she wondered what had possessed her to make such an intimate gesture. Had it been for Sterling's benefit, or had it been the result of genuine affection? Either way, it had been ill-considered and decidedly ill-bred. Meri had seemed to receive the kiss with surprised pleasure, but she hoped he didn't read anything more into it than a passing impulse. Clare bit her lip as she glanced back at him. He was following her progress from the ballroom with his gaze and looked so handsome her knees grew weak. Perhaps she'd meant more by the kiss than she was willing to admit...or then again, perhaps she'd simply lost her mind.

She wandered through the house, admiring all the lovely possessions Lord Greeley had acquired during his lifetime. In the spacious dining room, an enormous quantity of china and crystal was laid out for inspection. Although many of the items had already been spoken for, she did buy three porcelain teacups and saucers—one featuring violets for her mother and two painted with Parisian street scenes for Nell and Dora.

The library held a rich treasure trove of beautifully bound volumes. Clare spent twenty minutes or so selecting several novels—first editions of Lewis Carroll's Alice novels for her, and an edition of Mary Shelley's *Frankenstein* for Nell. The cost was so much less than what she would have paid at a bookstore, she almost felt guilty.

She moved on, pausing every so often to listen to buyers negotiating fantastic prices for items. The auction company clerks were accepting amounts for things she knew were worth ten times as much. Although Lord Greeley would undoubtedly be grieved to see the sum of his possessions sold off for a song, perhaps Meri was right about the items being put to good use. The teacups and saucers she'd bought would give her mother, sister, and Dora a great deal of pleasure, certainly, and she would look forward to reading her books by firelight once winter set in.

In the drawing room, her eyes were drawn to a lovely spinning wheel in the corner. As Clare knelt down to admire its graceful lines and beautiful finish, Lottie appeared.

"Please don't touch that. It's mine." She dropped a SOLD tag over the distaff.

Clare gritted her teeth as she stood. "You've been very busy shopping today."

"I take my pleasure where I find it."

"Indeed, you do. Whether entitled to it or not."

"As Mrs. Sterling Yates, I'm entitled to it now." The girl's smile never reached her eyes. "None of the most prominent ladies of High Wycombe will visit me because of you. They resent me on your behalf."

Already tired of the confrontation, Clare stepped back. "I'm sure you're mistaken. Excuse me."

She moved off, making her way over to the beautiful piano on the opposite side of the room. Although she had little interest in the gleaming instrument, it was a good excuse to get away from Sterling's insufferable wife. Like a bad penny, unfortunately, the young woman followed.

"Dora and Nell are very good friends." Lottie's glance was

sly. "I was surprised to learn Lady Yates intends to sponsor your sister at Court next spring. I'm sure your family is respectable, but you haven't much money. How can Nell expect to compete with the other girls?"

Lottie's presumptuousness was breathtaking.

"We'll manage to turn her out properly, I'm sure."

"I might be able to help…with the proper inducement."

"Help?" Clare peered at her, confused. "What are you suggesting?"

"Lord and Lady Yates might be willing to give Nell a clothing allowance if *I* ask them. All I need you to do is return to High Wycombe for a short while, to introduce me to local society."

The notion of feigning friendship with the woman was so revolting, Clare could scarcely keep her countenance.

"I have the feeling you're used to getting what you want." She lowered her voice. "By hook or by crook."

The girl shrugged. "It's always easier for people to do what I ask. I've been known to make trouble otherwise."

"I see." Clare refused to be blackmailed, threatened, or cajoled by Sterling's wife. "My answer is no."

Lottie's lips curled into a sneer. "If Nell doesn't have the right clothes, she'll end an old maid—like her sister."

"Thank you for your concern, Mrs. Yates, but I won't be returning to High Wycombe any time soon. Please give my best wishes to the entire Yates family. I've always been exceedingly fond of them."

With as pleasant an expression as Clare could manage under the circumstances, she sailed from the drawing room.

THE AUCTION

*M*eri had difficulty concentrating on the task at hand. As he walked around the room examining the paintings, he struggled to interpret what Clare's innocent kiss had meant. Her gesture had seemed genuine and heartfelt. Even now, the possibility she might have feelings for him sent his spirits soaring.

In the next moment, he censured himself for his fanciful daydream. Giddy speculation regarding her esteem—if true—mattered little because he could not reciprocate. Even if he yearned to court the lady, he couldn't give her his name. Knowing as much, he shouldn't have asked for her friendship. How on earth was he to return their footing to a more neutral stance?

On the other hand, to imagine she could care for him after such a short and adversarial acquaintance was the height of arrogance on his part. Hadn't Franklin often commented on his overblown opinion of himself? Undoubtedly he'd attached too much significance to the kiss because he wished it could be more than it actually was.

He forced his attention back to the artwork, making notes

in the margin of his auction booklet regarding items of interest. His time piece indicated the bell was less than ten minutes away, so Clare should be returning soon. As he glanced toward the door, he noticed Sterling a few yards off, staring fixedly in his direction. Since Meri could just as easily wait for Clare in the corridor outside the ballroom than put up with hostility from her former fiancé, he turned on his heel to leave.

Sterling caught his arm before he'd covered more than a few paces. "I'd like a word with you if you please, Mr. Holcraft."

Meri's eyes narrowed at what was most certainly a deliberate mispronunciation of the name.

"It's Holcroft." He removed his arm from Sterling's grasp. "How can I help you?"

"Have you a profession, sir?"

"I don't see what business it is of yours, but I own a livery stable in Stroud."

"I see. And what are your intentions toward Miss Ladd?"

"My intentions?" The fellow's sheer audacity nearly took Meri's breath away. "Forgive me, but Miss Ladd is no longer your concern, sir."

"I beg to differ. In fact, she's a dear friend and her welfare is uppermost in my thoughts."

Meri couldn't suppress a laugh. "You must be out of your senses. I suggest you tend to your wife and leave Miss Ladd alone."

"If you do anything to hurt Alice, I'll—"

"You'll do *what?*" Meri struggled to hold his temper in check. "I think you've said quite enough."

"Have I?" Sterling's face was so pale, it practically blended in with his shirt collar. "Do you know to whom you are speaking? I'm the son of a baron!"

Sterling Yates was an officious idiot who needed to be set down. Although Meri would have liked nothing better than to perform the task, he decided to walk away from a public confrontation that would most certainly lead to blows.

"The son of a baron? I'm in rarified company indeed." His bow was sarcastic. "I do hope your family is in excellent health, sir. Excuse me."

Meri strode off, fuming. Sterling had lingering sentiment toward Clare, obviously, despite having jilted her. But he was married now and had no right to express his opinion regarding her associates. Furthermore, how dare Sterling attempt to intimidate him with his rank!

When he emerged into the corridor, he spied Clare and raised his hand to wave. When she waved back, a sensation of warmth filled his chest. Despite that, he reminded himself to rein in his emotions. Nothing good would come of a flirtation except to inflict injury on them both.

He gave Clare a polite nod as she drew near. "The bell is about to ring for the auction. We should take our seats."

BECAUSE THE AUCTIONEER managed the bidding like a maestro, Clare found the event even more exciting than she'd anticipated. To bid, a buyer raised his auction booklet with the number visible. If he were fortunate, few others would participate and he would get a very good value. If several people wanted the same item, the auctioneer managed to extract often astonishing prices. The competition would occasionally become so furious, Clare couldn't follow who'd bid what. After several beautiful landscapes were sold without Meri putting in a bid, however, she was confused. In between items, she leaned closer to whisper, "Didn't you care for any of those last few paintings? I thought them quite lovely."

"I only purchase portraits." He gave her a crooked grin. "It's a quirk of mine."

As the auction progressed, Meri bid on three different portraits, but prevailed on only one. His demeanor throughout was impassive, whether he won or lost, and Clare suspected she could never remain so calm.

When the *Alice* painting was brought up for auction, the room seemed to stir. Clare knew Sterling would bid on it for Lottie, and she ardently hoped someone else would bid against him. After a flurry of initial bids, Sterling's opponents dropped out and it seemed as if he would prevail. Mr. and Mrs. Yates were sitting in the row behind her, off to the right. Out of the corner of Clare's eye, she could see Lottie practically bouncing in her chair with excitement. The conniving young woman's proximity set Clare's teeth on edge and engendered a flurry of uncharitable thoughts. Why did the undeserving always seem to get whatever they wanted, while others struggled from day to day?

Just when the auctioneer was about to bring down the gavel, however, Meri raised his booklet. Clare was taken aback, but she tried to emulate her escort's passionless demeanor. *Alice* wasn't a portrait, so she didn't quite know why he might wish to acquire it. Nevertheless, she welcomed any development that would keep the painting out of Lottie Yates's clutches. The eagle-eyed auctioneer seamlessly acknowledged the bid and kept the contest going. When several more rounds of bidding ensued, Clare assumed Meri was driving up the price deliberately, perhaps out of loyalty to her. To show her appreciation, she would have to ask Mrs. Gallagher to bake him another blueberry cake.

Once the bidding exceeded one hundred pounds, however, Clare's palms began to grow moist inside her gloves. Should Sterling decline to top his last bid, Meri would be obligated to pay a huge sum of money for something he didn't really want. Her neighbor was well-off, from what she'd observed, but surely he couldn't afford to spend a tidy sum on a whim. By contrast,

Lord Yates and his son, by extension were in possession of a vast fortune. Although she was unsure exactly how much of it was at Sterling's disposal, surely his credit was worth more than the owner of a livery stable could command.

The bidding neared one hundred twenty pounds, with Meri always seeming to wait until the last possible moment to raise his booklet.

Lottie made a sound of disgust. "Somebody make that man stop!"

For once, Clare had to agree with her. As the price of the painting climbed higher and higher, more people crowded into the ballroom to watch the contest. So many bodies filled the space, in fact, clerks were obliged to open the doors to the balcony to admit fresh air. As a slight breeze circulated through the room, she stole a glance at Meri. A fine sheen of perspiration was visible on his brow and upper lip, but whether it was from worry or the heat she couldn't say. Although she was tempted to murmur something to restrain him, she kept still. Some instinct told her he was not the sort of man who would welcome her interference.

Once the price of the painting topped one hundred thirty pounds, Clare wondered if she were in the midst of a nightmare. A brand-new carriage could be had for such a sum, and yet the bidding continued to increase. At last, Sterling seemed to balk.

Lottie dug her elbow into his ribs. "Go on, then! He can't go much higher!"

"Hush, dearest."

A smile played around Meri's lips at the commotion behind him, but Clare was baffled at his amusement. Had the man lost his mind? She cast a glance back at Sterling, whose face was pale and coursing with perspiration, and sent up a fervent prayer that he would put in one last bid to save Meri from financial ruin. With an expression of defeat, Sterling caught the auctioneer's eye and shook his head ever so slightly.

The gavel came down and Clare nearly fainted.

"*Sold* for one hundred forty pounds."

The onlookers burst into spontaneous applause, even as Lottie shot to her feet and stormed off. Although Clare sensed something inside Meri uncoil, he kept his countenance. Did the man have ice water in his veins? As *Alice* was taken off the dais in favor of the next item, Sterling rose and followed his wife from the ballroom.

The auctioneer called for a short break, and as the tension in the room dissipated, Meri gave Clare a smile.

"How do you like the auction so far?"

He was behaving as if nothing extraordinary had just occurred, and she didn't know what to make of it. With all eyes focused in their direction, she chose her reply carefully.

"It's not for the faint-hearted."

"No, I suppose not."

She bit her lip. "Are there any other portraits upon which you wish to bid?"

"Actually, no. Have you had enough fun for one day?"

"Indeed, I have."

"In that case, after I speak with one of the clerks, we'll be off."

"I'll have my purchases brought around and meet you in the entrance hall."

"See you in a few minutes, then."

As she hastened from the ballroom, she tried to relax her shoulders and breathe normally, but her heart was still racing. She may have just had enough fun to last for quite some time.

～

THE CLERK PRESENTED Meri with a bill of sale for the two paintings. "Thank you, Mr. Holcroft. We'll deliver your items Monday morning, first thing. The auction company is waiving your delivery fee, as a courtesy."

"Excellent. That's very kind of you."

When Meri turned away, he discovered Sterling waiting for him. The man had the air of a fellow who was either performing a task reluctantly or who was standing in a ripe sewer trench in his bare feet.

"I wish to acquire that painting from you, Holcroft, and I'm willing to make it worth your while."

Meri peered at him. "You had your chance. Why wait until now?"

Sterling's cheekbones turned rosy. "If I'd arranged for a larger letter of credit, I would have outbid you. Unfortunately, my wife wished to purchase a rather expensive Phaeton and a horse, so I was tapped out. Nevertheless, I'm good for it. Alice—Miss Ladd—will vouch for me."

"Will she?" Meri gave the man a good-natured smile. "Be that as it may, I'm not inclined to sell."

Sterling frowned. "Be reasonable. I'm offering you a great deal of money to take it off your hands."

"I'm quite happy with my acquisition, thank you."

Meri tried to brush past, but Sterling blocked his path. "My wife wants the painting, sir. Name your price."

"Your money is no good to me, Mr. Yates."

"Surely the owner of a livery stable needs funds."

"You've no idea what I need. Some things are inestimable, sir."

Sterling's eyes narrowed. "So this is about Miss Ladd?"

"My motivations are none of your concern. But now that you mention it, I have little use for sons of barons who jilt their fiancées." Meri touched the brim of his bowler. "Good day."

As he walked off past the gaping clerk, Sterling muttered an oath. A chuckle emerged from Meri's lips and he shook his head. In his university days, he'd known many spoiled aristocrats who'd tried to get their way by asserting rank and wealth. Fortunately, he'd hadn't been intimidated by them then and he wasn't intimidated by Sterling Yates now.

~

As Meri drove his rig away from Lord Greeley's estate, he glanced over at Clare. "You're awfully quiet."

"I'm not sure I've recovered from the auction." She shook her head. "I don't understand why you bought that painting."

"Did you want Mr. and Mrs. Despicable to have it?"

Not even his joke could lift the corners of her lips for more than a moment. "No, but neither did I want to watch you ruin yourself financially."

Comprehension dawned. "I see now. You don't understand how a man who lives in a relatively modest home and who makes a living from a livery stable could afford to thwart a wealthy fellow like Sterling Yates?"

She lowered her gaze to her hands, which were folded in her lap. "It's none of my business, of course, but I confess, I did wonder."

"Don't worry about me. If I were concerned about money, I could have sold the painting to him for more than I paid for it just now." He paused. "Would you have preferred that?"

Clare frowned. "No...to be honest."

"You might also be wondering if I bought the painting on your behalf, and whether you ought to feel obligated in any way."

He felt her eyes on him. "The thought did occur to me."

"I bought the painting as an investment. I occasionally deal in the artwork I've purchased at estate auctions. If Sterling Yates will pay in excess of one hundred forty pounds for the painting, so will others. You're under no obligation to me whatsoever."

"I see." A dull flush rose from her collar. "You must think me quite vain for having imagined otherwise."

"Not at all. In fact, I think you're quite...estimable."

Clare finally laughed. "Thank you. And although I hope *Alice* turns out to be a profitable venture, I'm grateful you kept it out of Mrs. Despicable's grasping hands. In that one thing, at least, she was disappointed."

"I'm glad to be of service." He paused, casting about for a more diverting topic of conversation. "I've a dreadful memory for lyrics, and I've been trying for some time to recall the Major-General's song from *Pirates of Penzanze*. Would you know it?"

"Why, yes. Papa likes to sing it at our Christmas gatherings, after he's had a cup or two of brandy punch. Unfortunately, whenever he attempts it, he gets all twisted up."

"Here we go, then." Meri cleared his throat. *"I am the very model of a modern Major-General..."*

The time passed in a delightful fashion as he and Clare worked out the Major-General's patter together. He discovered the lady had a beautiful voice of her own, as well as a pleasing laugh. After he was finally able to sing the entire song without a mistake from beginning to end, she applauded madly.

"That was brilliant!"

"I shan't ever forget the words again."

Moments later, she pointed. "Robbins Nest, dead ahead!"

Crestfallen, Meri frowned. "I can't believe we're here already."

"Did you take a shortcut?"

"No. Pleasant company always makes time fly, I suppose."

"That must be it."

Although he'd vowed to behave in a more reserved manner toward Clare, Meri cast about for some excuse to see her again.

"Do you and your housekeeper plan to attend church tomorrow morning? If so, I could take you in my carriage."

"Would you? I was beginning to wonder if we'd have to walk."

He was buoyed by her acceptance. "It's usually just my manservant and I, so we'd be glad for company. Franklin is an expert in horticulture, should you require advice about your garden."

Her eyebrows rose. "An expert, did you say? He's a rather unusual manservant then."

"He's more than a manservant, actually. Franklin was my guardian after my parents' accident. He's been with me for over twenty years."

"It sounds as if you depend on him."

"Indeed, I do."

Once they'd arrived at Robbins Nest, Meri carried Clare's parcels into the house. Dinah trotted over when they came through the door, wagging her tiny tail. As Clare knelt to pick her up, Meri touched the brim of his hat.

"See you tomorrow, then."

Clare rose with Dinah in her arms. "Meri, I…"

She was standing so close, he wondered if she meant to kiss his cheek again. The possibility seemed to hang in the air for a long moment before she spoke.

"I probably shouldn't have kissed you in Lord Greeley's ballroom."

"Probably not." A smile played on his lips. "It left me rather unsteady."

Her eyebrows drew together. "Unsteady?"

"I felt that kiss all afternoon." He tapped the left side of his face. "I don't think you should kiss one cheek without balancing it out on the other."

She glanced at him from underneath her lashes. "Is that what you want?"

Even though his manner was teasing, his blood began to warm nevertheless. "I confess, I do."

"In that case, here." Clare foisted Dinah into his arms, and the puppy promptly showered him with kisses. "Now you'll be steady for hours."

"Thanks." He laughed, even as his chin grew wet. "Very considerate of you."

"You're welcome." Clare gave him smile. "Good night."

Meri lowered the puppy to the ground and let himself out of the house. As he drove the remaining distance to Phoenix Downs, he wondered how best to explain his exorbitant purchase to Franklin. Despite what he'd said to Clare about buying the painting as an investment, he had no intention of selling *Alice*. Although it wasn't his usual acquisition, the piece represented a sweet victory over Sterling Yates—a victory he could enjoy whenever he glanced at it. More importantly, however, *Alice* reminded him of his neighbor, whom he could describe as…estimable.

After Clare heard Meri drive off, she called out to her housekeeper. "Mrs. Gallagher, I have news!"

The woman hastened from the kitchen with a worried frown. "Welcome home, Miss Ladd. Does Dinah need to go outside?"

"No, it's nothing like that. We're to ride in Mr. Holcroft's carriage to church tomorrow morning."

The housekeeper smiled. "Isn't that kind o' him!"

"Yes. We'll be sharing the carriage with his manservant, Mr. Franklin."

The woman's bright green eyes widened. "Mr. Franklin?" A violent blush spread from her collar to the mob cap on her tresses. "Oh, my."

"Are you unwell, Mrs. Gallagher? Perhaps you should sit down."

The woman shook her head, but she sank onto the stairs anyway. "Mr. Franklin is ever so distinguished."

Clare cocked her head. "You esteem him, then?"

The woman gave her a sheepish glance. "At my age, 'tis silly to get giddy o'er a man."

"It's probably silly for a lady to become giddy over a man whatever her age, but I understand completely."

"Mr. Franklin has such an air o' tragedy about him. He's not got the use o' but one hand, but he manages beautifully all the same." She sighed. "I've admired him ever since he came to town these nine years."

"You've never spoken with him?"

"Every so often we exchange pleasantries, but nothing more."

"That's a good start, wouldn't you say?"

Mrs. Gallagher snorted. "He'd ne'er look twice at the likes o' me."

"Why not?"

"I'm a spinster, I am."

"I thought you were a widow."

"Housekeepers always take on the title o' missus, but I've ne'er been married. Ne'er even been kissed if ye want to know the truth of it."

"Society considers me a spinster, too." Clare sat next to her on the stairs. "I'm beginning to wonder, however, if spinsterhood is more about how we view ourselves rather than how others view us."

"Do ye think so?"

"I do. Doesn't life experience have its own beauty and charm? I refuse to value myself less just because I'm not fresh from the schoolroom and hopelessly naïve."

"Hear, hear." Mrs. Gallagher stood and threw her shoulders back. "I may be five and thirty, but I still have a lot to offer."

"Indeed you do. We must be fearless English women." Clare gave her a crooked grin. "In fact, come Monday morning, I'm planning to purchase a bicycle."

Mrs. Gallagher gasped. "Ye aren't!"

"I've made up my mind." She laughed. "I'll join the Rational Dress Society of London, and whenever I ride my bicycle around Stroud, I'll be exceedingly modern and scandalously independent."

"Ye inspire me to be brave, too." The woman gave an emphatic nod. "I'll wear my best dress to church tomorrow, and Mr. Franklin won't be able to resist my charms."

She caught Clare's eye and they both dissolved into laughter.

Meri went out into the hallway and followed the smoke. To his increasing alarm, the haze grew thicker the closer he came to his parents' bedchamber. His eyes stung as he burst into the room and stared—unbelieving—at the scene within.

An oil lamp had broken against the wall next to the bed, allowing flames to blacken the flocked wallpaper and catch hold of the bedclothes. He stood stock still, shaking his head. None of it was real, and he was having a nightmare...

Meri flinched awake and sat up with his face wet from tears. Almost without missing a beat, he threw off his bedclothes, grabbed a towel from the washstand, and hastened down the stairs of the house. As he dashed from the house and across the lawn, he knew he needed his pond more than ever before.

BEAM AND MOTE

The following morning, Mrs. Gallagher had donned a pretty fern-patterned gown and her red hair was carefully arranged, but her ordinarily light-hearted conversation was limited to monosyllabic responses. In addition, she brought out a rack of toast with no butter or marmalade at all and forgot to set out the sugar bowl.

Clare peered at her. "Are you unwell, Mrs. Gallagher?"

"Oh, er, perfectly fine, Miss Ladd."

"Your apron is inside out."

The woman glanced down. "So 'tis. Um…I may have a cold coming on."

"A cold?"

"Er…yes, that's it. I'm going to stay home from church with a cup o' tea this morning, just to make sure."

Clare cocked her head. "What happened to fearlessness? Truly, your gown and hair are quite handsome, so you have no reason to be apprehensive."

Her face fell. "I'd like to be brave, but I'm just not ready to meet Mr. Franklin. I couldn't bear it if he disliked me."

Mrs. Gallagher's tone and manner were so pitiable, Clare relented.

"All right, I'll make excuses for you to Mr. Holcroft and Mr. Franklin. A headache or some such thing."

"Thank ye, Miss Ladd." The housekeeper heaved a huge sigh of relief. "Bless yer heart."

She bustled out, leaving Clare without a butter knife.

MERI, Franklin, and Clare climbed into the landau after the church service had concluded. As the driver turned onto the road, Meri's thigh accidentally pressed into Clare. Although the sensation was pleasant as far as he was concerned, he could make no such assumptions for his neighbor.

"Beg pardon, Miss Ladd. I don't mean to crush you."

"You're not at fault."

In the facing seat, Franklin was practically beaming in approval, and Meri could barely restrain himself from kicking the man in the shins. Would the fellow ever give up his futile attempts at matchmaking?

Franklin ignored Meri's scowl. "Well, Miss Ladd, how did you like the sermon? Our vicar is rather clever, in my opinion."

She smiled. "Indeed, I think I prefer him over our clergyman in High Wycombe. I also enjoyed the scripture reading very much. The Judgment of Solomon has always been one of my favorite biblical passages."

"I wouldn't say it was a particular favorite of mine." Meri frowned. "Solomon wouldn't have cut that baby in two, I don't imagine, but the real mother must have been exceedingly distressed when she saw his sword. I always thought the whole episode rather a nasty and brutal trick on Solomon's part."

Clare nodded. "Although his tactic was deceptive, admittedly, I've always found the story itself enlightening. Oftentimes when we're forced to make a critical choice, that's when we discover who we really are."

Franklin nodded. "I believe that's the most insightful comment I've heard in a long while."

"Gardening has turned me into a philosopher, I'm afraid." She laughed. "I have a great deal of time to ruminate on the mysteries of the universe when I'm weeding."

"I do the same thing whenever I'm training my bonsai trees, Miss Ladd, but I've not solved a single mystery yet."

"How about you, Mr. Holcroft?" Clare regarded him with a smile. "What deep thoughts do you have when you're hard at work?"

"Physical labor allows me to avoid introspection altogether. Perhaps that's why I'm fond of it."

She frowned. "You sell yourself rather short, sir. In my opinion, many of your observations are exceedingly thoughtful."

"In Mr. Holcroft's case, insight and hard work aren't mutually exclusive." Mr. Franklin chuckled. "I've never seen a man so happy as when he was digging his pond. Day after day he would dig until he was drenched with sweat and staggering with exhaustion. For that short period of time, at least, he slept like a babe."

"Franklin." The single word was meant as a warning. "Why don't you ask Miss Ladd about her roses?"

Clare brightened. "Oh, I'm so glad you mentioned that. Could I press the two of you to stop by Robbins Nest to advise me about my garden? As a further inducement, my housekeeper is planning to bake ginger biscuits today."

Meri was confused. "I thought you said she had a headache?"

"I imagine a cup of tea set her right again. Nothing keeps her down for long."

Although Meri yearned to spend time with Clare, he knew it was a foolish indulgence on his part. Why torture himself with visions of something he could never have?

"I have something to which I must attend, but you're free to stay, Franklin."

"Splendid." The older fellow practically wagged his tail in delight. "I adore ginger biscuits, especially on Sundays."

Clare's smile revealed a pair of dimples. "I'm so glad. My housekeeper, Mrs. Gallagher, has been a godsend."

Franklin's eyes widened. "Mrs. Gallagher, did you say?"

"Yes. Mrs. Iverna Gallagher used to work for Grandmama, and now she works for me. She's such a pretty and amiable lady, I consider myself quite fortunate to have her in my employ."

To Meri's puzzlement, Franklin grew quite pale and began to fidget in an uncharacteristic manner. Even more unusual, the fellow seemed to have no ready quip or witty rejoinder on the tip of his tongue. He wiped his brow with a handkerchief and then cleared his throat.

"I'm afraid I'm going to have to beg off, Miss Ladd. I've a letter to write to my sister that simply can't wait. Perhaps I might visit Robbins Nest some other time?"

Clare's shoulders drooped slightly. "Yes, of course. I should have given you more notice."

Although Meri respected Franklin too much to contradict him in front of Clare, he knew the excuse was specious. Franklin had a sister, but he didn't care for her overmuch. He usually wrote her twice a year—on her birthday and at Christmas—and neither occasion was nigh. Since Franklin seemed to like Clare very much indeed, what reason could he possibly have for begging off?

Once Meri had escorted Clare into the cottage, he returned to the carriage and gave Franklin a shrewd glance.

"What was that all about?"

"I don't know what you mean. My letter to Sarah is long overdue."

"You and I both know that isn't so. Do you have some previous quarrel with Mrs. Gallagher? I thought you might keel over in a dead faint when Miss Ladd mentioned her name."

The older man drew himself up. "Certainly not. I've never even been formally introduced to the lady."

Meri was mystified. "If I didn't know better, I'd say you were behaving almost like a bashful suitor."

Franklin stared out the window with pursed lips.

"Oh." The exclamation was soft and drawn out as Meri put two and two together. Mrs. Gallagher must be the secret object of the man's affection.

Franklin scowled. "There's no 'oh' involved, and I beg you not to interfere. You're merely cross because I mentioned your nightmares to Miss Ladd."

"Indeed you did, and you should have known better."

"A blind man can see the attraction between the two of you. I don't understand how you can shut her out entirely."

"I don't understand why you don't call on Mrs. Gallagher."

Franklin angrily yanked off his left glove, revealing the crippled hand underneath. Several fingers had been amputated, and the skin appeared melted. The remaining part of the hand, which was held in place by a strap around his wrist, had been fashioned of wood.

"It's awfully difficult to warm the cockles of a woman heart with *this*."

Meri had seen the grievous injury on several occasions, but it never failed to send a shock to his core.

"You ought to give the lady a chance to decide that for herself. You're so much more than your imperfection."

"And you're so much more than your name, *Mr. Holcroft*." A muscle worked in Franklin's jaw as he donned his glove. "Might I respectfully suggest you remove the beam in your eye before attempting to remove the mote in mine?"

Meri acknowledged the remark with a nod of his head. "Touché."

~

CLARE BIT into a freshly baked ginger biscuit as she climbed the stairs to her room. Dinah had learned to climb, albeit with great effort, and cheerfully scrambled from one tread to the next in an attempt to follow. From time to time Clare paused to murmur encouragement, and when the puppy reached the top, the little creature wiggled with pride. Clare finished her biscuit before kneeling to chuck her under the chin.

"There's a brave girl."

After she changed from her Sunday dress into a cool, tailored shirtwaist of gray pinstripes, she examined her reflection in the mirror with a vague sense of disappointment. Both Mr. Franklin and Meri had declined to stay after church, and on the flimsiest of pretexts. Not only did she feel as if she'd failed Mrs. Gallagher somehow, but she had to admit her feelings were bruised. Maybe Meri regretted asking for her friendship yesterday and had decided to interject more distance between them?

So be it. Considering the fact their dispute remained unsettled, his refusal was sensible and desirable. Furthermore, if Meri didn't want to spend time in her company, she didn't want to spend time with him either. What sort of brave spinster would she be if she yearned to have a man hanging about, waiting to be fed, cajoled, caressed…and kissed? Gah! She shook herself from that dangerous line of thought and stroked Dinah's fur instead.

"At least you're not a poodle."

She brought the pup downstairs to the sitting room, so she could compose a letter to her sister regarding Lottie Yates. What unflattering impressions could she relate about her former fiancé's wife that wouldn't reek of jealousy? In all likelihood, her sister had already had the opportunity to meet the girl and form an opinion as to her character. Perhaps she should write about the estate sale and auction, and mention having met

Sterling and Lottie there. Although she yearned to also mention the bicycle she planned to purchase, she dare not put Nell in the position of having to conceal her secret. How many times had Papa railed against members of the High Wycombe Ladies' Bicycle Club?

"Look at those vulgar hoydens pedaling about with their knees in the air!" Sir Andrew would shake his head in disgust. "No doubt they'll demand the vote next."

The memory made Clare shudder. No, she would definitely not confide her resolve to acquire a bicycle to Nell, but it would be safe to tell her about the tea cups and books she'd bought. As she sat at the desk and readied a piece of stationery, she regretted answering Dora's letter so very quickly. Upon Sterling and Lottie's return to Bramble Manor, they would certainly tell the family all about meeting her and Meri. If Dora also happened to share Clare's letter, everyone would conclude she and Mr. Holcroft were courting. Nothing could be further from the truth, of course, but tongues would wag. Perhaps she could nip the gossip in the bud with her letter to Nell and hope her sister passed the information along to Dora.

Clare bent over the stationery and began to write. In the end, she mentioned Mr. Holcroft's offer to purchase her property, and her refusal to consider it. That characterization of their relationship should cast them in the roles of adversaries rather than friends and put the lie to any rumors.

MERI SPREAD A QUILTED blanket on the grass next to his pond and picked up his kite. After unfurling a few yards of line from the spool, he ran across the lawn until the mid-morning breeze seized the sails and dragged the diamond skyward. The red bows attached to the tail danced as he played out the line, and when the kite had reached a satisfying height, he finally sank down on the blanket and watched the kite swoop and dip like a living creature. If he released the line, would the kite fly off, never to return?

As he gazed upward, his recent quarrel with Franklin weighed on his mind. The man believed no lady could possibly be attracted to him because of his injury, but that simply wasn't the case. Whenever Meri and Franklin were out together, the older man always received his share of admiring glances from ladies who'd passed the first blush of youth. Was Franklin so convinced of his own inferiority that he simply couldn't see what was in front of him? Or perhaps he was so worried Mrs. Gallagher would be repulsed by his deformity that he'd rather admire her from a distance. If Meri knew of some way to encourage the relationship, he wouldn't hesitate to act. Unfortunately, Franklin had already practically accused him of being officious.

The line grew taut, and he began to fear the kite would tear free in the high wind. As he reeled it in, Franklin appeared.

"I haven't seen you fly a kite in a long while."

Meri shrugged. "I thought it would be fun."

"Is it?"

"Not as much as I'd hoped." He got to his feet and offered Franklin the spool. "Care to have a go?"

"No, thank you. Two paintings were delivered just now." He held up a manifest. "This indicates a purchase price on *Alice* of one hundred forty pounds."

A shrug accompanied Meri's reply. "What of it? I've plenty of money."

"That's not the point. Do you not understand that by paying so much for a painting of questionable worth, you've brought unwanted scrutiny upon yourself?" He handed Meri a calling card. "Mr. Herbert Watson is a newspaper reporter who heard about your acquisition and wishes to conduct an interview with you."

"How ghastly." A sigh escaped Meri's lips. "I can't talk to any reporters, obviously, so send him away." He peered at the card. "What a curious coincidence his name should be Herbert Watson. My father had a stable boy working for him by the name of Bertie Watson."

"Caught that, did you? It's not a coincidence."

"Are you serious?" Meri gasped. "Did he recognize you?"

"Of course." Franklin's mouth quirked up on one side as he gestured with his black-gloved hand. "I don't exactly blend in."

Meri began to pace. "There's no need to assume Bert knows who I am just because he remembers you. After all, that's why I go by the name of Holcroft."

"Come, now, Meri. Bert knew the Holcrofts and he's worked out who you are. In fact, he says he's interested in writing a series of articles about your father."

"He'll have to do it without my cooperation." A muscle fluttered in Meri's jaw. "Tell Bert that Mr. Holcroft is not at home."

"As you wish." Franklin paused. "In the future, perhaps you might want to be more circumspect about your public expenditures. I'm sure there are other ways to impress Miss Ladd."

A shaft of heat shot down Meri's spine. "It had nothing to do with her and I resent your implication!"

"I believe I implied nothing but stated my observation openly. Should you choose to ignore it, that is your prerogative."

As Franklin strode back toward the house, Meri reached down to snatch the blanket from the grass. If Bert Watson wished to publish an article about how Mr. Meriweather Holcroft of Stroud had paid a stupidly large sum of money for a painting, there was nothing he could do to prevent it. Nor could he stop Bert from writing articles about the Pallinger murder—save for refusing to give any interviews on the subject. The friction between Meri and Franklin, however, was another matter. Their previously cordial relationship had soured, and he felt powerless to do anything about it.

~

As Clare walked home from Stroud with a brand-new cycling costume in her carryall, she had a skip in her step. Her new bicycle would be delivered with her next order of groceries, and she couldn't be more pleased. The cycling costumes which featured actual pantaloons were far too daring for her to contemplate as yet, but she'd selected a very pretty bottle green suit featuring a specially designed skirt. From the front, the garment appeared to be a normal wool skirt—albeit several inches shorter than the usual length. When she pulled the fabric to one side in the back, however, it was obvious the skirt was actually a pair of trousers. In her carryall was also a small packet of lead weights to be sewn into the hem for modesty. She'd also purchased black leggings to cover her lower extremities. Clare giggled as she imagined herself proudly riding her bicycle into town. Her newfound freedom would allow her to shop at the merest whim, or to visit the library whenever she liked. Although the occasionally steep streets might prove challenging, it was an exciting moment.

An unfamiliar gig was parked in front of the cottage when Clare arrived. As she stepped through the front door, Dinah trotted from the parlor, begging to be petted.

Mrs. Gallagher hastened from the kitchen. "Miss Ladd, there's a gentleman waiting for ye in the parlor." She gave Clare a calling card and leaned close to whisper, "Mr. Herbert Watson's a reporter for a London newspaper, he says."

"A reporter?" Clare wrinkled her nose and dropped the card in her carryall. "Why would he want to speak with me?"

"Something about a painting at the auction." Mrs. Gallagher shrugged. "I didn't know what he was going on about."

"All right."

She gave her housekeeper the carryall, took Dinah into her arms, and joined her visitor in the parlor. A neat black bowler was resting on the sofa, but its owner—a man in his mid-thirties —was standing next to a table where she'd stacked her newly acquired books.

"I'm Miss Ladd. How can I help you, sir?"

He glanced up from her copy of *Alice's Adventures in Wonderland,* and his thick handlebar mustache twitched into a smile. The fellow's shrewd gaze immediately put her on her guard.

"Hello, Miss Ladd. I'm Mr. Watson." He held up the bookmark she'd left on top of the stack, embroidered with her full name. "Your middle name is Alice?"

She nodded. "My father named me after the character in the novel. Er...my housekeeper said you came to ask me about a painting, but you're wasting your time. I didn't bid on anything and left before the auction was over."

He returned the book and bookmark to the table. "Your neighbor, Mr. Holcroft, paid a great deal of money for an obscure work. That's newsworthy."

Clare was bewildered. "I can confirm Mr. Holcroft bought two paintings at the auction, but that's all. If you'd like to know more, you must ask him."

"I wish I could, but he wasn't at home." He shrugged. "It's of little consequence, really, since one of the auction clerks already told me what I needed to know for my article. I just wanted to meet you in person."

"I'm sorry I can't be of more help." She took a half step backward. "If there's nothing else, I'll have my housekeeper show you out."

Again, his handlebar mustache twitched. "I know the way." He reached for his hat. "Thank you for seeing me, Miss Clare Alice Ladd." His eyes crinkled at the corners. "You're as lovely as I was told."

Clare's lips parted, but no sound emerged. After Mr. Watson departed, she nuzzled Dinah with her cheek. The man's visit was inexplicable, by any measure. Who would be talking of her, especially to say she was lovely? Perhaps he'd mistaken her for someone else.

Mrs. Gallagher hastened into the parlor with a plate of biscuits. She blinked in surprise when she realized Clare was alone.

"Oh, has Mr. Watson gone? I meant to offer him some refreshments."

"He just left." Clare lowered Dinah to the floor. "Did you put my carryall upstairs? I want to try on my new riding costume."

The housekeeper's face lit up. "Ye bought a bicycle then?"

"I did indeed." Clare giggled. "And as soon as it's delivered, I'm determined to set propriety at naught!"

The older woman nodded. "That's the spirit."

UNFOLD

High Wycombe

Sir Andrew passed Nell an envelope at the breakfast table. "You've had a letter from Clare."

"At last!" Nell wiggled with delight and tore the letter open. "I hope she's not put out about my going to London with the Yates next spring."

Lady Ladd glanced up from spooning marmalade onto her plate. "I'm certain Clare is rejoicing in your good fortune."

Sir Andrew lowered his newspaper. "Taking Nell to London is the least the Yates can do under the circumstances. My gratitude toward them is limited."

Nell frowned. "What do you mean, Papa? Their offer is exceedingly kind and generous."

"The Yates may feel remorseful over Sterling's poor treatment of Clare, but their generosity toward her younger sister is a terribly small measure of recompense. In addition, it's self-serving, since any criticism of the Yates will be calmed by their actions."

Nell shrugged. "I suppose you're right, but I'm still glad of it."

She opened the letter without delay and focused her attention on her sister's handwriting.

"Ugh." She grimaced. "Clare encountered Sterling and Lottie at an estate auction. She said Sterling was decent enough, but Lottie wasn't at all friendly."

Lady Ladd frowned. "I'm not surprised. Has she any other news?"

Nell bent over the letter. "Er...Clare was escorted to the event by her neighbor, Mr. Holcroft. She writes the man is frightfully attractive, and she worries the Yates might have taken away the wrong impression about their relationship."

Her mother made a dismissive sound. "I hope they did. Sterling deserves to believe Clare has other suitors, even if it isn't true. Furthermore, Lottie Yates deserves to be put in her place. I've never met a young girl who thought so well of herself with so little justification."

"Clare says she bought presents for you and me at the estate sale." Nell beamed. "I wonder what they are."

"Almost anything, I imagine. I went to an estate sale when I was about your age and came away with a pretty jet bead necklace and a decorative biscuit tin from France."

Nell's eyes fell to the page once more. "Ha! It seems Mr. Holcroft wishes to purchase Robbins Nest, but Clare doesn't wish to sell. Isn't that awkward!"

"It's unfriendly, at any rate." Lady Ladd frowned. "I shouldn't like to live next door to a fellow who wants to buy my property out from under me."

Sir Andrew glared at his newspaper. "What in blazes?"

His wife peered at him with widened eyes. "Is anything amiss?"

Nell froze. "England isn't at war, is it?"

"Far worse than that. Clare is in the news." He gripped the paper with shaking hands and began to read aloud. "Little-known artist William Learned vaulted into the celestial realm of the art world when one of his whimsical paintings sold at auction for the princely sum of one hundred forty pounds. The newsworthy sale, however, is the least interesting part of the story. The painting, inspired by Lewis Carroll's novel *Alice's Adventures in Wonderland*, would not ordinarily have fetched such a handsome sum if it weren't for the presence of Alice herself. No, I refer not to the eponymous character in the fantastical tale, but a real-life uncommon beauty by the name of Miss Clare Alice Ladd. The bidding on the painting was a modern-day joust on the lady's behalf, with Mr. Meriweather Holcroft emerging as her champion."

Nell managed a squeak, but Lady Ladd could only gape.

"By all accounts," Sir Andrew continued, "Mr. Holcroft and The Honorable Mr. Sterling Yates were practically at fisticuffs after the gavel came down. This reporter, having met the lady in person, concurs she's an English rose worth fighting for." He folded the newspaper with a disgusted snap. "The story is entitled, 'Auction Row or Romance?' The writer might as well have entitled it 'Licentious Miss Ladd Leads Men Astray.'"

Nell recoiled. "Papa!"

A soft groan escaped his wife's lips. "Upon my word!"

Nell wore an expression of disbelief. "Sterling and Mr. Holcroft were fighting over her? That's unlikely. Sterling is married now, and Clare can't have known Mr. Holcroft more than a few days."

"The reporter must be exaggerating." Lady Ladd shook her head. "If there was some sort of *contretemps* at the auction, it isn't Clare's fault whatsoever."

"Besides which, it's rather nice for Clare to be mentioned in the newspaper." Nell shrugged. "All our friends will see the story and be madly jealous. I confess, I'm a trifle envious myself."

"Except for births, marriages, and obituaries, the best families endeavor to stay out of the papers." Sir Andrew scowled. "This publicity, whether Clare's fault or not, has subjected our family to unwanted scrutiny." He threw down his napkin. "I mean to get to the bottom of it."

Lady Ladd drew back. "How?"

"I've long worried that Clare's independent streak would cause trouble sooner or later. I'm going to Stroud forthwith, to fetch her home."

"Fetch her home?" His wife's lips formed a straight line. "You'll do no such thing, dear."

Both Sir Andrew and Nell stared at her in shock. Lady Ladd was almost always soft-spoken, but her assertion was laced with steel.

"To do otherwise would be to abrogate my responsibility as a father!" He pushed back his chair and stood. "I'm leaving forthwith."

Lady Ladd practically glared. "Sit down."

Sir Andrew was so surprised, he nearly collapsed into his chair. "What?"

"As Nell said, the article was nothing but flattering toward our daughter. And if indeed a romance with Mr. Holcroft is in the offing, you must let it unfold. I won't have you stand in the way of her happiness!"

"But her reputation has been called into question!"

"Don't be absurd." Lady Ladd stabbed a bite of pickled peach with her fork. "I understand invitations to Dora's eighteenth birthday party are going out soon. I'll call on Lady Yates to ask if Mr. Holcroft might be included."

A broad grin spread across Nell's countenance. "What a wonderful idea, Mama! I'd love to meet the man who may have caught Clare's fancy."

Sir Andrew's eyebrows rose. "How do you know the fellow has caught her fancy?"

"Clare described him as handsome in her letter, and she's not inclined to exaggeration." Lady Yates rolled her eyes. "Really,

Andrew, sometimes I don't think you don't know your daughter at all."

Nell hid a smile behind her napkin, but Sir Andrew continued to scowl. "Why would Lady Yates be inclined to invite the man who argued publicly with her son?"

"She wishes to convey the impression that we've forgiven Sterling, of course." She paused. "And I have the impression she wouldn't mind vexing Lottie in the bargain."

CLARE SWALLOWED the last mouthful of Devonshire cream and fresh strawberries, reveling in its wholesome sweetness. When she turned the page of her morning newspaper and saw the headline, 'Auction Row or Romance?' however, she nearly bit her tongue. Stunned, she skimmed the article, and then read it twice more. Mr. Watson had intimated—without any evidence whatsoever—that Meri and Sterling harbored romantic feelings toward her. Why would that reporter invent such an embarrassing falsehood? Even if an argument had occurred between the two men, it was likely over the painting and nothing else. Evidently, such salacious nonsense sold more newspapers.

Her heart was pounding so loudly, she could scarcely hear herself think. Meri hadn't mentioned anything about an argument with Sterling, so the article must be wholly invented. On the other hand, she'd not told him about her private and rather nasty conversation with Lottie Yates either, so perhaps that proved nothing. What should she do now?

First, she ought not panic. The Season was in full swing, and most people would be searching for articles about wealthy and interesting people, not about estate auctions or the eldest daughters of prominent retired barristers. Nobody would read the story, presumably, and even if they did, the stupid thing would be instantly forgotten. Furthermore, there were probably a dozen Clare Alice Ladds in England, so nobody would necessarily assume she and the lady in the article were one and the same. Why would they? She was merely a country spinster, too old to be considered 'an uncommon beauty,' and of no consequence whatsoever.

Her shoulders and hands relaxed, and she managed to laugh. Thank heavens she could reason this crisis through and not lose her head! She pushed the paper aside and returned to her breakfast with a lighter heart. Although she wouldn't mention the article to Meri, if he should happen to see it, he'd probably laugh as well. Sterling, on the other hand, took himself far too seriously to shrug it off. He and Lottie were traveling, though, so in all likelihood he wouldn't read it either.

Once she was done with her breakfast, she brought the newspaper into the sitting room and cut the article out with a pair of shears. She must revel in her tiny bit of infamy while she had the opportunity. After all, the next story about her printed in the paper would likely be her obituary.

In a moment of fancifulness, she drew a piece of stationery toward her, dipped a pen in ink, and wrote out two names— Mrs. Clare Ladd Holcroft and Mrs. Meriweather Holcroft. Then she wrote a new monogram in decorative letters. CHM. The monogram looked very well indeed, and far better than the CYS she'd picked out of her linens. Clare sighed, crumpled the stationery into a ball, and wiped the nib of her pen on the blotter. The only monogram she would ever have was the one she had at present. CLA.

IN A CLOUD OF UMBRAGE, Meri folded the newspaper and tossed it next to Franklin's breakfast plate.

"Have you seen this story?" He pointed an accusing finger at the page. "It's a disaster!"

Franklin put down the small spoon he was using to eat his soft-boiled egg and peered at the paper instead.

"'Hail Kills Six Horses in Rapid City, South Dakota.'" He glanced up with a grimace. "Oh, dear. Are lethal hailstorms a common problem in that part of the world?"

"No, not *that* story." Meri turned the paper over. "The article about the auction."

"Hmm." Franklin's eyes darted back and forth as he read. "Hmm."

"Is that all you can say?"

The man glanced up with a gleam in his eye. "Did you get into an argument with Mr. Sterling Yates?"

"Indeed, I did. He's an arrogant idiot."

"Yates." Understanding dawned. "Would he be the S.Y. of the mysterious monogram?"

"Yes, and our disagreement was within earshot of one of the auction clerks, who must have told the reporter what he'd heard." Meri sighed and shook his head. "The clerk should have been more discreet."

"And you and Mr. Yates were fighting over Miss Ladd?"

"N-Not exactly. He wanted to buy *Alice*, but I declined to sell it to him because he'd jilted Miss Ladd." Meri scowled. "The ridiculous popinjay threw his former fiancée over in favor of a grasping, selfish schoolgirl. I wouldn't have sold him a sweaty handkerchief."

"This article is very complimentary toward Miss Ladd, I must say." Franklin chuckled. "It almost casts her as Helen of Troy."

"She's a lovely girl who doesn't deserve ill treatment!"

"Do I detect growing sentiment on your part?" The inquiry earned Franklin a level glance, which he waved off with a gesture of exaggerated surrender. "I merely asked a reasonable question."

Meri combed his fingers through his hair, exasperated. "It

doesn't matter if I have enough sentiment to fill a moat. Meriweather Holcroft cannot marry."

"No, but Meriweather Barnabas Pallinger can." With a frown, Franklin lifted his injured hand. "Was my sacrifice for nothing?"

"No! You have my everlasting gratitude, as you're well aware."

"That's not enough any longer." Franklin's lips were compressed as he stood. "I'm going to stay with my sister in London for a few days."

"Don't be ridiculous. You're not fond of your sister."

"Our quarrels have moderated with age. At any rate, I'm going to visit a physician while I'm in town."

Fear gripped Meri by the throat. "You've been hiding an illness from me. That's why you're so thin."

"I've been having pains in my stomach for some time now, so I've arranged an appointment with a physician." He shrugged. "For good or for ill, I'd like to know what I'm facing."

Meri folded his napkin with bloodless fingers and dropped it on the table. Franklin had been growing steadily thinner the last few weeks, but Meri hadn't wanted to admit it. Now, faced with the prospect of losing his friend, the room seemed to close in on him and he couldn't breathe.

"I'll go along." He choked out the words. "We'll stay at the best hotel, you and I, with every possible comfort. And if we don't like what your physician says, we'll seek out a better one."

"Thank you, but no." Franklin shook his head. "My sister is expecting me, and I'll return to Phoenix Downs soon enough."

Meri searched Franklin's countenance. "What can I do?"

"Court Miss Ladd. If I'm to die, it would set my mind at ease knowing you won't be alone." He averted his eyes. "I'd like to be on the eight o'clock train tomorrow morning."

From the set expression on the older man's face, Meri realized he would not change his mind.

"Of course I'll take you to the station." He paused. "I can't lose you, Franklin."

"That eventuality is out of our hands. Excuse me while I go pack my things."

He ambled off and Meri was left alone with ghosts…

Gasping for air, he backed from his parents' bedroom and ran, even as a bell began to peal downstairs in alarm. He fled into his bedchamber and into the cool dark closet, squeezing his stinging eyes shut and pressing his hands over his ears to block out the shouting and screaming. If he could go back to sleep, he'd wake up in the morning and run to his mother so they could laugh together at the idiotic dream he'd had. He even started giggling hysterically at the stupidity of it all.

Eventually, the shouting and ringing bell stopped, but the smoke continued to seep under the door sill. Meri lowered his hands from his ears and raised his night shirt over his mouth so he could breathe. The door suddenly flew open and a familiar man bent down to grab him by the shoulders.

"Thank heavens you're all right!"

"Franklin?"

"I'd despaired of finding you, lad." A thick lock of dark hair fell down over the valet's forehead as he hauled Meri to his feet. "Come along."

The man took him by the hand and pulled him into the hallway, but after being folded for so long, Meri's legs didn't want to work properly.

"I can't walk!"

Without hesitation, Franklin threw him over one shoulder and carried him down the stairs. As they darted out the front door, they passed a line of men passing buckets of water from the pond nearby in a futile attempt to extinguish the blaze. A crowd of female servants were huddled on the lawn, haphazardly clothed in whatever they could grab when the bell sounded. Although it was the dead of night, they were illuminated by the eerie, flickering glow coming from the fire. Some of the ladies resembled ghosts, clad as they were in their white shifts along with their long, unbound tresses.

Franklin lowered Meri to the ground. "Where is your mother?"

His face crumpled. "She's dead. Father is dead, too."

"How do you know that?"

"I saw them. I saw their bodies."

The valet staggered backward for several moments, as if he'd been struck full across the face. Finally, his gaze settled on Meri once more.

"I'll be right back."

Meri caught his sleeve. "Don't go into the house!"

Franklin pulled away. "I must save your future."

The valet disappeared into the cavernous, smoke-filled structure and Meri was forced to hobble across the gravel courtyard in his bare feet. He'd taken only a few painful steps before the head coachman hastened over to lift him up.

"I've got ye, Master Meriweather. Are ye injured?"

"My chest and my eyes hurt, Mr. Holcroft, but my mother and father..." Meri trailed off and burst into tears.

The elderly coachman gave him a comforting hug. "Don't ye fret none, lad. Yer parents are around here somewhere. Until they're found, me and Mrs. Holcroft will take care of ye."

He pulled one of the stable boys from the bucket line. "Bert! Take Master Meriweather over to the pump so he can wash up, and then bring him to Mrs. Holcroft. I've got to see where Mr. Franklin's gone off to before he gets himself killed."

The boy's bright gaze rested on Meri. "Yes, sir."

"And once you've done that, saddle a horse and go fetch the surgeon. I daresay we're going to have need of his services tonight."

"Right away, sir."

Bert led Meri to the pump and worked the handle until a stream of water spewed forth. Although the liquid was shockingly cold, Meri was glad for the chance to rinse the smoke and ash from his face and hair.

He straightened afterward, sputtering and wiping moisture from his eyes.

"Here." Bert gave him a handkerchief. "It's not fancy, but it's the best I got."

Meri tried to remember his manners. "Thank you, Mr. Bert."

"It's just Bert."

After Meri dabbed his face as best he could, he gave the handkerchief back. As the stable boy stuffed the damp square into his pocket, his expression was full of pity.

"Come along, let's get you to Mrs. Holcroft so I'm free to fetch the surgeon."

"I can find my way." Meri glanced over his shoulder and gulped. The magnificent house he'd always called home was spewing forth heat and smoke. "I think you'd best hurry."

WITH FRANKLIN AT HIS SIDE, Meri drove the gig away from Phoenix Downs. "Do you have enough money with you? I'll give you a little more once we're at the station."

The older man chuckled. "You sound like a worried hen."

"I *am* worried. You've not gone off on your own for more than a few days since I can remember, much less in a medical crisis."

Franklin glanced at him. "I expect that's the problem. It's time for both of us to shake things up a bit to see how they sort out." He paused. "You had another nightmare last night."

"What makes you say that?"

"The dark circles under your eyes."

"I can't fool you." Meri frowned. "Do you ever regret what you did for me?"

"My only regret was in not dodging that falling beam. I should have been more careful, but I was distracted by the situation."

The man lapsed into a thoughtful silence. As Meri drove past Robbins Nest, Franklin stirred.

"Stop!"

"What's wrong?" Meri pulled back on the reins. "Did you forget something?"

"Yes. Give me a moment, will you?"

The man climbed down from the rig, straightened his jacket, and marched up the walkway to the front door of the cottage. Meri watched, curious as to what was about to unfold. When Mrs. Gallagher answered the door, Franklin doffed his bowler, sketched a bow, and said something Meri couldn't hear. Whatever it was made the housekeeper smile and bat her eyes. The man was forty-five if he was a day, yet he flirted as if he were in his prime. The couple chatted for a very short while before Franklin bowed again and returned to the gig. Meri gave the reins a snap and they were on their way into Stroud once more.

"Well done." Meri slid his friend an approving glance. "What did you say to the lady, if you don't mind my asking?"

"I mentioned we were neighbors and I wanted to introduce myself." A slight smile lifted the corners of his mouth. "Mrs. Gallagher seemed pleased to make my acquaintance. When I told her I'm off to visit my sister for a few days, she invited me to correspond."

Meri's eyebrows rose. "That's fast work."

Franklin tugged on the rim of his bowler. "I'm nothing if not efficient."

A chuckle escaped Meri's lips. "Ever the wit, you are." His smile faded. "I hope you have a nice visit with your sister and let me know as soon as you have news. I shan't rest until you do."

"The physician might not be able to fit me in for a few days, so don't expect to hear from me right off." He cleared his throat. "Now that I set a good example for you with Mrs. Gallagher, I hope you'll follow it."

Meri forced a jocular note to his reply. "You think I need to follow your lead where Miss Ladd is concerned?"

"Of course. It's always good to learn from the best."

ALTHOUGH IT WASN'T the proper time of year to prune roses, Clare removed several obviously dead canes to good effect. She'd just settled down to weed when she heard a rig pull into her drive. Moments later, Meri appeared around back with a box of groceries. The sight of him sent a pleasurable tingle across her entire body.

"Hello!" She stripped off her gloves and hastened to open the kitchen door for him. "Pressed into service once more?"

His smile was strangely muted. "I volunteered again." He stepped into the unoccupied kitchen and lowered the box onto the counter. "Where's Mrs. Gallagher?"

"Cleaning upstairs. Dinah's with her, chasing the dust mop. My housekeeper is in quite a good mood since Mr. Franklin stopped by yesterday. Considering her congenial nature, that's saying something."

Even as Meri chuckled in response, Clare could see a cloud over his head. Was he that troubled about the article in the newspaper, or did he have other problems on his mind?

"Erm...did you happen to read the paper the day before yesterday? It mentioned your purchase of *Alice*."

He winced. "I did. I confess, I was rather put out."

She felt her cheeks begin to burn and moved to unpack the groceries. To be linked to her romantically would likely be distressing to any eligible gentleman.

"I comprehend your feelings completely. I was mortified as well until I realized nobody would read the silly article." She shrugged. "I found the reporter's remarks about me to be amusing, but I don't intend to give it another thought."

"I wasn't amused."

"I can see that." She bit her lip. "Perhaps it's my fault. Mr. Watson stopped by to have a chat with me, and discovered my middle name is Alice. He may have used that fact to add a salacious edge to an otherwise dry story, but I hope you don't think I encouraged him."

His eyebrows drew together. "I didn't blame you whatsoever. Forgive me if I made it seem otherwise."

"You didn't." The box was empty, so she returned it to Meri. "We shall go on as before and soon it will be forgotten."

He grasped the crate with one hand. "You've quite the most marvelous ability to deal with life's challenges with aplomb." For the first time since he arrived, a genuine smile emerged. "Speaking of challenges, I have your new bicycle on the back of my rig."

She gasped. "It's here? Show me."

He opened the door and made a sweeping gesture with the crate. "After you."

Heedless of propriety, Clare picked up her skirts and ran outside. Two bicycles were tied onto the back of Meri's dog cart —one designed for a lady and the other for a man. As he joined her, she gave him a quizzical glance.

"To whom are you delivering the other bicycle?"

"Myself. I was thinking we could learn to ride together."

"You're joking! When?"

"No time like the present."

She grimaced. "Oh, I'm bound to make a dreadful fool of myself!"

"So am I." He winked. "'What fools these mortals be!'"

"What fools, indeed." She regarded him. "All right, then, if you'll unload our new contraptions, I'll go change into my riding costume."

"A harder bargain was never driven."

Clare dashed into the house, suddenly filled with a sense of joy. Not only would she learn to ride, but she'd have a friend with whom to ride. At that moment, she wouldn't have had a dozen blue and silver filigreed carriages for anything in the world.

THE INVITATION

*L*ady Yates gave Sterling and Lottie a serene glance. "Well I know your time in Kingscote was well spent because of the pretty things you had delivered. But did you enjoy Bath?"

Sterling nodded. "Oh, yes, the town is always great fun."

Dora smiled. "Bath is almost my favorite place other than London. Sterling, do you remember all the occasions you escorted me to the matinée when I was younger?"

He chuckled. "Oh, yes. I enjoyed that just as much as you did, I think."

"I adored Sydney Gardens, personally, but two days isn't long enough to see much of anything." From her perch on a sofa, Lottie leaned forward to admire her new spinning wheel. "I would have liked to attend the theater while we were there, but we only visited a few stuffy museums instead."

Sterling frowned. "But you knew it would only be a quick jaunt, dearest. I thought you wanted to visit London before the Season is over?"

The young woman brightened. "Oh, yes, of course! We must bring Nero and my new phaeton, so all eyes will be on us."

Lord Yates's eyes flickered toward his wife. "Er...Lottie and Dora, will you excuse us for a little while? Delphine and I would like to have a word with Sterling."

Dora seemed relieved to be excused. "Yes, indeed. I've letters to write."

She hastened from the drawing room. Lottie followed more slowly, with a sulky expression on her face. As soon as she disappeared from view, Lord Yates nodded to Sterling.

"Close the door, lad."

Sterling did as he was asked and came to sit down in a chair across from his mother. He gave his parents a wary glance.

"I sense some sort of scolding coming just around the corner."

His father maintained an impassive expression. "Since you've been traveling, I take it you didn't see the London article mentioning you at the Greeley estate auction?"

"No, I only had access to the *Bath Chronicle* over breakfast at the hotel." Sterling's eyebrows drew together. "Why would anyone make mention of me in the paper?"

Lady Yates regarded him. "The article details your argument with Clare's neighbor, Mr. Holcroft."

He recoiled. "That conversation was private!"

"No longer. Everyone must be aware of it by now." Lady Yates retrieved a folded newspaper from a writing desk next to the window and dropped it into his lap.

Sterling read the article, clearly aghast, then glanced up with a grimace. "Keep this article away from Lottie. She's jealous enough of Clare as it is."

Lady Yates frowned. "I'm not certain that Lottie is temperamentally suited to take anything in stride yet."

Lord Yates crossed over to the bar cart, to pour himself a short glass of port. "I imagine she'll mature...especially if the proper pressure is brought to bear."

Sterling made a sound of exasperation. "This is all exceedingly stupid. Lottie wanted the painting desperately. After Mr. Holcroft won the bid, he refused to sell it to me out of some sort of loyalty to Miss Ladd. I call that boorish behavior, but one can't expect anything more from the owner of a common livery stable."

His father gritted his teeth. "Never mind Mr. Holcroft. You were prepared to pay one hundred forty pounds for a painting above and beyond what you'd already spent on a horse and carriage?"

"Not to mention other items." Lady Yates gave the spinning wheel a pointed glance. "Dearest, it would behoove you to take your wife in hand."

Lord Yates nodded in agreement. "Furthermore, the newspaper article makes it seem as if you're unhappily married."

"I am, rather." He scowled. "I-I was trapped into it."

"Come now, Sterling!" Lady Yates bristled. "You had a choice before you took up with Lottie and one could argue that you chose wrongly. Nevertheless, she is your wife now, and I cannot permit you to speak poorly of her."

Sterling averted his eyes. "You're right, of course."

Lord Yates sighed. "Your mother and I have been discussing what's best to be done going forward. I've friends in the banking industry who would be willing to give you a position. You'll have to leave England for a few years, but I believe the change will be especially beneficial for Lottie."

"You want me to work?" Sterling's nose crinkled, as if he'd smelled something unpleasant. "I'm the son of a baron! Why would you have me go into trade?"

"Why indeed?" Lady Yates rolled her eyes. "You've been back in England for only a few weeks, and already you've exceeded your allowance several times over."

"But Lottie needs things! She was raised with very little."

"Be that as it may, your mother and I believe the discipline of living on a salary would better prepare you to properly manage the estate when I'm gone." He exchanged a brief glance with Lady Yates. "I've written you a letter of introduction. You'll depart for New York on the first of September."

"*New York?*" Sterling's lips parted in shock. "How will I get Lottie to agree to that?"

"You're a future baron, lad." Lord Yates lifted one eyebrow. "You'll manage."

"This is your influence, isn't it?" Sterling's level gaze rested on Lady Yates. "You're not my mother—not really—and I can't help thinking you'll enjoy my absence."

At that, Lady Yates grew pale, and her lips began to tremble. "Oh, Sterling."

Lord Yates bristled, swelling up like an angry cat. "How dare you! Delphine has always treated you as if you were her own flesh and blood."

His wife had tears in her eyes. "I adore you, Sterling. I would have thought you knew that by now."

A myriad of expressions crossed his face, as if he were struggling with himself. "I-I do. Forgive me. I don't know what I'm saying."

He strode from the room with the newspaper crushed in his fist.

Lord Yates pulled his wife into a comforting embrace. "I'm sorry for Sterling's behavior. He's not completely happy with Lottie, but he has no right to abuse you as a result."

She sighed. "I'm beginning to feel like a fairy-tale stepmother by sending him away. Tell me we're doing the proper thing, Edwin."

"I've no doubt of it."

"Nevertheless, I feel cruel."

"You're not." Lord Yates pressed a tender kiss to her forehead. "We must turn our attention to getting Dora properly wed."

Lady Yates relaxed into his arms. "Family is very important

to me. As an only child, I've no relatives but you and the children."

"Hopefully, we'll have grandchildren soon. That should make up for everything."

~

Lottie's mouth was compressed into a thin line as she glared at her husband. "Why don't you stand up to your parents? You're a future baron, for mercy's sake!"

"Why does everyone continually remind me of that?" Sterling spread his hands expressively. "You must be reasonable, dearest! I've very little money of my own, and no way to support you unless I do what they ask. We must think of New York as an adventure."

He moved over to where she was perched on the bed and attempted to caress her cheek with his fingertips, but she jerked her head away.

"I can't think of anything less appealing than sailing across the Atlantic Ocean to live amongst Americans. Do they have any culture at all?"

"I'm informed there's a great deal of wealth in New York City. Through my father's connections at the bank, we'll have the opportunity to socialize with the best of society."

She frowned. "Perhaps so, but this is absurd nevertheless. We must leave England just because I spent a little money? I can only assume there's something else you're not telling me."

Sterling pursed his lips. "Well…a bit of bad publicity about the auction cast me in a poor light."

Her eyes gleamed. "You were in the newspaper? I want to read the article!"

"You won't like it."

When he produced a crumpled square of newsprint from his pocket, Lottie snatched it from his hand. She bent over the article with avid interest, but moments later her expression registered disappointment.

"Why isn't my name mentioned? You were attempting to purchase the painting for *me*, not Clare Ladd. The reporter got it all wrong." She studied the article once more. "I should write Mr. Herbert Watson a letter to tell him so."

Sterling grimaced. "No, dearest, I beg you to leave it be! My mother and father are aghast at the publicity as it is."

Lottie pouted. "But it's not fair! Anyone reading this article would think Clare was some sort of outstanding beauty, when nothing could be further from the truth."

"I forbid you from contacting that reporter." He extended his hand. "Give me the newspaper so I can burn it."

A slow smile curved her lips as she put the paper behind her back. "Come and take it, dearest." She glanced at him from underneath her lashes. "If you can."

A spark of desire lit his gaze. "You minx."

In the romantic clinch that followed, Lottie surreptitiously dropped the newspaper to the floor and nudged it out of view under the bed.

IN THE CARRIAGE HOUSE APARTMENT, Meri sat limp as elderly Mrs. Holcroft stripped him of his smoke-permeated night shirt and gave him one of her husband's old flannel ones instead.

A woman appeared in the doorway, clad in her nightdress and wrapper. As usual, her mousy brown hair was pulled into a low bun at the nape of her neck.

Her cool gaze fell to Meri. "I see the young master has survived."

Mrs. Holcroft scowled. "Aye, no thanks to you, Miss Lapin. Why did you leave the poor lamb behind?"

The woman bristled. "He wasn't in his bed! What would you have me do, wait around until I was burned to a crisp like his parents?"

Mrs. Holcroft seemingly swelled with umbrage. "Who says they're burned to a crisp? They might be wandering around the estate in a daze, and here you are scaring this poor lad out of his wits."

Miss Lapin sniffed. "Nobody's seen hide nor hair of Lord and Lady Pallinger. They're gone all right." The nanny's eyes narrowed. "I'm not staying around here to get blamed for anything. Plenty of other jobs to be had."

She turned on the heel of her high button boot and fled.

"Good riddance to her," Mrs. Holcroft muttered. "Miss Lapin was always prim and proper when your mother was around, but she was probably in her cups when the fire started." She patted Meri's cheek. "Maybe she's wrong about your parents, lad. There's a great deal of confusion just now."

Meri hung his head. "She's not wrong. I saw—"

The crowd of servants on the lawn cried out as a great roaring crash sounded. Mrs. Holcroft gazed out the window and made a tsking noise with her tongue.

"Part of the roof caved in, and the rest is sure to follow."

Seized with panic, Meri scrambled to his feet. "Mr. Holcroft and Franklin are inside!"

"Surely not!" The woman grew pale and gripped the windowsill as she peered through the windowpane. "Wait...they're coming this way. Mr. Holcroft is helping Mr. Franklin across the lawn, but from the way the man's holding his arm, I think he's hurt."

"Bert's gone to fetch a surgeon." Tears began to flow anew. "I told him to hurry."

A few minutes later, Mr. Holcroft and Franklin staggered into the apartment. The coachman had a carved mahogany box under one of his arms, and he was supporting the valet with his other arm.

"Let me take that." Mrs. Holcroft took the box from her husband. "You help Mr. Franklin."

Mr. Holcroft assisted Franklin into the nearest chair. The man's handsome face was contorted with pain and his breathing was labored. Mrs. Holcroft glanced down and flinched.

"Merciful heavens. I'll get the laudanum."

"No!" Franklin's voice was hoarse. "No laudanum."

When Meri saw the condition of the man's injured left hand, he grew woozy and his stomach contracted. He rushed from the apartment and leaned over the railing, retching over and over again until his stomach was empty...

Meri rolled from his bed and lunged for the chamber pot, but as he drew air into his lungs, he managed to avoid vomiting. He wiped away prickling perspiration from his brow, and closed his eyes, trying to clear his mind of the lingering horror.

Franklin's absence was playing havoc with his equanimity. The man had written to say he'd arrived in London, but that was all. Until Meri could assure himself of his friend's continuing good health, it wasn't likely he'd enjoy an entire night's rest. The only time his anxiety eased was when he was in Clare's company. Fortunately, she lived next door and he could visit her at a moment's notice. Hopefully, he wasn't making a nuisance of himself.

CLAD IN HER NIGHTGOWN, Clare threw open her bedroom window and leaned out to enjoy the morning air. As she surveyed her garden and the meadow beyond, she gave a happy sigh. Dinah—who was growing larger by the day—was running up and down the pathways, chasing insects. Her rose garden was already looking far tidier and vibrant. Next spring, she would prune the bushes more properly and wait for the roses to bloom. With Mrs. Gallagher's recommendation, she'd hired a gardener to tend the grounds and trim the hedges. Robbins Nest no longer appeared abandoned and was even beginning to display a bit of charm.

One unfortunate result of the tall grass having been cut, however, was her direct view of the diminished stream.

Although she yearned to hear and see the water flowing past, neither she nor Meri seemed eager to broach the topic of the dam. Should she press the issue? The two of them had been getting along so very well, she was reluctant to spoil things.

A vague sense of unease made her smile slip.

Why was she attempting to justify her inaction? A modern, independent woman wouldn't allow herself to be swayed by sentiment. She ought to confront Meri, tell him she'd definitely decided not to sell her property, and press him to remove the dam. And yet because of her increasing regard for the man, she'd done nothing.

She sat down to brush her hair. As she gazed at her reflection in the mirror, she was forced to admit she admired Meri far more than she'd ever admired Sterling. Furthermore, to her pleasurable and unanticipated delight, her entire body felt far more alive when she was with him. Such heated sensations and desires had been foreign to her until now, but she was beginning to realize how consuming a passionate and loving romance could be.

For a few long moments she closed her eyes, the better to remember the look of Meri's muscled torso when he was chopping wood. A delicate shudder came over her and she gave a deep sigh of appreciation. It was unlikely she'd ever view him in *dishabille* again, but the sight had provided a veritable banquet for her imagination. In fact, she would enjoy seeing him that way every night. Was it so very wicked to picture herself as his bride? No, her fantasies weren't shameful, but wild imaginings were not reality, and only a schoolgirl would confuse the two. Meri had given her no indication beyond their occasional flirtations that he had marriage on his mind.

Even though their time together had been agreeable, she could put off asserting her riparian rights no longer. If her neighbor grew cold and distant as a result, he wasn't truly a friend. She would just have to pick the right moment and say what was on her mind. After all, hadn't Meri said he appreciated her lack of guile? Still, even as she knew what had to be done, her resolve was weak.

After she dressed and went down to breakfast, she found the morning post included an invitation to Dora's upcoming birthday party, along with a personal note from the baroness.

Dearest Clare,

We're all counting on you to attend Dora's eighteenth birthday party at Bramble Manor. I hope it wasn't too forward of me, but I took the liberty of sending an invitation to your neighbor, Mr. Holcroft. Since Sterling and Lottie will be attending, I was hoping the presence of your own special friend might set your mind at ease. The occasion should be delightful fun.

Sincerely,

Delphine Yates

Clare wasn't sure whether she should be overjoyed or appalled to learn Lady Yates had invited Meri to the party. What if her neighbor assumed the invitation had been sent at her request in order to draw him in?

She gave herself a shake and reached for her tea. Why should she be overly concerned about Meri's erroneous assumptions? If he felt uncomfortable with the idea of attending any social function, he was a grown man and could certainly decline the invitation. On the other hand, it would be marvelous if he accepted. She could introduce Meri to her family and friends, even as Sterling and Lottie scowled in the background. Despite his admittedly lowly rank, no man at the party could possibly compare to Mr. Meriweather Holcroft in looks and bearing. With such an escort by her side, she needn't endure anyone's pity or scorn.

With a sigh, Clare tossed the invitation aside. Since Meri had acknowledged his mortification at being linked to her romantically, her daydream was the silliest of fancies. Nevertheless, the notion of attending the party in all her spinster glory was too depressing for words. The image of a gloating Lottie flashed before her eyes and made her push her bowl away. Nobody would blame her if she declined the invitation—and that's exactly what she intended to do.

~

STILL UNSETTLED FROM HIS NIGHTMARES, Meri could only manage tea and toast for breakfast. He had a tray brought to the table on the back patio, where he had a direct view to his pond. To a lesser extent, he could catch glimpses of Robbins Nest through the trees. A faint line of smoke rising from the cottage chimney told him the residents therein were astir, and that knowledge made him feel a little less lonely.

Although he wasn't ordinarily prone to building castles in the air, he took a few moments to picture Clare as his wife. They would breakfast together here on the patio, where she would sit close enough for him to enjoy the wonderful fragrance of her skin and hair. He would lean closer to nuzzle her cheek until she turned her head and allowed him to claim her lips. And if he managed to coax a blush to her face with his kisses and meaningful glances, he would thereafter take her by the hand and lead her to their bedchamber to express his ardor in a more physical and passionate manner...

Meri wrenched his thoughts away from that particularly slippery slope, and instead fixed his attention on the puffy white clouds dotting the morning sky overhead. He might as well stare at the sky the whole day long than to yearn for things he couldn't have.

The maid brought him the morning post, but the welcome distraction slid into bewilderment when he spotted an envelope from Lord and Lady Yates on the salver. The missive was so out of place, Meri double checked the addressee to make sure it hadn't been delivered to him by accident. Inside the envelope, he was puzzled to discover an invitation to their daughter's birthday party. Why would the Yates want him to attend any social function at Bramble Manor, especially after his unpleasant altercation with Sterling?

Polly reappeared with another envelope. "Excuse me, sir, but the postman forgot to deliver this with the others."

"Thank you."

His stomach tightened as he stared at the familiar writing, but he was obliged to wait until the maid was out of sight before reading the letter. The message therein was to the point, and after he read it, he squeezed his eyes shut against the pain.

PICNIC

Clare brought an armful of freshly trimmed and fragrant blooms to her room and was arranging them in a vase when Mrs. Gallagher appeared in the doorway.

"Miss Ladd, ye've a visitor. Mr. Holcroft has come to call."

Clare's stomach lifted and her pulse began to race. "I'll be down in a moment."

She steeled her resolve and practiced aloud what she'd been meaning to tell him about his offer.

"I'm not selling my property, Meri, and it's past time for you to remove your dam."

Mrs. Gallagher stuck her head in the doorway. "Excuse me, Miss Ladd, but I was walking away and didn't quite hear ye."

Feeling foolish, she shook her head. "No...I was talking to myself I'm afraid."

The housekeeper grinned. "I do that daily, so I do."

Mrs. Gallagher left, and after Clare checked her hair in the vanity mirror, she descended the stairs. Meri was sitting on the carpet in the parlor, playing with Dinah.

"Hello." Clare gave the puppy a rueful glance. "I'm not certain Dinah doesn't prefer your company to mine."

"She has good taste in gentlemen, that's all." He rolled to his feet. "I came to carry you off to a luncheon picnic—with your willing consent, of course."

"Oh?" Her eyebrows rose. "Do we walk or ride our bicycles?"

"It's just across the stream next to my pond, so walking will do." He glanced down at Dinah. "The puppy told me she'd like to come, and one ought not argue with pups. They have the strength of their convictions."

His last quip reminded her again of what she meant to say. "So should we all." She cleared her throat. "Meri, I've something to tell you. I—"

"If you wait until we reach the picnic, I promise to pay rapt attention to every word."

His pleading expression was so boyish and sincere, she could only smile. "All right. Let me speak with Mrs. Gallagher and then I'll fetch my hat."

CLARE AND MERI ate their picnic sitting on a blanket in the shadow of a towering yew bush. Afterward, he sent a kite aloft, pressed the spool into Clare's hand, and sank down next to her. The kite tugged on her arm, but even more powerful was the delicious surge of heat she felt at the man's nearness. To avoid giving her feelings away, she focused her attention on the flying object overhead.

"I haven't flown one of these since I was very little." Her eyes flickered toward him. "It's amazing how kites stay aloft, just with a bit of breeze."

"Perhaps it's magic." He winked.

"Indeed, perhaps we're in Wonderland after all."

Dinah ran across the manicured lawn as fast as her legs would carry her, barking at nothing in particular. Nearby, the pond's smooth surface reflected the sky, making the water appear to be full of marshmallow clouds.

Meri removed his spectacles and set them aside. "Did you get enough to eat?"

"You must be joking. I believe I ate more than you did."

"Not true at all, but I'm glad you enjoyed the food." He shrugged his jacket off and hung it on a yew branch. "I meant to ask you about the invitation I received this morning from the Yates."

She felt warmth creeping across her face. "For Dora's birthday party, yes. I received an invitation this morning as well."

"I was a bit taken aback by it, to be honest. Sterling Yates and I didn't get along when last we met, and I've no idea why the Yates would welcome my presence in their home."

"From what I gather, Lady Yates must have seen that newspaper article and made an erroneous assumption about our relationship. You needn't accept if you'd rather not. In fact, I'm planning to decline."

"Might I know why?"

"For the same reason I left High Wycombe in the first place." She shrugged. "After I was jilted, my friends and family felt sorry for me. I didn't relish being the object of pity, and nothing has changed."

He frowned. "Perhaps if you had the proper escort, you'd be more inclined to accept." He met her gaze. "A gentleman who needn't earn his own living, for example."

Her lips parted in astonishment. "No…that's not it at all! I'd be pleased and proud to have you escort me anywhere, Meri. If you must know, I didn't think you'd want to attend, and I refuse to go alone."

"So you wouldn't be ashamed of me?"

"Not in the slightest. I've no doubt I would be the envy of every woman there."

His eyes seemed lit from within. "In that case, I insist on escorting you. And in case you were wondering, I *do* own a set of evening clothes."

"I never had any doubt of it."

"It's settled then." Meri lay down on the blanket and closed his eyes. "Thank you for being here, Alice. I confess, I've not been this relaxed in a long while."

"It's a very peaceful place."

"I think it's the pleasant company."

Meri stirred slightly when Dinah trotted over and curled up against his body, but thereafter his breathing grew deep and regular. Clare slowly reeled the kite in, set it aside, and watched as her neighbor slept. Her gaze roamed from his ruggedly handsome features, across his broad chest, and then down his muscled arms. His hands were rough, calloused, and far from those of a gentleman, yet she found them more attractive than Sterling's soft, white ones. His masculinity, when coupled with his obvious intelligence, education, and wit, was irresistible. Meri fancied her physically, she suspected, but his appreciation for her charms was useless unless he proposed. Unlike Lottie Yates, she'd no interest in dragging a man to the altar with seduction and lies.

Nearby, the afternoon breeze sent ripples across the serene pond, drawing her attention toward the stream. Perhaps for the sake of neighborly relations, she should just capitulate on the dam. If Meri had befriended her with that as his goal, he'd succeeded admirably. Although her romantic affections were unrequited, the extraordinary way he made her feel when they were together was worth something to her...and the cost just might be the stream. Still, she'd not known the man very long, and perhaps she oughtn't give up hope he might propose someday. Yes, she'd given her heart away far too easily, and he was obviously not equally incautious. Should his feelings for her ever deepen, however, he would be a man worth waiting for.

As the minutes passed, Meri's sleep became increasingly restless. He flinched and groaned—as if he were having a terrible dream that was worsening by the moment. She leaned forward to listen as he whispered, "I'm sorry," over and over again. Although she called his name, he continued thrashing so hard that Dinah bolted from his side. What sort of ghastly nightmare had him in its grip?

~

AT THE INQUEST, Meri swore on the Bible to tell the truth. As he finished with the oath, perspiration began to prickle across his forehead. He desperately wanted to lie and say he hadn't seen anything, but if he did, he'd burn in Hades forevermore.

The magistrate, Mr. Leeds, frowned at him. "What did you see, if anything, the night of the fire?"

"Well, er, I didn't really..." His mother's face swam in front of his eyes. She was in Heaven right now, listening, and if he didn't tell the truth, she'd be terribly sad. "I was awakened by a loud noise, but I couldn't find my nanny. So I went to my parents' room, where I—"

Tears filled his eyes and he hated himself for it. Hadn't his father always told him that big boys don't cry? Meri swallowed hard and forced himself to keep talking.

"Mother was lying on the bed and her spectacles were on the floor. My father was sprawled on the carpet with a pistol in his hand. His h-head was half gone, and it looked like he'd knocked over a lantern when he shot himself because the wallpaper and bedclothes were on fire. I-I ran and hid."

Everyone in the courtroom gasped. His grandmother slumped in her seat, and his grandfather enveloped her in his arms. Aunt Dee removed her spectacles and buried her face in her hands.

Meri gave the periwigged judge a mortified glance. "I thought I'm supposed to tell the truth?"

"You've done nothing wrong." The judge sighed and pressed the

bridge of his nose with his thumb and forefinger for a moment before fixing Meri once more with his gaze. "In your opinion, what had gone on just before you entered the room?"

"My father killed my mother and then himself. I think the fire was an accident."

A keening cry was torn from Meri's grandmother's throat. His eyes welled up as he watched the older woman suffer.

"I'm sorry, Grandmother." He gulped. "Don't cry."

"Get thee behind me, spawn of Satan!" The woman glared at him as she shot to her feet. "You're the very picture of your murdering father and the sight of you makes my skin crawl."

She fled the courtroom, past reporters who were scribbling on scraps of paper with pencils. Aunt Dee wavered for a moment before following in her mother's footsteps. Although his grandfather remained, he wouldn't meet Meri's gaze.

"I'm sorry." Meri drew his sleeve across his wet face. "Grandfather, please don't be mad at me. I'm sorry."

The judge cleared his throat. "Some provision must be made for the boy, Mr. Fortescue. He'll require a legal guardian, a place to live, and proper management of his estate."

Meri's grandfather shook his head. "Under the circumstances, you see it's impossible. Every time we look at him, we'll be reminded of Primrose's murder."

Mr. Leeds peered at Mr. Fortescue. "You're the child's only living relatives!"

"No." The older man stood. "You'll have to make other arrangements."

Meri couldn't stop shaking. Before now, everyone had taken delight in his uncanny resemblance to his father. Now, he was saddled with the man's guilt.

"I'm sorry, Grandfather! I'm sorry!"

Mr. Fortescue left the courtroom without a backward glance, and Meri's apologies fell on deaf ears...

~

CLARE STROKED Meri's cheek with her bare fingertips and then shook him gently by the shoulders.

"Wake up."

"Alice?" He came to consciousness with a start, seemingly confused. "What's happening?"

"You were having a horrible dream."

Meri drew in a deep, shuddering breath. "Indeed, I was."

He reached for her hand, brushing his lips against the soft white skin of her palm. The gesture sent a delicious shaft of heat to her core and made her pulse race. Too soon, he released her and sat up.

"Thank you for waking me. I can't believe I fell asleep." He drew the sleeve of his shirt across his face. "My apologies, Alice. To be honest, I haven't slept very well since Franklin left. His health has me terribly concerned."

She met his gaze. "Is he ill?"

"Yes. He went to London to consult a physician, and I finally heard from him this morning." He gulped. "Franklin believes his condition is quite serious, so he's staying for more tests."

"How dreadful!"

"I-I honestly don't know how I'll manage without him. Franklin has sacrificed everything for me." He bowed his head.

Meri expression was so very vulnerable, she yearned to comfort him somehow. "Is there anything I can do?"

"That's what I asked him before he left. Unfortunately, I can't provide the one thing he wants. He wishes to see me settled before he dies, but I cannot marry. Please don't ask why."

Clare's heart sank at the realization her love was unrequited for an immutable reason. Nevertheless, Meri was helping her avoid humiliation by providing her an escort to the Yateses' party. The least she could do would be to return the favor.

"Tell Mr. Franklin we are engaged."

His eyes widened. "You'd have me deceive him?"

"In this case, would a small act of deception be a kindness? Just say our engagement is a secret until we can obtain my father's approval." She shrugged. "My father is quite stubborn, so our engagement could carry on for years."

He searched her face. "Alice, you'd truly do that for me?"

Clare gave him a tremulous smile. "Why not? Nobody else will have to know."

"You're the dearest, sweetest, kindest woman I've ever met." He leaned forward to press a kiss to her cheek. "I'll take down the dam."

"No, don't do that."

"Why not? I'm glad to."

"I haven't decided yet whether or not to sell my property, so destroying the dam may be precipitous."

Clearly he thought she was teasing, because he laughed. "The purchase offer will remain open, of course, but I hope you don't accept. I want to have you as my wonderful neighbor forever."

She averted her gaze. "We'll see. For now, however, I must go compose a reply to Lady Yates. I'll also send a letter to my mother, to let her know my plans."

Even as she whistled for Dinah, she knew the decision to sell had already been made for her. After Franklin passed away, she'd sign the offer and pack her things. Although she and Meri might always be friends, they could never be lovers—and she would never be satisfied with that arrangement.

NIGHTTIME PRESSED against the window panes of Meri's study as he blotted the ink on his letter to Lady Yates and readied it for the post the following morning. Before he began his reply to Franklin's letter, he reached for his snifter of brandy and allowed the strong drink to stiffen his resolve. Since childhood, he'd made it a habit to avoid deception, so composing a false-hood was difficult. Nevertheless, if an innocent ruse gave his old friend any measure of comfort, he would gladly comply.

Dear Franklin,

I confess your news was not what I'd hoped for, but perhaps your medical tests will provide more cheerful answers. As for me, I have plans of my own which hopefully will set your heart at ease. I've taken your advice and asked Clare to marry me. Until Sir Andrew Ladd gives me permission to marry his daughter, however, I must ask you to keep our engagement in the strictest confidence. The delay bothers me only a little because I have yet to fully share with my beautiful fiancée the nature of my colorful family tree. The least written about it here, the better, since you already know to what I'm referring.

I'm to travel to High Wycombe in a se'enight, to meet Clare's relations as well as attend a birthday party for The Honorable Eudora Yates. Out of respect for Clare, Sterling Yates and I must find a way to get along, so any sage advice will be welcome.

Please do continue to keep me apprised of your health or I will show up at your sister's door at the worst possible moment and embarrass you horribly until you tell me what I want to know.

Faithfully Yours,

Meri

As he read over the letter, the words *beautiful fiancée* made the breath catch in his throat. What wouldn't he give to turn the lie into reality? He sat back in his chair and drank the rest of his brandy, wishing he could find the key to unlock his living prison. If he closed his eyes and tried to examine the possibilities like he might study a chessboard, perhaps a novel solution would present itself. For example, what consequences would ensue if he told Clare who he really was?

She might not mind. In fact, her esteem for him might be so strong, she would berate him for not having told her sooner. Although he had no outward proof she cared for him in that way, she had regard enough to help him fulfill a dying man's wish, didn't she? If she returned his esteem, he would ask her to marry him in earnest and make her his bride as soon as could be arranged. His loneliness would be forevermore assuaged, and he would devote himself to making his wife feel treasured, loved, and happy. His past would fade into a distant memory, and their future together would be rosy and bright.

On the other hand, after Meri disclosed he was the son of an infamous monster, Clare might recoil in horror. She would be all politeness, of course, disclaiming any prejudice about his past, and then take her leave with undue haste. His offer to purchase her property would show up on his doorstep, signed, and a moving wagon would be parked in her driveway the same day. Indeed, how could she ever spend time in his company without wondering if his father's crime had been due to a madness that ran in the family? Any argument, however minor, might spark fear in her eyes as she wondered if he possessed hidden murderous tendencies. Meri opened his eyes and shook his head in despair. His king was checkmated and there was no way to win.

His temples were throbbing as he unlocked the deep bottom drawer of his desk and lifted out the slightly charred mahogany box containing the items Franklin had paid so dearly to save. He opened the lid to reveal a family seal, a large family Bible, and a crest signet ring. For the first time in his life, Meri slid the ring onto his finger…and was taken aback by how well it fit.

Several yellowed newspaper clippings had been tucked into the Bible, like bookmarks. Their lurid headlines regarding Barnabas the Butcher made Meri's skin crawl, so he ignored them in favor of the book itself. As he ran a fingertip down the pages in which generations of births, deaths, and marriages had been recorded, he discovered the date his father and mother had died was inscribed therein, in Franklin's handwriting. The fellow had always paid scrupulous attention to such details.

Although Meri was genuinely thankful to have proof of his

heritage, he could never resume his rightful place as a peer. First and foremost, he possessed little desire to carry on the name of Pallinger. Rejection by his extended family had made his identity even more unpalatable. After the inquest debacle, the Fortescues hadn't shown the slightest interest in his wellbeing. Albeit reluctantly, the magistrate had made Meri's living arrangements with the Holcrofts—and Franklin's guardianship—permanent. Meri had used the Holcroft name at school, and pretended he was the coachman's grandson. The Holcrofts had long since passed away, but at least he still had Franklin... for now.

He returned the ring to the mahogany box and picked up a small cloth bag containing a distinctive gold locket. Once opened, the name *Primrose Fortescue Pallinger* was inscribed on the left and a woven lock of golden hair with a strawberry glint filled the right side. The intimate memento had always made him feel a little more connected to his mother. Although he resembled his father in appearance, he'd had nothing else to remember his mother by except the weak eyesight he'd inherited from her side of the family.

An overwhelming hunger seized him to share this bit of personal history with Clare. It was strange to imagine that revealing something of himself might fill the crevasse in his soul, but perhaps this would be the first step in telling her the truth—and pray she didn't shrink away.

HIGH WYCOMBE

*M*eri used the excuse of Clare's weekly grocery delivery to stop by Robbins Nest. He came around to the kitchen door, but nobody responded to his knock. Dinah, however, began to bark in the vicinity of the former vegetable garden. As the pup came bounding over, Clare straightened up and waved.

"Hello!"

"Hello!" He lifted the crate in his arms. "I've brought your order from the Emporium."

"I'll be right there."

Dinah put her paws on his leg and begged to be petted, but he could only glance down and smile.

"Sorry, but I have my hands full at the moment."

Clare approached, rake in tow. Her broad-brimmed straw hat shaded her face, and the pretty blue ribbon band matched the color of her lightweight dress. He had an almost irresistible impulse to duck underneath the brim of her hat to steal a kiss, but he restrained himself.

"Every time I see you, you're busy with yet another industrious activity."

"I mean to plant some late summer vegetables as soon the soil is ready." She leaned the garden instrument against the cottage and opened the kitchen door. "Mrs. Gallagher is upstairs cleaning, but there should be bottled lemonade in that crate, and I think I can find some biscuits."

"I'd adore lemonade and biscuits, thank you."

He wiped his boots, entered the house, and lowered the crate to the counter. While Clare removed her hat and busied herself with the refreshments, he knelt to give Dinah a good long belly rub. Afterward, the puppy gave a great yawn and went over to curl up on the blanket in the corner.

"That belly rub should hold her for a while, I imagine." He rose and crossed over to the sink to wash his hands. "Franklin sent a reply to my letter regarding our engagement. He said he couldn't be more delighted, sends his best wishes, and hinted he'd like to be my best man."

"I'm so glad he's happy."

Clare opened a tin of biscuits and began to arrange them on a small plate. Meri mischievously came up behind her—intent on sneaking a biscuit—and found himself mesmerized by the heady scent of her fragrance.

"Vanilla."

She turned. "What?"

They were inches apart.

"You smell like vanilla." He leaned in even closer to take a deep whiff. "Sugar and spice and all that's nice…that's what little girls are made of."

Clare rested her hands on his chest but made no move to push him away. "Frogs and snails and puppy dog's tails…and that's what little boys are made of."

Meri made his voice conspiratorial. "Don't tell Dinah about the tails. I don't think she'd like it at all."

She lowered her lashes. "I expect you're smelling the biscuits."

"Let me see." He slid his hands around her waist and nuzzled her neck with his nose. "Mmm...I think—"

The sound of Mrs. Gallagher singing as she approached the kitchen made Meri release Clare and step backward.

The housekeeper appeared with a basket full of laundry. "Oh, Mr. Holcroft! I see ye brought a delivery." She put the basket next to the crate of groceries and began to unpack them.

Meri felt his face flush. "Er, yes. Miss Ladd has been kind enough to offer me refreshments for my trouble."

Clare gave him a sidelong glance. "Mr. Holcroft enjoys the smell of your biscuits, Mrs. Gallagher. They drew him all the way across the room, in fact."

"That would be the vanilla, I warrant. My dear mother used to say extract of vanilla attracts a man like catnip attracts a kitten."

Meri tried not to smile. "I hadn't heard that."

Oblivious to his mirth, the woman continued to unpack the crate. "I had a letter from Mr. Franklin this morning. He's enjoying the sights of London with his sister's family, so he is."

Meri exchanged a brief glance with Clare. Apparently, Franklin had chosen not to share his condition with the house-keeper and was spinning tall tales instead.

"I'm glad to hear it, Mrs. Gallagher. Franklin has never taken enough time for himself."

"His letter said he brought the little ones to the Palace for skating. Better him than me, I must say. Gliding over ice is unnatural, in my opinion."

Clare spoke. "I hope Mr. Franklin returns soon. A great many people are missing him."

Mrs. Gallagher's face grew pink. "Truer words were ne'er spoken." She began carrying items into the pantry.

Clare picked up the plate of biscuits. "If you'll bring the lemonade bottles, Mr. Holcroft, we can have our refreshments sitting in the garden."

Meri was glad for the suggestion. "What a good idea."

Meri brought a square gardening basket over to the bench and turned it upside down to use as a makeshift table. He joined Clare on the garden bench in the dappled shade of the rickety arbor and took a sip of lemonade. Although the beverage wasn't ice cold, it was sweet and refreshing.

He jerked his head toward the cottage. "It's Franklin's business, of course, but I wish he wouldn't lead Mrs. Gallagher astray as to his health."

Clare nodded. "She's going to be cruelly disappointed when she learns the truth, but I suppose we must keep his confidence. I daresay he'll tell her about his condition when he feels the time is right."

"I agree." He drained his bottle and then set it aside. "Speaking of confidences, may I share something with you?"

Meri produced the gold oval pendant from his pocket and put it in her hand. The decorative pattern on the gold glinted in the sunlight and brought an admiring smile to Clare's lips.

"How lovely!"

"It contains my mother's hair. She gave that locket to my father on their wedding day."

Clare opened the locket. "Her hair is a gorgeous color! It resembles liquid gold in this light." She peered at the engraving. "Primrose Fortescue Pallinger." Her glance flickered in his direction. "Not Holcroft?"

"No. Pallinger is my actual last name, but because of the negative association, I haven't used it since I was a child."

He braced himself for Clare's reaction.

"I don't blame you. If my name had been Pallinger, I would have been tempted to change it as well." Her eyes widened. "Wait…you're not related to Barnabas the Butcher, are you?"

Clare's response, although not wholly unexpected, made Meri's heart sink. "N-No, of course not." He shrugged. "I might be a very distant cousin. You never know about these things."

She sighed. "That whole case was terribly tragic."

"Indeed, it was. At any rate, I found the locket last night and wanted to share it with you."

Her dimples showed as she smiled. "What a wonderful memento."

"Yes. I can't recall her features distinctly any longer, but I have the impression she was a beautiful woman. Unfortunately, I resemble my father rather remarkably. I always have."

"Why should that be unfortunate? I'm sure he was a terribly handsome man."

He was dismayed at his slip. "Oh, I meant only that I was closer to my mother, and it would have been comforting to see a little of her in the mirror each morning."

"I imagine you're more like her than you know. May I ask how you came by the name Holcroft?"

"The Holcrofts were a kind couple who took me in after my parents died."

Clare studied him. "I'm very glad you chose to confide in me." She pressed the locket back into his hands. "You remind me of a rosebud."

The incongruent comparison made him laugh. "How so?"

"Your petals are unfolding, bit by bit, and I'm finally getting to see who you really are."

Since he hadn't managed to be straightforward with Clare after all, Meri knew differently. Nevertheless, he covered his guilt with a mischievous grin and reached for a biscuit.

"Perhaps it's due to the vanilla."

ALTHOUGH SHE FEIGNED CALMNESS, Clare's thoughts and pulse were racing. She rose from the bench, walked off a few paces, and then slid Meri a probing glance.

"My father is a retired barrister, you know. He's always been interested in notorious criminals…and in the Pallinger tragedy in particular."

Meri broke his biscuit in half. "I can't imagine why." He returned the broken biscuit to the plate, uneaten.

"Papa thought the facts fascinating and even filled a box with newspaper articles. I used to amuse myself by reading the clippings and discussing them with him."

His complexion went pale. "How dreary."

"Not at all. My heart always went out to the little boy. Do you recall his name?"

He stood. "Meriweather. Meriweather Barnabas Pallinger, to be precise."

"Yes, that's it." A surge of emotion in his eyes brought moisture to her own. "I yearned to reach out to him somehow and let him know I cared. I imagined him to be a brave little man, but I didn't realize just how brave until now."

A muscle worked in his jaw. "I'm sure he would have treasured your friendship. He grew up exceedingly lonely."

"Oh, Meri, I'm sorry I called your father Barnabas the Butcher. I'm usually not so rude, but after I saw your mother's name in that locket, it took me a few moments to put the puzzle together."

"I'm quite used to the epithet, I assure you." He walked off a few paces and took a deep breath. "I'm glad you know."

"I wish you'd told me sooner."

Meri gave her a sharp glance. "What?"

"I can understand your reluctance to be open with strangers, but I would have liked to help. The very thought of your bearing this burden alone grieves me terribly."

He peered at her. "Do you mean to say you're not put off…or afraid of me?"

"I'm not put off in the least, and I daresay I'm more afraid of Mrs. Gallagher than of you."

When Meri reached out his arms to envelope her in an intimate embrace, warmth spread throughout her body and she closed her eyes in bliss. Nothing in her life had prepared her for the complicated rush of emotion that ensued as she relaxed against his strong, muscular frame. This man made her feel protective yet protected…strong yet vulnerable. He was simply the most wonderful, magnetic, vibrant, complex man of her acquaintance, and she hoped he would never let go.

"Marry me, Alice."

The words were muffled as he buried his face in her neck, and she couldn't be quite sure she'd heard him correctly. Puzzled, she pulled back far enough to look into his eyes.

"We're already engaged."

"I'm quite serious. I'm asking you to become Mrs. Meriweather Holcroft. I wish I could make you Lady Pallinger, but you know that's impossible." A tender smile lit his face. "Say you'll marry me."

"This isn't just for Mr. Franklin's benefit, is it?"

His gaze grew smoky. "Despite my regard for Franklin, the benefit is all mine."

The sentiment was underscored by fervent kisses and yet she could scarcely believe it.

"But, Meri, you said you could never take a bride."

"And so I could not, not under false pretenses. I never imagined I would meet the perfect woman who could accept me along with my scandalous family history."

He kissed her again with such tenderness and passion as to drive all doubts from her mind.

"I will marry you." She squealed with delight when he picked her up in her arms and twirled around.

"My adorable Alice! I'll ask for your father's blessing when we're in High Wycombe."

He sat down on the bench, holding her on his lap. Clare slid her arms around his neck, reveling in his masculine strength and the depths of his ardor.

"And suddenly, I'm the most fortunate man alive," he murmured between kisses.

"And I'm the most fortunate lady."

~

MERI GLANCED out the rain-spattered window of their train compartment. "Ordinarily, I might make a disparaging remark about the inclement weather, but ever since you agreed to marry me, everything has been turned on its head. Even a torrential downpour lifts my spirits."

Clare beamed as she reached out to squeeze his hand. "I understand exactly how you feel. I can't seem to stop smiling." She paused. "I *do* miss Dinah."

"I'm sorry you had to leave her behind."

She sighed. "So am I, but the thunderstorm sent her streaking under the bed in a fright. When she shrank from me, I didn't have the heart to force her."

"We'll return soon enough."

"Yes, Mrs. Gallagher will sleep in one of the spare rooms while I'm away, so the puppy won't be lonely."

His eyes sparkled. "Tell me, is your father terribly fearsome? You said he's a barrister, so I daresay he must be formidable."

"He values candor and abhors deceit. As a result, for example, Sterling may never get back into his good graces."

"When I'm at the party, I'll make sure to thank Mr. Yates for his moral failings. After all, if he hadn't behaved abominably, you and I would never have met."

"You're teasing, of course. At any rate, Sterling will likely give you a wide berth, so I shan't worry about it."

Meri laughed, but as he contemplated his impending introduction to Sir Andrew, he felt a flicker of anxiety.

She peered at him. "You're troubled, I can tell."

He winced. "I don't want to marry you under false pretenses, but I'm concerned your father will toss me out of the house the moment I disclose my true identity."

"You've nothing about which to be concerned. My father has always been fair."

A lightning bolt light up near the train, and the instantaneous peal of thunder caused Meri and Clare to jump.

She laughed nervously. "That struck a bit too close, wouldn't you say?"

"Yes, but I've every confidence we'll arrive in High Wycombe intact."

THE WEATHER HAD CLEARED by the time Clare and Meri arrived at High Wycombe. As Clare stepped off the train alongside Meri, she spotted her father on the platform immediately.

"Hello, Papa!" She waved.

Sir Andrew hastened over with a smile. "Alice!"

He kissed her cheek even as he gave Meri an appraising glance. Clare bit back a smile as she introduced the two men. Although her father was cordial, she could see his manner was far more gruff than was usual. Evidently, he assumed she'd brought home a suitor and was determined to scrutinize him accordingly.

Sir Andrew nodded at her. "Let's claim your luggage and get on with it. Lady Ladd will have tea waiting when we arrive."

Meri smiled. "Excuse me a moment, will you? I must make arrangements for my trunk to be taken directly to the hotel."

He bowed and hastened off while Sir Andrew engaged a porter to retrieve Clare's bags. While she and her father were waiting, he gave her a sidelong glance.

"I'm glad we have a few minutes to ourselves, Alice. After that newspaper article appeared in the paper, I was determined to bring you home."

She groaned. "I was hoping it might have escaped your notice."

"It did not." He paused. "Are you and Mr. Holcroft courting?"

Her face grew warm. "We are."

"I feared as much." Sir Andrew's tone was flat. "Alice, need I remind you the man owns a livery stable?"

She bristled. "He does very well for himself *and* he deals in art."

Her father harrumphed. "For which he greatly overpays. I'm not particularly impressed by his business acumen, and I'm not inclined to think a working man is good enough for you."

Clare's fists clenched. "How can you condemn him without making his acquaintance? I thought you fairer than that."

"I'm not necessarily condemning him personally. You must understand that Nell is to accompany Dora to London next spring, where she'll likely meet quite a few eligible gentlemen. Since I haven't a great deal of money to settle upon her, our prestige as a family must be as pristine as possible."

She peered at him, aghast. "So I'm to sacrifice my happiness in favor of Nell's?"

Sir Andrew glanced around to make sure they weren't being overheard.

"I care about the happiness of both my daughters, and I cannot be seen as favoring the elder over the younger by allowing her to marry down, willy-nilly."

Fury swept over Clare, but she forced herself to make a measured reply. "Sir, I beg you to withhold judgment until you've given Mr. Holcroft the opportunity to sway you to his side."

"I'm not heartless, Alice. After your sister is advantageously married, you might consider Mr. Holcroft. Until then, however, I suggest you put your courtship with him in abeyance."

Clare's stomach was tied into knots, so she said little else thereafter. Although her father asked her several questions about Robbins Nest, she answered in monosyllabic replies. Finally, he made a sound of exasperation.

"Alice, if you continue to act resentful, Mr. Holcroft will assume we've quarreled."

Her temper flared. "So we have. You must promise to give him a chance to impress you, Papa!"

He sighed. "I shall endeavor to keep an open mind. Will that do?"

"I suppose I have little choice."

"By the by, Nell has heard something from Dora that will cheer you considerably."

Her interest was piqued despite herself. "Oh?"

"Sterling is to take a banking position in New York City. He and Mrs. Yates are departing in September."

She couldn't help but smile. "That *is* good news, albeit unexpected. I wonder what's behind it."

"It's rather obvious, to my way of thinking. Lord and Lady Yates are inclined to help Dora put her best foot forward next Season, you see. The absence of the scandalous Mr. Yates will aid them considerably."

Clare realized full well his point was aimed at *her*. "In your opinion, my alliance with the lowly owner of a livery stable is akin to a scandal?"

Her father held up his hands, as if in surrender. "I've promised to set aside my judgment until I'm better acquainted with the man. You'll have to take me at my word."

Clare fell silent. Perhaps Meri's charm and manner would win her father over in much the same way he'd handily won her heart. If not, she might have to wait years until Nell decided to settle down. Oh, why was Papa being so beastly?

QUARREL

On the drive to Ladd House, Meri couldn't help noticing Clare's strained expression and reticence. Although they were unable to converse freely due to the presence of Sir Andrew, he did manage to slide her a surreptitious, quizzical glance. She answered with an uninformative frown and a tiny shake of her head. What had her father said at the train station to transform her recent sunny attitude to one of unease?

As the carriage rolled through rain-moistened streets of High Wycombe, Sir Andrew drew his attention to the hotel at which he would be staying as well as a few other landmarks. For his part, Meri paid the town several deserved compliments. Sir Andrew's subsequent responses were polite, but nothing more.

Clare finally joined in the conversation. "If you're in want of furniture, High Wycombe is the place to shop. When I was a little girl, Her Majesty came to visit. Her coach passed underneath a magnificent arch of chairs built over High Street in her honor. More recently, an even larger chair arch was erected to mark the visit of the Prince of Wales."

"I should have liked to see that." Meri sought his memory.

"Didn't the late Prime Minister Disraeli have a home hereabouts?"

"Hughenden Manor." Sir Andrew nodded. "A magnificent residence with splendid grounds."

When they turned down a lane, Clare pointed to a grand house up ahead. "That's Bramble Manor, where the Yates reside. Ladd House is within a very easy distance."

"Since you've spoken so highly of the Yates, I shall look forward to meeting them. You're fond of Miss Yates in particular?"

"My sister is closer in age to Dora, but we all get along quite well."

Sir Andrew's hands tightened on the reins. "Mr. Holcroft, I gathered from a newspaper article that you and Sterling Yates locked horns?"

Meri was unapologetic. "I confess we did. Considering the fellow's officious and arrogant manner, I believe I set him down creditably."

The corners of Sir Andrew's lips crept upward. "Excellent."

Meri chuckled, but Clare rolled her eyes. "There is no reason for you to resent Sterling any longer, Papa."

"Once a father's resentment has been earned, it's implacable."

Sir Andrew punctuated his pronouncement with a cool glance in Meri's direction. He took it as a warning and responded accordingly.

"In that case, I shall endeavor to earn your good opinion."

The man's mustache twitched. "Anything's possible."

Despite Sir Andrew's critical manner, Meri rather liked him. After all, if they had a mutual dislike of Sterling Yates in common, that was a good start.

The carriage stopped in front of a tidy, well-kept house made of brick, and Clare flashed Meri a smile. "Here we are."

"Alice, why don't you show Mr. Holcroft inside? After I drive the rig to the carriage house, I'll join you directly."

"Do you need help, Sir Andrew?" Meri asked.

"Thank you, but no." The older man shook his head. "My manservant will take care of the rig and bring in the luggage."

Meri jumped down and assisted Clare to the pavement. As Sir Andrew drove on, she caught Meri's arm.

"Avoid any discussion of the Pallingers at present."

He peered at her. "But you said yourself your father abhors deceit."

"And so you *shall* tell him the truth when the time is right. Let's just have a nice, pleasant conversation over tea…and perhaps you can speak with him tonight at the party. Men always go off to have brandy and cigars at these things, so you'll have the perfect opportunity."

"As you wish, Alice."

Even as he assented, however, Meri felt a surge of apprehension. A lie of omission was still a lie, and Sir Andrew had all but warned him against earning his pique. Still, Clare knew the man better than he did. If she felt it would be better to wait a few hours, then wait he would.

As Meri and the Ladd family sat at the dining table for afternoon tea, Clare's mother gave him a twinkling smile.

"We've been looking forward to meeting you, Mr. Holcroft."

The older woman poured amber liquid into his cup. Although a sumptuous array of finger sandwiches, cakes, and biscuits had been laid out, he and Clare's mother were the only ones who were eating much of anything. Sir Andrew had his arms folded across his chest and Nell was staring at her hands. Only Lady Ladd seemed to be making an effort to be welcoming and hospitable.

"Thank you, Lady Ladd. I never had the pleasure of meeting your mother, but she apparently had quite the lasting impact in

Stroud." He dropped a spoonful of sugar into his tea. "My attorney informs me she was a famous beauty."

Lady Ladd fluttered with obvious pleasure. "Mama would be happy to know she's been so fondly remembered."

Out of the corner of his eye Meri could see Clare's sister stealing timid glimpses at him. The girl had scarcely spoken since he entered the house, so he tried to draw her out.

"I understand you had a rather significant birthday recently, Miss Nell?"

She blinked. "Y-Yes."

"Congratulations are in order."

Clare gave her sister a fond smile. "Indeed, Nell is to accompany Dora Yates to town next Season. I can't imagine anything more exciting."

Nell finally came alive. "I can't wait!"

Meri was relieved the girl's reserve had slipped. "I'm very happy for you. Are you to be presented at Court?"

"Lady Yates has offered to sponsor me, but I'm not certain I should accept. The notion of being in Her Majesty's presence makes me feel faint." Nell selected a raspberry tart from a platter and put it on her plate.

Meri nodded. "I understand completely, but such opportunities are few and far between. Just think of the stories you will have to tell your family and friends."

"I agree." Clare's nod was emphatic. "I long to hear everything about St. James's Palace, how the debutantes are dressed, and your impressions of the royal family."

"I might work up the courage to do it, then, for your sake." Nell took a big bite of her tart.

Sir Andrew had said little, but Meri was under no illusion his reticence was due to timidity. Ever since they met at the train station, the man's scrutiny of him had been intense. Their mutual dislike of Sterling Yates had brought them together for a brief moment, admittedly, but that particular topic was spent.

He'd made inroads with Clare's mother and sister, but how best could he engage her father in conversation?

Meri opened his mouth to speak, but Sir Andrew beat him to it. The man proceeded to pepper him with questions touching upon where he'd matriculated, his pastimes, his politics, and even his taste in literature.

Finally, Lady Ladd intervened. "Now, now, dearest. Our guest is not on the witness stand and we're not in court."

The older fellow didn't seem at all abashed. "Yes, quite."

Meri seized the moment. "Sir Andrew, Miss Ladd tells me you've an interest in notorious criminal cases?"

The older man frowned. "I admit to some fascination with the subject, yes."

"Perhaps we'll have the opportunity to discuss the Pimlico Poisoning Mystery at some point. The defendant's acquittal did nothing to answer certain lingering questions, but one must pay homage to her attorney's expertise."

A flicker of interest crossed Sir Andrew's face. "I have particular admiration for Sir Edward Clarke, whose defense of Adelaide Bartlett was impeccable."

"A well-known physician, Sir James Paget, made an amusing quip once the verdict was announced. Do you happen to know it?"

"I do." Clare's father began to chuckle. "'Now that she has been acquitted for murder and cannot be tried again, she should tell us in the interest of science how she did it!'"

Meri and Sir Andrew shared a hearty laugh while Lady Ladd frowned.

"If Mrs. Bartlett got away with murder, Andrew, I cannot understand how anyone can think it anything other than a miscarriage of justice!"

"So it was, dearest." Despite the reproof, however, her husband continued to laugh.

Meri gave Clare's mother an apologetic glance. "Forgive me,

Lady Ladd. I suppose Sir Andrew and I share a similar sense of dark humor."

His gaze flickered toward Clare, who was seated to his right. Her shoulders had relaxed, fortunately, and she'd stopped twisting the napkin in her lap. As he watched, she picked up the minced chicken sandwich on her plate and took a nibble. If Clare was comfortable enough to eat, she must have confidence he was doing well.

Sir Andrew cleared his throat. "Mr. Holcroft, tell us about your family."

Clare froze. Cognizant of her request, however, Meri had already formulated a benign response.

"I've been on my own for some time, I'm afraid. When I was a boy, my parents perished the night a horrific fire broke out in our home."

Nell gasped, wide-eyed. "How perfectly dreadful!"

He acknowledged her comment with a nod. "Yes, it was. I had no relatives to help me, so a local farrier and his wife took me in. Although I inherited my father's considerable wealth, I've eschewed the life of a gentleman and developed a successful business in the livery trade instead."

"And you have an avid interest in art," Clare prompted.

"It's more an interest in ancestors than art. You see, every painting in my parents' home was destroyed in the fire, so I acquire portraits of other people's family to make up the lack." Meri averted his eyes. "Works of art are not an adequate substitute for actual relatives, but it's the best I can manage."

Lady Ladd peered at him; pity etched on her features. "Your predicament saddens me, Mr. Holcroft."

"Please don't distress yourself." He glanced at Clare, whose eyes were brimming with emotion. "Lately, I've been looking forward to the future more than ever before."

The maid appeared in the doorway. "Er...Mr. Holcroft's cab has arrived."

"I'll be along directly." Meri gave the Ladd family a broad smile. "I can't tell you what a pleasure it has been to meet you.

Lady Ladd frowned. "I'm sorry we can't ask you to stay with us here at Ladd House, but we've no spare rooms. In fact, the girls had to share while Mama was living with us."

"Don't trouble yourself, Lady Ladd. I'm sure my accommodations will be more than adequate." Meri folded his napkin and put it by his plate. "Miss Ladd, shall I call back for you at seven?"

"Oh, yes..." Clare bit her lip. "If that's all right with you, Papa?"

Sir Andrew nodded. "I suppose there's no harm in a short drive across the street."

The Ladd family accompanied Meri outside. As he stepped into his cab and waved good-bye, he was cautiously optimistic. Although it was too soon to tell if he'd ingratiated himself, at least he hadn't been ordered from the premises. Tonight, when the opportunity presented itself, he'd take Sir Andrew aside and disclose the truth of his background. When and how he would ask for permission to wed the man's daughter would depend on his reaction. No matter what, Meri didn't intend to leave High Wycombe without making Clare his fiancée.

CLARE WATCHED Meri's cab roll down the street, missing him already. As the Ladds returned to the house, she gave her father a hopeful glance.

"Well? Do you approve of Mr. Holcroft now?"

"The man impressed me favorably, I'll admit it, but..." his gaze flickered toward Nell "...I've not decided one way or the other."

"I liked Mr. Holcroft very well indeed." Lady Ladd beamed. "He far surpassed my expectations."

A smile spread across Clare's face. "And what about you,

Nell?" To her utter shock, her sister was scowling at her. "What's wrong?"

"Oh nothing, I'm sure." Her lips tightened. "You're horribly selfish, that's all!"

She gaped. "What?"

Nell fled upstairs, leaving Clare nearly speechless. She turned to her mother, wide-eyed. "Have I said something to offend her?"

Lady Ladd grimaced. "It's not you, exactly. It's Mr. Holcroft."

Clare was bewildered. "He said nothing untoward. In fact, I thought his visit went uncommonly well!"

"That's the problem. I think she was unprepared for the deep regard you and Mr. Holcroft obviously have for one another." Her mother sighed. "Ever since Nell learned she was to have a Season, she's been predisposed to think ill of him, I'm afraid."

Suddenly the conversation Clare had had with her father on the train platform made sense. Apparently, her younger sister was making her influence felt.

"I see." Her eyes narrowed. "Fortunately, it's not up to Nell."

Lady Ladd frowned. "Do try to smooth things over, dearest. You mentioned gifts in your letter. Perhaps now would be a good time to give them to Nell?"

She bit her lip. Although she didn't appreciate her sister's lack of support, it would do no good to engage in an argument —especially within hours of a social function.

"All right, Mama. I'll try."

Clare tapped on her sister's door with a tea cup and saucer in one hand and a book under her arm. When she received a muffled response, she opened the door.

"I brought you presents, Nell."

Her sister, who'd draped herself across the bed, pushed herself up into a sitting position. "Tell me you're not planning to marry Mr. Holcroft."

Clare put the gifts on the dresser. "I can tell you no such thing. Why are you so determined to dislike him?"

"I don't dislike him personally, but I can scarcely boast about a brother-in-law who's in trade. The sort of circles in which Dora and I will travel won't understand."

"So you'd be ashamed of me."

"Oh, I hate it when you're difficult! Lottie says Mr. Holcroft is an unpolished ruffian who's obviously twisted you around his finger."

"You're taking advice from Lottie?"

Nell tossed her head. "I want to marry well, Clare, and I finally have a good chance to do exactly that."

"And I prefer to marry for love!"

"With that unrealistic attitude, it's no wonder you're an old maid!" Nell clapped her hand over her mouth and her eyes grew wide. She dropped her hand after a few painfully long moments. "I'm sorry. I didn't mean that."

"I think you did." Tears stung Clare's eyelids. "Now that I understand you care more about yourself than you do about me, I must act accordingly."

She backed from her sister's room without another word. Although she closed the door quietly, her hands were shaking with fury. Nell had called her horribly selfish, but it was abundantly clear her sister was the one guilty of defending her own interests above everything else. If that was indeed the case, Clare vowed to think only of her own happiness. Should her father fail to grant his permission for her and Meri to wed, they would elope. Further, should the scandal follow Nell to London, so be it.

Lady Ladd was laying out her shoes and gown for the evening

when Clare entered her bedchamber. She put the floral-painted tea cup and saucer on the table near the window.

"Here is your gift, Mama. I hope you like it."

Lady Ladd's face lit with pleasure at the sight of the pretty china. "Isn't that lovely!" She caught sight of Clare's dour expression. "Oh, dear. You and your sister have quarreled, I take it?"

"Nell feels Meri is not elegant enough as a brother-in-law, and I believe she's persuaded Papa to see things her way." She sank down onto a settee. "Now that the Yates have taken Nell up, she sees herself far above her company I fear."

Her mother wrinkled her nose. "I don't imagine Lottie Yates's influence has done her any good. I'll be quite glad when that girl has set sail." She sighed. "For what it's worth, I think Mr. Holcroft everything worthy, and I'd welcome him as a son-in-law."

Her sentiments brought a smile to Clare's lips. "Oh, thank you, Mama! I knew you'd be on my side. I can say without equivocation that Meri is truly the most wonderful man in the world."

Lady Ladd bent to kiss her cheek. "Perhaps it's because my own origins were relatively humble, but I've never shared the general prejudice against the working class. I'll speak to Nell about her attitude. She's been swept away by the notion of a London Season, but I don't believe she intends to be hurtful." She paused. "What did you bring to wear tonight?"

"A beige satin dinner gown."

Her mother made a sound of disgust. "You're not going to a church social, Clare! You've got a trousseau at your disposal, so why don't you pick out something more festive?"

"I thought you'd stored my trousseau in the attic?"

"I didn't want the gowns to get crushed and musty, so the bags are still hanging in your closet. Be sure to wear something with an enticing décolleté."

"Mama!"

Lady Ladd giggled. "Run along and get dressed! Your young man is calling for you at seven."

CLARE DRAPED her trousseau across her bed and sorted through it until she reached one of the gowns she'd planned to wear on her honeymoon with Sterling. The underdress was the palest blue silk, and the delicate lace overlay hugged her bodice and waist before fanning out in a luxurious waterfall of fabric. Tiny cornflowers appeared at the top of the shoulders, and dainty puffs of tulle formed the sleeves. As she held the gown up to examine her reflection in the mirror, the daring neckline made her lips quirk up. Yes, the gown would do very well.

Once dressed, she sat down at the vanity table to style her hair. She'd just tucked a jeweled comb in her sleek sable twist when Nell burst into her room without knocking.

"Help me with my sash, will you? I can't seem to get it to lie down smoothly." She peered at Clare's dress. "Isn't that from your trousseau?"

"Indeed, it is." Clare's tone was decidedly cool. "I might as well get some use out of it."

"But you're wearing it in front of Sterling?"

"Since he's never seen it, he won't know the difference."

"That's a bit cheeky, but you do look lovely."

Clare rose. "Turn around so I can tie your sash."

A frown crossed Nell's face as she complied. "Mama told me I'd spoken out of turn regarding Mr. Holcroft, and I apologize. I oughtn't to have said anything."

After Clare re-tied the pink sash with a snap, she fanned the loops out. "No, you ought not. I'm rather disappointed you've chosen to put your happiness above mine."

As Nell whirled around, her bell-shaped white silk skirt flared out at its flounced hem. "That's unkind!"

"But not untrue."

Her sister studied her a long moment, as if struggling with her response. Finally, she sighed. "Yes, you're right. Mama encouraged me to see Mr. Holcroft through your eyes, and I shall endeavor to do so."

"I'm glad."

She giggled. "He *is* frightfully attractive. Perhaps you can convince him to give up his livery business. If he cares for you, it shouldn't be too hard."

So her sister wished her to change Meri to make him more acceptable to society? As far as Clare was concerned, he was perfect exactly as he was.

"I wouldn't dream of it."

Nell's smile faded. "You've grown exceedingly difficult since you went away."

Clare was unmoved. "And you've grown supercilious."

Nell's jaw jutted out. "I take it back. You're not difficult, you're horrid!"

"It's horrid for me to marry the most decent man of my acquaintance?" She shook her head. "Don't distress yourself, Nell. I'll be departing High Wycombe in due course and you won't have to see your horrid sister for a very long time."

"Hmmpf!" Nell swept from the room.

With a roll of her eyes, Clare returned to her toilette. Although she had no wish to quarrel with her sister, the apology Nell had tendered just now was tinged with insincerity. Was her selfish attitude the result of Lottie's influence? If so, the vicious girl had indeed successfully taken her revenge. Clare could only hope her sister would come around sooner rather than later.

NEIGHBOR FROM STROUD

Clare picked up Dora's newly wrapped teacup and saucer, draped a short evening cloak over one arm, and joined her parents in the parlor downstairs. Lady Ladd wore a sumptuous magenta satin dinner gown with white stripes. A heavy turquoise necklace graced her throat and her upswept hair featured a jeweled comb. Sir Andrew was sporting traditional evening wear with a ruby stickpin in his lapel.

He beamed as Clare entered the room. "I cannot believe I'm so fortunate to escort three such splendid ladies this evening."

"Thank you, Papa." She set down her brightly wrapped package and adjusted the fit of her *peau de soie* evening gloves. "Mr. Holcroft is escorting me to the party, so you must content yourself with only two splendid ladies."

He glanced over her shoulder. "Where is Nell?"

Although Clare was still put out with her sister, she tried to keep her tone civil. "I'm sure she'll be along directly." She smiled at her mother. "You look beautiful, Mama."

"Thank you. This will be the first social event I've attended since coming out of mourning for my mother, and it's rather

191

refreshing." She nodded at Clare's dress. "I'm so glad you're wearing that gown. It was the prettiest one of your trousseau."

"I do hope Meri likes it." She heard the arrival of a carriage outside, and her breath caught in her throat. "That must be him."

Sir Andrew reached for her cloak. "Let me help you with that."

As Clare donned her outerwear, she tried to calm her nerves. Although Meri said he owned evening clothes, would he show up dressed in a bowler hat and a sack coat? Even if he did, she vowed not to care a jot. Whatever he wore, he would be extraordinarily handsome.

Bess appeared in the doorway and cleared her throat. "Mr. Meriweather Holcroft."

Once the maid stepped back, Clare was struck dumb at the tall, handsome gentleman who entered the room. His evening clothes were impeccable and showed his athletic frame to perfection. The top hat in his hand was indistinguishable from that of any aristocrat, as were his shoes, gloves, and elegant white silk-lined cape. No one who met him thusly attired could ever imagine him as the lowly owner of a livery stable. Of course, she was the only one who knew he was actually Lord Pallinger.

Her heart swelled with pride as she curtsied. "Mr. Holcroft."

"Miss Ladd." Meri bowed. "Good evening, Lady Ladd and Sir Andrew." He glanced around. "Where is Miss Nell?"

"Still in her room." Clare forced a smile to her lips. "May we go, Papa?"

Sir Andrew nodded. "Go on ahead. We'll drive over to Bramble Manor as soon as your sister comes down."

Lady Ladd gestured toward the package Clare had set near the door. "And we'll bring your gift for Dora as well."

"Thank you, Mama."

As Meri accompanied Clare through the entranceway, footsteps on the stairs heralded Nell's arrival. The shocked expression on the younger girl's face when she glimpsed Meri brought Clare a great deal of pleasure. After everything her sister had said about him earlier, her stupefaction served her right.

~

As Meri escorted Clare outside to the cab, he felt his blood stir. "You look exquisitely beautiful, Alice."

She gave him a sidelong, teasing glance. "How can you tell without your spectacles?"

"Believe me, I can tell." He attracted the driver's attention. "Bramble Manor, if you please."

The man touched his hat. "Yes, sir."

After the cab left Ladd House behind, Meri leaned over to caress Clare's lips with his. "Not only do you look beautiful, but you taste delicious."

Clare slid her fingers in his. "I'm glad. Oh, Meri, if Papa won't give his permission for us to wed, may we elope?"

He frowned. "I hope that won't be necessary. I thought I'd been ingratiating myself with your family creditably."

"Nell has been influenced by Lottie Yates, I fear. Unless I can make a prominent marriage, she wants me to remain unwed until she makes a good match."

"I *am* a viscount." He chuckled. "Wouldn't she'd be proud to have the son of Barnabas the Butcher as a brother-in-law?"

"Don't tease." She sighed. "I never would have imagined my own sister could be ashamed of me, but I shan't let her opinion shape my future."

"I haven't given up hope of obtaining your father's permission, nor should you. An elopement is unseemly and a trifle ungentlemanly, in my opinion."

"And if Papa says no?"

"Should we have no other choice, we'll elope, but I hope it doesn't come to that."

A twinge of pain behind his eyes made him wince.

Clare peered at him with an expression of concern. "What's wrong?"

"Oh, it's nothing. Whenever I go without my spectacles for any length of time, I get a headache."

"Put them on, for heaven's sake." She squeezed his hand. "You're just as handsome with or without your spectacles. In fact, I prefer you with them."

"Franklin teases me incessantly about my vanity, but I can't seem to help it." Meri leaned in for another kiss. "Never fear, I have the spectacles in my pocket. After I meet everyone, I'll don the wretched things—if only to see you more clearly from across the room."

The cab arrived at their destination shortly thereafter and joined the end of a short carriage queue. Meri retrieved his spectacles long enough to admire the residence.

"Bramble Manor is indeed a magnificent estate. Now I understand more fully why Mrs. Despicable finds Mr. Despicable so terribly attractive."

Clare suppressed a smile. "I have some good news on that topic, by the way. The newlyweds are very shortly to sail to New York."

His eyebrows rose. "Is the move permanent?"

"I cannot say, but since Sterling will be working in the banking industry, his absence will no doubt be lengthy."

"The son of a baron is to work, is he? It sounds as if your former fiancé is being banished."

"I expect you're right. Dora will have a far easier time in society without her elder brother around to remind everyone he's a jilt."

"Perhaps Mr. and Mrs. Despicable will form an attachment to New York City."

"What a pleasant notion."

The cab discharged its two passengers in the courtyard. As Meri helped Clare descend, he gave her a wicked grin.

"Shall I carry you inside?"

Her lips parted in a gasp. "Don't you dare! The Yates would definitely not be amused."

"That's not terribly sporting of them."

Meri chuckled as he escorted Clare up the granite steps and into the spacious entrance hall, where dozens of splendidly clad guests were chatting in small groups. He checked their wraps and his hat with a servant before ushering Clare toward the receiving line. Sterling received Clare more warmly than did his wife, but his manner definitely cooled when he addressed Meri.

"Mr. Holcroft." Sterling's lips quirked up to one side in a mocking smile.

Meri couldn't resist a subtle gibe. "I understand you're to quit England soon, Mr. Yates. I'm sorry you and I won't have the opportunity to become better acquainted. We were off to such a promising beginning."

Sterling gave him a withering glance. "It's a devastating circumstance, sir, but we must bear it the best we can."

Clare hastened Meri along, introducing him to a young lady clad in a feminine gown fashioned of pink silk with puffy chiffon sleeves.

"Miss Eudora Yates, this is Mr. Holcroft."

As the girl curtsied, her burnished fair hair reflected the illumination from the gaslit fixtures on the chandelier overhead. Her features were slightly blurred—a casualty of Meri's weak eyesight—but she was obviously pretty.

He smiled. "Thank you for inviting me to celebrate your special day, Miss Yates."

"You're very welcome, sir. Clare has written about you in her letters."

"Miss Ladd and I are quite fortunate to be neighbors."

Dora giggled. "Oh, Clare, Grandpapa and Grandmama have come for a visit. They come to Bramble Manor so infrequently, I feel quite honored." She glanced around. "I don't think they've come down yet, but I'll be sure to introduce you when they do."

Clare smiled. "I look forward to meeting them at long last."

The handsome older woman standing next to Dora gave Clare a kiss on the cheek.

"Hello, dear." Her gaze flickered to Meri. "May I assume this is your neighbor from Stroud?"

"Yes indeed, Lady Yates, this is Mr. Holcroft."

"Welcome to Bramble Manor, sir." She turned to the white-haired gentleman to her right. "Dearest, this is Mr. Holcroft. Mr. Holcroft, allow me to present my husband, Lord Yates."

Lord Yates was significantly older than his wife, Meri discovered, but from the way he glanced at the baroness, his affection for her was obvious.

"I'm quite pleased to make your acquaintance." Meri gave him a warm smile. "Bramble Manor is an impressive home."

"Thank you, sir. I understand you have an interest in art." His eyes twinkled. "Perhaps Miss Ladd will show you the many fine paintings in our gallery? I warn you, however, none are for sale." He winked.

Evidently the baron found Meri's argument with Sterling amusing. In a way, they had that in common.

"I would be happy to tour your gallery, Lord Yates. Let's hope I don't discover any portraits I can't live without."

The older man's laugh was hearty. "If so, I shan't ask Sterling to negotiate the price."

～

OVER HORS D'OEUVRES and mulled wine punch, Clare introduced her handsome escort to curious acquaintances, from her former church circle to the leading members of the local gentry. Most of the women, be they youthful or mature, reacted to Meri in a coquettish manner. Was it any surprise they found him as attractive as she did?

She leaned close to whisper, "You're much admired this evening."

"You're too kind." His smile seemed fixed. "I'm not used to socializing with so many people, I'm afraid. I've been a bit of a hermit my entire adult life." He reached up to rub his eyes.

"You really must don your spectacles, Meri."

"I can hold out awhile longer."

She sighed. "Come with me to the gallery for a little peace and quiet. I imagine we'll have it to ourselves and you can give your eyes a rest."

He smiled. "You're an angel."

Clare led him to a long wide corridor with high ceilings, chandeliers, and a wall of windows on one side. On the other wall, portraits and other paintings covered the white wood paneling. A sleek ebony baby grand piano filled the far end of the corridor.

Meri finally donned his spectacles and glanced around. "What an impressive gallery! One could use the space as a ballroom."

"Actually, the Yates often use this gallery for dancing. They hosted a rather large party here when Sterling turned one and twenty."

"We've no music, but that's no reason we can't waltz." He bowed. "May I have a dance?"

Pleased at any excuse to be in his arms, she sank into a deep curtsy. "Thank you, sir. I'm honored by your request."

To her delight, Meri began to sing "Dance a Cachucha" from the newest Gilbert and Sullivan comic opera, *The Gondoliers.* She joined in the fast-paced song as they danced madly across the floor.

"Oh, what a good idea!" Dora's voice rang out. "I'd love some music."

Clare and Meri, breathless from their dancing, paused to discover the birthday girl poised in the entranceway of the gallery.

"My grandparents have joined the party, so I came to fetch you, Clare. But now, I shall bring the party in here!" She whirled around and dashed off.

Clare sighed. "So much for peace and quiet."

MERI DEPOSITED A LINGERING kiss on Clare's lips before releasing her. "Thank you for the dance."

"It was wonderful fun while it lasted."

"The night's not over." He removed his spectacles and stored them away in his pocket. "Shall we view some paintings before we are overrun? Lord Yates is bound to ask me my impressions."

She gestured toward the nearest one. "Behold…a cat sitting in the sun."

Meri peered at the painting. "This reminds me of an oil that was hanging in my grandparents' house." He laughed and stepped closer. "It's not an uncommon subject, I suppose, but it's very like the other one. It always made me yearn for a cat of my own."

"Did your grandparents collect art?"

"They weren't well off enough to collect fine art, but they did commission several portraits of family members—one each of their two daughters, and one of the entire Fortescue family. My mother had an artistic bent and she gave them several pieces of her own."

"So it was from your mother you inherited your interest in art?"

"Certainly more interest than ability." He laughed. "When I

was eight years old, Mother gave my aunt a study of lily pads she'd painted. Although I had no artistic discernment at that age, I thought it was cleverly done nevertheless."

Clare made a sound of surprise. "Why we passed something quite like that. Let's have a look."

Meri accompanied her as she led him back toward the entrance, where the hum of voices was becoming increasingly louder.

"A tidal wave of guests is approaching. Perhaps we'd best hold on to something or we'll be swept away."

Clare giggled as she pointed at the wall. "There's the lily pad painting, which I consider to be rather fine. Was your mother's work similar?"

As he gazed at the painting, Meri had the strange sensation of being pulled backward violently through the eye of a needle.

"Meri?" Clare's voice seemed to touch him physically. "You look as if you've had a shock."

He wrenched his eyes from the painting. "It's hers."

"What?"

"This doesn't make any sense. How did my mother's painting end up at Bramble Manor of all places?"

Her expression was one of gentle compassion. "Meri, hasn't it been an awfully long time since you've seen your mother's painting? There are only so many ways to depict a lily pad after all and—"

He jabbed his finger at the artist's signature. "Look. It's signed by Primrose Fortescue."

When Clare peered more closely at the painted scrawl, he could hear her quick intake of breath.

"I think you must be right!"

A crowd of chattering people swept into the gallery, but Meri only had eyes for his host. When the baron entered the room, Meri touched Clare's arm.

"Excuse me, Alice, but I must speak with Lord Yates."

"I'll come with you."

Meri led the way through the crowd and managed to pull the baron aside. "Sir, that painting—the one depicting the lily pads —how did you come by it?"

The older man was clearly taken aback by the abrupt inquiry. "I knew you might find something you like, but as I said, it's not for sale." His glance at Clare was accompanied by a smile. "Dora insists that we have dancing and games. I trust you're feeling light footed tonight?"

Clare brushed the question aside. "Lord Yates, forgive me but this is terribly important. Do you know the provenance of the painting? Mr. Holcroft is intimately connected to the artist."

"Er…the painting belongs to my wife, actually."

Meri frowned. "I must speak with Lady Yates, then."

"Some other time, sir. My wife is quite occupied with her other guests just now, but if you call on her tomorrow after-noon, perhaps she might answer your questions."

As somebody began to play a few exploratory bars of music on the piano, Dora approached with an elderly couple in tow.

"Clare, I promised to introduce you to my grandparents, Mr. and Mrs. Fortescue."

As Meri stared at the couple, his headache returned with a sickening vengeance. The last time he'd seen the Fortescues had been from the witness stand in front of the magistrate. His grandfather was nearly bald, his grandmother's hair had grown white, and both their bodies were shrunken and wizened. Despite that, Meri would have recognized them anywhere. Judging from the hate-filled expression on his grandmother's face, she recognized him as well. Meri donned his spectacles and prepared for battle.

Oblivious, Dora continued with her introductions. "Grand-mama and Grandpapa, this is Miss Clare Ladd and her friend—"

Mrs. Fortescue's shrieks filled the gallery like the report of a cannon. The piano music broke off and everyone stopped to stare.

"Get thee behind me, Satan!" The elderly woman's faded blue eyes latched onto Meri, even as she shook her walking stick in his face. "You're a murderer, Barnabas Pallinger, and an unholy devil!"

Dora gulped. "Grandmama, you're mistaken! This is Mr. Holcroft."

An ashen-faced Lady Yates rushed over. "What is wrong, Mama?"

Mr. Fortescue tried to pacify his wife. "Think what you're saying, dearest. Barnabas has been dead for years." He squinted at Meri. "You must be Meriweather Pallinger, of course. Gah, but you're the dead spit of your father, save those spectacles."

Meri bowed, ever so slightly. "I wish I could say our meeting is a happy one, sir, but I'm afraid I cannot."

Dora's hands crept up to her mouth as she stared at Meri, and she took a half-step back.

"Meri?" Lady Yates fumbled in her pocket for her own pair of spectacles, peering at him with dawning comprehension. "It can't be!"

"The spawn of Satan has come back to haunt us!" Mrs. Fortescue collapsed into her husband's arms, sobbing.

"Come, dearest, let's retire. You're overwrought." The elderly man was close to tears as he led her from the gallery.

Lady Yates turned on Meri. "How dare you worm your way in here under false pretenses!"

Fortunately, numbness cushioned the impact of her verbal blows.

"I can assure you, Aunt Dee, had I realized who you were, I never would have accepted your invitation. With all due respect, I've no interest in renewing our acquaintance whatsoever."

Whispers of "Barnabas the Butcher" crescendoed around the room, adding to the nightmarish atmosphere. Several yards away, Sir Andrew was shaking his head sadly. No doubt Clare's father thought him the worst sort of deceitful scoundrel, yet Meri still felt nothing. His brutal unmasking amongst dozens of people had left him savaged, but his emotions seemed to have been frozen in place.

Dora clutched at her father's sleeve. "Please, Papa, *do* something! My party will be ruined!"

Lord Yates regarded Meri with pity. "Forgive me, Lord Pallinger, but I must ask you to leave. Your presence is upsetting my family and guests."

Clare's hand crept into his, and as Meri met her gaze, he realized he'd no right to make her partake of his humiliation. He brought her gloved hand to his lips before releasing it.

"I'm sorry, Alice. I'm sure your father will see you home."

Sterling Yates strode over, quivering with indignation. "Allow me to show you out, Mr. Holcroft."

Meri longed to slap the superiority from the man's face. "The name is Lord Pallinger, and I can find my own way."

The crowd drew back as he left the gallery, leaving pandemonium in his wake. He went to the entrance hall to retrieve his cape and hat, but as he strode toward the front door, Sterling loomed into view.

"Just who are you really?" His fists were clenched at his sides.

Meri made no effort to hide his bitterness. "Meriweather Barnabas Pallinger, the black sheep of the family and your reluctant cousin."

Sterling frowned. "I've been told my stepmother has no siblings."

"Aunt Dee is your stepmother? You and I are relieved of the burden of being actual blood relatives, then." Meri sketched a mocking bow. "Please convey my deepest regrets to Miss Yates for spoiling her birthday celebration. I shan't darken your doorstep ever again."

He burst from Bramble Manor like a bull on a rampage.

THOR

*D*elphine Yates and the Fortescues were the relatives who'd abandoned Meri so long ago? Clare was so stunned by the revelation she was rendered almost immobile. Nearby, Lottie was smirking with ill-concealed delight, the party guests were abuzz with gossip, and Nell appeared to be completely bewildered.

"My apologies!" Lady Yates sang out to everyone within earshot. "Mama was quite confused and upset, but it's over now. Shall we continue with our music?" She slid a pointed look at Dora, who nodded and hastened toward the piano.

Clare was appalled. Lady Yates could have extended a friendly, familial hand to her nephew, but apparently couldn't be bothered. Did she truly care nothing for Meri?

Meri!

Startled out of her stupor, Clare darted from the gallery and sped down the corridor, praying she could catch him before he left. When she reached the entrance hall, Sterling was leaning against a pillar in the entrance hall with his arms folded across his chest.

"Where is he?" Desperation bled through her question. "Did he come this way?"

Sterling's lips flattened. "Yes, but he was in no mood to talk."

She made a sound of frustration, picked up her skirts, and fled the house. The darkness outside precluded her from spotting anyone, but he couldn't have covered too much distance on foot in such a short period of time.

"Meri!"

Although he made no answer, she was determined not to lose him. Heedless of the damage her shoes and gown might suffer, she ran across the courtyard and down the gravel driveway. A flash of white—the lining of his cape—caught her eye. If she hurried, she could catch him before he passed through the gate. She forced herself to move more quickly than she thought possible, even though the breath caught in her chest and her legs felt leaden.

"Meri...wait!"

To her relief, he paused his footsteps and waited. His expression was extraordinarily grim as she approached.

"Meri, I'm going with you." Her words were barely audible in between her gasps, but he seemed to understand her well enough.

"No." He shook his head. "I hoped if nobody knew who I was, you and I would have a chance together. Now, that my identity has been revealed, it's too late. I can never marry you, and any association with me will bring you misery. Stay away from me, Clare."

Without warning, he swept her into his arms and kissed her with such passionate desperation, her heart nearly broke. Then, without another word, he let her go. As he disappeared into the night, he took all her hopes, dreams, and emotions with him.

Completely numb, Clare had no choice but to return to Bramble Manor to collect her things and walk back to Ladd

House. After everything she'd learned, she could not remain at the party and pretend to enjoy herself.

As she ascended the stairs to the entrance, she noticed Sterling sitting at the top. Although she meant to sweep past without addressing him, he rose to his feet and blocked her way.

"I regret if I seemed flippant in the entrance hall. What I said didn't come out right and I didn't mean to make a bad situation worse."

Clare glanced over her shoulder toward the road. "Nothing is coming out right lately."

Sterling hunched his shoulders. "I was shocked to discover my stepmother hasn't been entirely forthcoming about her family connections."

She met his gaze. "Lady Yates accused Meri of coming here under false pretenses, but nothing could be further from the truth. Neither Meri nor I had any notion your stepmother was his aunt or that his grandparents would be in attendance." Clare shook her head. "Lady Yates has opened old wounds tonight and disappointed me cruelly, I'm afraid."

Sterling frowned. "It's an ugly business all around, to be truthful. I must admit, I feel sorry for Pallinger. And here I was, prepared to hate him."

"Why would you hate him?"

His laugh was sardonic. "Mostly because he's everything I'm not." His smile faded. "Furthermore, he won your heart, which isn't something I was ever able to accomplish."

"Oh, Sterling…" Her voice trailed off.

He averted his eyes. "I never really apologized properly for jilting you, Alice. I am sorry."

Although his expression of remorse improved her opinion of him somewhat, her anger had long since been assuaged.

"Your apology does you credit, but I don't believe either of us were truly in love with one another. I should have recognized my feelings sooner and released you from your promise."

A flicker of pain passed over his countenance and he swallowed hard. "Will you and Pallinger marry, do you imagine?"

The inquiry was nearly Clare's undoing. "Now that he's been exposed, he won't have me." She failed to keep the anguish from her reply.

His frown was laced with sympathy. "I'm sorry, Alice. I wish there was something I could do."

"So do I." Emotion pooled in her eyes. "I just want to go home."

As Sterling accompanied her into the house, she was surprised to see her family in the entrance hall, collecting their things from the coatroom.

Nell hastened over. "Oh, thank heavens you came back. Now we may all drive home together."

"I'll ring for your carriage to be brought around." Sterling sketched a bow. "Excuse me."

After he left, Clare gave her sister a cool glance. "Don't leave the party on my account."

Her sister blushed. "I deserve that, I suppose. But once Papa explained what had happened between Lady Yates and Mr. Holcroft...er, Lord Pallinger, I mean...I didn't want to stay another moment."

"If you leave, the Yates might rescind their invitation to sponsor you next Season."

"I wouldn't accompany them for anything, Clare. If society people treat their family in such a horrible fashion, I'm content to go lower." Her smile was sheepish. "I've been giving myself airs and graces, I'm afraid, and lost sight of what's important. Please forgive me."

Clare said a silent prayer of thanks as she gathered Nell in her arms. After all the horrendous events of the evening, at least she had her sister back.

〜

WHEN STERLING RETURNED to the gallery, a raucous game of musical chairs was underway. A matron was playing "Three Little Maids From School Are We" from *The Mikado*, as Dora led a procession around a short row of chairs. The music suddenly stopped, and shrieks of protest came from the players who couldn't find a seat.

As the music commenced once more, Lottie sidled over. "Where have you been?"

He ignored the inquiry and nodded toward the ongoing game instead. "Why aren't you playing?"

"Oh, I was caught out almost straight off. I've never been very good at these sorts of games."

"Neither am I."

She leaned in to whisper. "Your stepmother is better at games than I'd given her credit for. If I were related to Barnabas the Butcher, I wouldn't want anyone to know either." She giggled. "I wonder if we can turn that information to our benefit somehow?"

A flash of anger ensued. "This stops now, Lottie. No more troublemaking, do you hear? If you don't behave, I'll cash in your ticket to New York and you'll be obliged to sail across the Atlantic in steerage."

She recoiled. "You wouldn't dare!"

"Wouldn't I?" His eyes narrowed. "Oh, and that newspaper article you slid under the bed, hoping I'd forget about it?" He paused for emphasis. "Burned."

"You didn't!" Her lower lip protruded, and she tossed her head. "In that case, you can sleep in your own bed from now on."

"I think not." Sterling held Lottie's gaze for several moments. "Perhaps you'd like to pay a long visit to your father in India instead of accompanying me to New York?"

Her spine stiffened. "I thought you said you weren't good at playing games."

"I'm learning quickly."

The corners of Lottie's mouth turned up at the corners and she leaned into him. "I'm only teasing, dearest."

Sterling nodded. "Good. We're finally beginning to understand one another."

~

LADY LADD ORDERED tea brought to the parlor when the family arrived home. As they gathered together, Clare related what she knew about Meri's true identity and how he'd coped with the tragedy.

"I suspected he was being less than forthcoming, but I'd assumed it had something to do with a secret engagement." Sir Andrew glowered. "I don't like being misled."

"Meri wanted to tell you his name right away, Papa, but I implored him to wait until you'd become better acquainted."

Albeit grudgingly, her father nodded. "To be fair, it's not the sort of thing one can just blurt out."

"For my part, I never took Mr. Holcroft—er, Lord Pallinger —for a working man," Lady Ladd said. "From the start, there was something in his bearing that was a cut above an ordinary."

"Agreed." Sir Andrew glanced at his wife. "Delphine Yates hushed up the connection rather well, I must say."

"I'd no idea Lady Yates even had a sister." Nell shook her head. "I don't believe Dora did, either."

"Sterling didn't," Clare said. "He told me so tonight, and he would have no reason to mislead me."

Conversation broke off when Bess arrived with a tray. Lady Ladd dismissed the maid and poured the tea herself.

"Lord Yates must have been so eager to acquire a mother for his son, he didn't delve too deeply into her ancestral tree." Lady Ladd stirred sugar into her tea. "The Fortescues are not a prominent family, so few people would contradict them."

"After tonight, everyone in England will know of the connection," Nell said. "Nobody was talking about anything else at the party."

Clare blotted her tears with a handkerchief. "Now that Meri's secret has been revealed, he's broken our engagement. He doesn't wish to burden me with his past."

Sir Andrew sighed. "He has a point. Meriweather Pallinger might as well be the direct descendant of Robespierre for all the notoriety his father's crime engendered."

"I don't understand." Nell frowned. "Can't Clare and Meri go on as Mr. and Mrs. Holcroft?"

Clare gloom lifted ever so slightly. "Yes, hang the name and the title. I don't need to be married to an aristocrat to be happy."

"I guarantee you'll be found out." Her father shook his head. "Lottie Yates will never stay silent, for one."

"The Fortescues must be terribly evil people." Lady Ladd passed her husband the sugar bowl. "How could anyone revile their own grandson?"

"Thank you, dearest." He lifted a spoonful of sugar into his tea and blew gently across the hot liquid to cool it. "Perhaps they were driven mad with grief after they lost their daughter in such horrific circumstances."

"Mad or not, the Fortescues have treated Lord Pallinger dreadfully." Lady Ladd's lips tightened. "And I'll never forget how Lady Yates spoke to him tonight. His expression remained unchanged, but all the color left his countenance."

"Indeed, he was exceedingly brave." Nell put her tea cup down. "I'll never forget how everyone drew back away from him, as if he were some sort of leper."

A jagged pain went through Clare. "All this is Meri's worst nightmare. Everything he feared has come to pass."

Sir Andrew cleared his throat. "Alice, there's nothing to be done to improve his situation. All things considered, it's time for you to sell your property to him and come home."

"No!"

Her mother leaned forward. "Clare, imagine how Lord Pallinger will feel going forward, with you living next door. Since he broke your engagement unwillingly, the torture will be unbearable."

As Clare was forced to acknowledge the truth of her mother's assertions, her hopes withered away and turned black, like a tender flowering vine in a hard winter freeze. If no future with Meri were possible, living at Robbins Nest would be a punishment for her as well.

"Yes." Clare swallowed hard. "Of course, you're right. I'll return to Stroud, sign the purchase offer, and pack up my things."

Nell leaned forward. "You don't have to do this alone." She offered her sister a sympathetic nod. "We'll come with you."

Lord Yates and his family stood in the entrance hall, seeing the last of the party guests out. As soon as the front door closed, Lady Yates's smile disappeared and her shoulders drooped.

"I need some brandy."

"I need some hemlock!" Dora quivered with indignation. "Why did you choose my birthday party to let our skeletons out of the closet? It was so horrendous, it might as well have been All Hallows Eve!"

Sterling laughed. "An apt description, if ever I heard one."

His sister scowled. "This isn't funny!"

Lottie smirked. "That depends on your perspective, I suppose."

Her remark drew Sterling's sharp glance. "You're welcome to go to bed, dearest."

She folded her arms. "Oh, no. I wouldn't miss this for anything."

"Shall we retire to a more private location?" Lord Yates held out his arms, as if to herd his family along. "The walls have ears."

Moments later, Lady Yates entered the drawing room and headed directly to the bar cart. Her hand shook so badly, she had trouble removing the glass stopper from the decanter.

Lord Yates appeared at her elbow. "I'll get it, Delphine."

"Thank you."

As she sank into a wing chair, Sterling gave her a level look. "A little disclosure is in order, Mother."

Lottie kicked her shoes off, curled up on the sofa, and gazed at Lady Yates with rapt attention.

"My elder sister, Primrose, had the misfortune to marry Barnabas the Butcher and get herself killed." Lady Yates swallowed. "Thereafter, my parents pretended I was an only child to avoid the scandal and protect my chance to make a good marriage. I'd no idea my nephew would show up to spoil everything, and now Dora's marriage prospects are ruined!"

Dora blinked. "So Mr. Holcroft and I are truly cousins?"

"He's Lord Meriweather Pallinger, not Mr. Holcroft." Sterling moved over to the bar cart to pour himself a whiskey. "And he's not a bad chap."

His stepmother peered at him. "Not a bad chap? Through him, Barnabas has had his revenge on us from the grave!"

Sterling shrugged. "That's not Meri's fault. As far as I can tell, he's not to blame for anything that's happened. In fact, he has my utmost sympathy."

"Mine as well." Lord Yates brought a snifter of brandy to his wife. "I wished I hadn't asked him to leave tonight, but for Dora's sake, I didn't feel as if I had much choice."

His wife accepted the brandy, even as she gave him a bewildered glance. "You seem awfully sanguine about this situation. It's almost as if you aren't surprised at all."

"The night I asked your father for permission to marry you, he and I met in his study over a celebratory quantity of spirits.

You might imagine my surprise when I noticed a family portrait featuring Mr. and Mrs. Fortescue and their two daughters. When I inquired about it, your father told me everything. He was so intoxicated, I doubt if he remembered our conversation the following day. Shortly thereafter, however, the portrait disappeared."

"But you never said a word! Didn't it matter to you that my brother-in-law was a notorious murderer?"

Lord Yates reached for her hand. "I loved you completely, Delphine. It wouldn't have mattered if you were related to Genghis Khan." He paused. "I only wish you would have taken me into your confidence."

A single tear slipped from the corner of her eye. "I'm sorry."

"Now that the cat is out of the bag, as it were, I suggest you find a way to turn circumstances to your advantage." Lottie laughed when everyone's eyes latched onto her. "You needn't stare at me as if I had two heads. I do know a little about these things."

Dora grimaced. "We're related to a murderer, Lottie. How on earth can you turn that into an advantage?"

"Because it's *interesting*, of course. Didn't you see everyone's eyes light up when they thought they were about to meet Lord Barnabas Pallinger's son?"

Lady Yates cocked her head. "What do you suggest?"

"I would have suggested you give an interview to that reporter who wrote the auction story." Lottie slid a withering glance in her husband's direction. "Unfortunately, the article is gone, and I cannot remember his name."

Sterling made a sound of impatience. "Meriweather was the victim of tragedy and has been horribly wronged by his family. Instead of looking for an advantage, why don't you seek to make amends?"

"I agree." Lord Yates nodded at his wife. "Nothing good has

come from trying to hide the truth. Perhaps it's time to seek forgiveness."

"Meri could never forgive me for shunning him all these years." Lady Yates bowed her head. "Truth be told, I can't blame him."

Although Lottie rolled her eyes at the remark, Dora and Sterling exchanged a sober glance.

Lord Yates patted his wife's knee. "Can you think of some sort of olive branch to accompany an apology?"

"An olive branch?" Her brow furrowed. "Now that you mention it, perhaps I can."

MERI SAT up all night in his High Wycombe hotel with a bottle of whiskey. The bottle remained untouched after the first glass, but he took solace in its presence nonetheless. As soon as possible the following morning, he paid his bill and hailed a cab to the train station. Few people spoke to him on the journey home, but he was not at all surprised. He felt quite unwell, and his unshaven, grim image could not have been less inviting.

When he arrived in Stroud, the sky was filled with dark clouds and the smell of rain was in the air. Meri flagged Gus down to take him home. The driver gave him a curious glance as he stowed his trunk on the cab.

"Are you all right, Mr. Holcroft?"

"Never better." Meri's throat was so sore, his reply sounded like a croak. "Has Franklin returned?"

"I haven't seen him."

Yet more bad news. The taxi left the station just as the clouds began to wring out their moisture. The dour homecoming was appropriate under the circumstances.

Gus growled in frustration. "I'll be glad when this weather passes."

"Yes."

All at once, Meri felt bone weary. His life had been one long storm, with only occasional moments of sunlight. Clare had been one such bright, shining moment, but the brief respite she'd provided had slipped away. Once Franklin died, Meri would have nothing to look forward to. A sorrowful sort of heaviness seemed to fill him up, much like the rain filling the roadside ditches. His grainy eyes closed for a split second before Gus was waking him up again.

"Sorry to disturb you, Mr. Holcroft, but we've arrived at Phoenix Downs."

Meri shook his head to clear it. "Thank you, Gus."

He paid the man, threw his trunk over his shoulder, and carried it into the house. As he lowered it to the floor, a maid hastened down the hall to greet him.

"Polly, has Franklin come back by any chance?"

"No, sir." She took his hat and overcoat. "I'll get one of the men to bring your trunk up to your room."

Reeling from lack of sleep and food, Meri wandered into the drawing room. *Alice* hung over the fireplace; the whimsical artwork seemingly incongruent when juxtaposed against the traditional architecture. A faint smile lifted the corners of his lips as he gazed at the painting, remembering how he'd felt like the master of the universe when he'd won the bid. Yet his triumph had had nothing to do with canvas and pigment and everything to do with Clare. His esteem for her had made him strong, perhaps for the first time in his life. Now, he had nothing whatsoever to offer her.

Well, that wasn't precisely true. He could give her the stream.

～

MERI GRIPPED the sledgehammer in his fist as he strode past his pond, which had breached its banks from the storm. Driving rain angled into his eyes, unhampered by the spectacles he'd left in the drawing room. After all, the task at hand required brute strength, not clarity of vision. Even before he reached the stream, he was nearly soaked through, but his single-minded purpose chased any other concerns from his mind.

The broad ditch had already been moistened by the continuing rains, and a sizable amount of water filled the bottom. The rains had swollen the stream on the far side of the dam, sending water gushing over the ruined section. Meri stood to one side, gripped the sledgehammer with both hands, and swung it with as much strength as he could muster. The sound of the hammer striking the stacked stone was reminiscent of thunder, and a grim smile found its way onto his lips.

"Better the avenging Norse god, Thor, than the wretched demon, Caliban."

Over and over again he drove the heavy hammer into the dam. The shock of the impact traveled up his arms and into his shoulders, but he didn't slow his effort to destroy the structure he'd built so carefully years before. Sharp chips of stone flew pell-mell, nicking his skin and drawing blood. Pink rivulets dripped off his body, but he continued to pound away at the wall. When at last a crack appeared—broad enough to allow water to pour through—he paused only long enough to gather his strength for a final assault.

"This is for you, Alice."

Meri slammed the sledgehammer into the base of the fissure with such force that his entire frame reverberated with the impact. He scrambled back as the wall gave way, but a huge gush of water knocked him off his feet before he could get clear. For several excruciating, horrible moments, his head was submerged, and he couldn't breathe. His body was swept along with the flow, despite his efforts to grasp hold of anything solid.

At one point he managed to raise his head long enough to draw air into his lungs, but then the mud under his feet made him lose his footing again. This time when he fell, he struck his head on a rock. Although he was dazed, he felt himself sliding downstream. Just before his body passed under the bridge over the road, something grabbed his arm and held him fast. A tugging sensation ensued, to little avail—the current was too strong to pull Meri free.

A familiar voice finally reached his consciousness. "Come on, lad, I can't do this by myself!"

Dimly aware Franklin was trying to effect a rescue, Meri straightened his legs and pushed himself in the direction of the man's voice. When he managed to crawl free of the water, he was coughing, dizzy, and so cold his teeth wouldn't stop chattering. Then, everything went black.

AWAKENING

*M*onday morning, the Ladds boarded a train to Stroud. Thereafter, Clare stared at the passing countryside through a prism of misery. Her sister's hands moved ceaselessly as she knitted a muffler, her mother's attention was focused on an embroidery hoop, and her father read a newspaper. Although genuinely grateful for her family's company, Clare was equally glad they were occupied. Considering the circumstances, she'd no wish to feign conviviality or make polite conversation.

Sir Andrew finally glanced up from his paper. "Have you decided what to do with your housekeeper?"

Lady Ladd smiled. "I remember Mrs. Gallagher! I wish we had a place for her at Ladd House, but we're fully staffed."

"As I recall, the woman was quite competent." Clare's father shrugged. "Give her a glowing letter of reference and then discharge her. People change their employment all the time."

"It's not that simple, Papa. She quit her last position to work for me, so I feel some obligation as to her welfare."

He gave her a shrewd glance. "I can negotiate for her to stay on in Lord Pallinger's employ as a condition of the sale. Will that do?"

"I'll ask Mrs. Gallagher her thoughts. If she wants to stay, you may write up an addendum to the contract."

"That's easy enough. How soon can you pack your things and be ready to leave?"

Clare glanced at Nell. "With help, I might be able to leave as soon as tomorrow. Besides what I had with me originally, I'll also be bringing Dinah and my bicycle."

"Your *what?*" He bristled. "I cannot abide women on bicycles!"

Nell's face lit up. "A bicycle? You must teach me how to ride it, Clare."

"Absolutely not!" Sir Andrew shook his head emphatically. "I'll have no daughters of mine making spectacles of themselves."

Lady Ladd gave her husband a sidelong look. "Your ideas regarding bicycles are outdated, dearest. Even the vicar's wife has one."

He peered at her. "You must be mistaken!"

"I've seen her riding it around town when she visits the poor."

"Just because the vicar can't keep his wife in hand is no reason to approve of the contraptions. The bicycle stays in Stroud."

"Papa, I absolutely insist on bringing my bicycle." Unbidden, rivulets of moisture began to spill down Clare's face. "I'll brook no opposition on it."

"Gah!" Sir Andrew seemed to struggle with himself before throwing up his hands. "If it means that much to you."

Nell wriggled in excitement. "I can't wait until the prissy Hancock sisters see me ride past their house. I'll wave and laugh myself sick at their horrified expressions!"

Clare couldn't bring herself to thank her father for allowing her to keep what was hers, but she did give him a misty smile. Still, now that she'd had a taste of freedom, how on earth could she move back into his home and live by his rules? It was too disheartening for words. Perhaps permanent residence in Paris was in her future. What a shame she hadn't paid better attention to her language tutor.

"*La plume de ma tante est sur la table,*" she murmured.

Nell gave her a quizzical look. "What was that?"

"Oh, nothing. Just practicing my French."

ALTHOUGH THE CLOUDS over Stroud were thin and white, the ground surrounding the train station revealed recent signs of rain. When the cab passed the Holcroft livery stable, Clare strained for a glimpse of the owner, but he was nowhere to be seen. Apprehension mixed with disappointment as she wondered if he'd decided to visit Franklin in London instead of coming straight home. If so, she might miss saying goodbye to him altogether. Undoubtedly, her father would pronounce that was for the best. For her part, she wasn't sure she could bear it.

On the drive through town, Clare remained largely silent. Ordinarily, she might have pointed out local landmarks or narrated a bit of history for her sister's benefit, but her flagging spirits left the task up to her mother.

When Robbins Nest came into view, Lady Ladd smiled with pleasure. "The place looks beautiful, Clare. Almost as if Mama never left."

Nell pointed at Meri's house. "That must be Phoenix Downs? It's lovely."

"Indeed, it is." Clare swallowed. "The garden-facing bedrooms on the upper level of Robbins Nest have a view of it."

Clare was the first to climb down when the cab arrived, so she could open the front door. Dinah came scampering through the hallway with a series of excited yips. The puppy, at least, provided a short burst of good cheer. She set the valise she'd brought with her at the foot of the stairs and picked the dog up to introduce her to the family.

"This is Dinah."

Her mother chucked the furry creature under her chin and cooed. "How sweet."

Nell exclaimed. "She's adorable! May I hold her?"

"Of course." Clare transferred the wiggling pup into her sister's arms.

Clearly charmed, Sir Andrew patted the dog on the head. "Dinah is a very pretty girl."

"Hullo, Miss Ladd!" Mrs. Gallagher hastened from the kitchen, wiping her hands on her apron. She was brought up short by the sight of visitors. "Oh, I didn't realize ye had company."

Clare introduced her family, and the housekeeper curtsied. "Hullo, Miss Nell. Hullo, Mr. and Mrs. Ladd. It's been a while since I've seen ye, but I remember ye from before."

"My father's been elevated to the knighthood, Mrs. Gallagher, so you may address my parents as Sir Andrew and Lady Ladd now."

The housekeeper's smile seemed oddly forced. "How grand!"

Despite Mrs. Gallagher's words, Clare could see from her demeanor the woman was under some sort of strain.

"Is something wrong?"

Her lower lip trembled. "It's poor Mr. Holcroft, so it is. I hate to be the one to tell ye, but he fell in the stream yesterday and nearly got himself drowned."

Clare grasped the staircase newel for support, but Mrs. Gallagher wasn't done.

"Mr. Franklin rescued him, but now he fears Mr. Holcroft has caught his death o' cold!"

Clare had no words to express her horror, but her feet seemed to have a mind of their own. She darted from the cottage without hesitation—nearly colliding headlong into the cab driver bringing in the luggage—and fled toward Phoenix Downs. Her father called out her name, but his voice was barely audible over the sound of rushing water. As she passed over the bridge, her consciousness registered the existence of the stream down below, but in her panic she didn't pause to investigate. Up the long drive to the Meri's house she ran, ignoring the stitch in her side and the burning of her muscles. When she reached the large red door, she employed the brass knocker until Franklin opened it. The sight of the man's grim, drawn expression made her burst into tears.

"Is Meri all right?"

"Come in." He stepped back so she could enter. "I'll take you to him."

THE DECOR of the large bedchamber was spare, but Clare only had eyes for the unconscious man lying in the four-poster bed. The unhealthy pallor of Meri's complexion made his unshaven whiskers look darker by comparison. A bandage was wound around his forehead, and his sunken eyes were closed. The realization he might die made her dizzy with dread.

"The doctor came last night and again this morning, but there's little he can do." Franklin's voice shook as he spoke. "I've never seen the lad this sick, not even when he was a young boy."

As Clare rested her hand on Meri's bare arm, she could feel his fever even through the fabric of her gloves. She tugged off the gloves, reached for the moist cloth resting on his forehead, and dipped it in the portable basin of water sitting on a bedside table.

"This water isn't nearly cool enough. Do you have any ice?"

"I'll bring some from the kitchen." Franklin darted from the room.

Clare removed her hat, picked up the basin, and pulled down Meri's bedclothes, not bothering to shrink from the man's nakedness. She moistened every bit of his exposed skin with the cloth, willing the heat to diminish with every breath she took. She was taken aback to see his hands and forearms marked by numerous scratches, and he'd even sustained similar injuries to his face. When Franklin arrived with a sizable chunk of ice, she put it in the basin with fresh water and sponged Meri again with a moistened washcloth. After she was finished, she draped a cold compress across his bandaged forehead and perched next to him on the bed.

"I'll stay here and sponge him with cool water until his fever breaks." Clare tore her gaze away from Meri's face long enough to meet Franklin's gaze. "Mrs. Gallagher said he fell in the stream. Did the dam give way due to the rain?"

"Not exactly."

Franklin told her what he'd seen, and of Meri's harrowing rescue after the dam broke apart. The story made Clare's blood run cold.

"Had you not been there at that moment, he might have died!"

"I only wish I'd come earlier. I don't know how long he was out there swinging that sledgehammer in the storm, but it was beyond foolish." Franklin shook his head. "If I didn't know better, I would almost have thought he was trying to do himself a mischief."

As her gaze returned to the man she'd grown to love so dearly, her eyes swam with heartache.

"Perhaps he was. You see, at the Yateses' party, he was

reunited with his aunt and grandparents in the most ghastly way, and there was nothing I could do to shield him."

"You're not serious?" Franklin peered at her, stunned. "You don't mean to say the Fortescues are acquainted with the Yates?"

"It's worse than that. Delphine Fortescue is married to Lord Yates."

He made a sound of disbelief. "What horrendous luck!"

"Indeed, Meri walked straight into the lion's den with no warning whatsoever."

Clare related what had transpired at Bramble Manor, from Meri's discovery of his mother's painting, to the confrontation with his grandparents.

"Elderly Mrs. Fortescue became absolutely unhinged at the sight of Meri, and Lady Yates was nothing but cruel. Meri bore up under the punishment amazingly well, but obviously it cost him dearly. When he left the premises, he said I should stay away from him." Her shoulders lifted up and down in a helpless shrug. "Considering *your* ill health, perhaps he simply couldn't face losing both of us at once."

With a groan, Franklin sank down into a straight-backed chair. "This is my fault. He won't lose me because…well, I'm not actually dying."

Her eyes grew wide. "What? I thought you were in London for medical tests and such!"

"I *was* visiting my sister in London, and I *did* visit a physician. Aside from the occasional touch of indigestion, however, I have no wasting ailments. I told Meri otherwise as leverage to encourage his courtship of you."

A strange growling noise came from the bed, and Clare jumped to her feet. Although Meri's eyes were still closed, he was stirring ever so slightly, and his lips were moving.

"What is it?" She bent to listen and then straightened, flushed with embarrassment.

Franklin peered at her. "Well?"

"As a lady, I-I can't repeat what Meri said, verbatim. Suffice it to say, he's not at all pleased with your deception."

The older man laughed. "Good. Perhaps the thought of my punishment will give him something to live for."

Clare fixed Meri with a fierce gaze. "I'll give him something else to live for." She grasped his hand. "Our wedding."

When Meri's fingers tightened around hers, the simple physical gesture seemed to light a flame of hope within Clare's breast.

~

One Week Later

CLARE SLIPPED into Meri's bedchamber and was pleased to find the invalid sitting by the window with Dinah in his lap. He was drawn, his hair was wild, and his face hadn't seen a razor in eight days. Despite his ragged appearance, however, she felt a wave of blessed relief he was on the mend.

"Good morning! You're up."

"Am I?" His smile was wan. "I'm out of bed, but I'm still not quite myself, I'm afraid." He glanced at his half-eaten breakfast tray. "I did manage some tea and toast."

"You've been quite ill, Meri. It's going to take time for you to get your strength back."

"Thanks to you and Dinah, I'm sure to be myself soon. She's slept in my arms the last three nights."

"So that's where the rascal has been!"

Dinah jumped off Meri's lap, stretched, and trotted over to greet Clare. She knelt to stroke the puppy's fur.

"You're a good dog to keep the master of the house company."

Meri cocked his head. "My lap is free at present, if you're so inclined."

Her eyebrows rose. "You must be feeling better if you're telling jokes."

"I'm not joking." He scratched his beard. "Although I suppose I'm too scruffy to appeal to a beautiful woman such as yourself."

"You might be surprised."

"Indeed, I would." He chuckled. "I've been a very dull host since you and Nell came to stay. Do you both have everything you need?"

"Oh, yes. My sister has been riding my bicycle into Stroud every day to shop and visit friends."

His eyebrows rose. "She's made friends already? That's fast work."

"Nell crossed paths with a Miss Cheryl Vanderpool while she was riding her bicycle. It seems Miss Vanderpool is fond of riding as well, so she and Nell had much to discuss."

Meri nodded. "The Vanderpools are a prominent local family. Miss Vanderpool should be about your sister's age."

"I believe she is, and Miss Vanderpool has offered to introduce Nell into her circle."

"And your parents? Are you sure they wouldn't be more comfortable at Phoenix Downs?"

"Actually, I think they are enjoying having the cottage to themselves. The sound of the stream is romantic, Mama says, and it's been rather like a second honeymoon."

He smiled. "You're making me blush."

"I can't tell under all that wild hair."

"I thought you found it appealing."

"I find *you* appealing, but that doesn't necessarily extend to your beard. That's why I ordered you a bath and a shave."

"Hello, hello!" Franklin wheeled in a cart weighed down by a large steaming vat. "Your savior is here with your hot water."

"My *other* savior, you mean." Meri gave Clare a fond glance. "I couldn't have survived this crisis without both of you."

Franklin chuckled. "I'll always think of Miss Ladd as your guardian angel."

Clare smiled. "And with that lovely thought, I'll take Dinah for a walk and give you some privacy." She knelt to coax the dog from underneath the bed.

Franklin picked up a silver salver upon which sat an envelope. "The post has arrived with a letter from The Honorable Sterling Yates."

Puzzled, Clare glanced over. "I wonder what Sterling has to say for himself?"

"I can't imagine." Meri fumbled for his spectacles and slit the envelope open. Moments later, he frowned. "He regrets the way we parted and says he and Dora are coming for a visit." His expression reflected astonishment. "What on earth can either of them have to say to me?"

Clare shrugged. "Sterling was shaken to learn about your connection to his stepmother. Perhaps he and Dora merely wish to deepen their acquaintance with you."

"I'm in no fit state to entertain anyone, must less the Yates siblings," Meri groused. "I would write back with a refusal, but they are arriving late this afternoon. I'll just have to make the best of it, I suppose."

"It would help if you were clean." Franklin wheeled the cart toward the bathroom. "Come along, lad. Your water is cooling."

"I'll let you get on with it, then." Dinah finally emerged from her hiding place, so Clare scooped her up. "Dinah, Nell, and I are spending the day at Robbins Nest."

"Given me up as a lost cause, have you?"

Clare laughed. "Hardly. No, we're working in the garden. I've not given up hope of late summer vegetables." She paused. "I'm enjoying the view of the stream very much, Meri, even though I'm sorry it cost you so very much."

"You're worth it."

Filled with happiness, she hastened from the room. Like

Meri, she could not imagine why Dora and Sterling wished to visit, particularly without a proper invitation. One thing was certain, however—if they meant to stir up trouble, she'd toss them out herself.

~

As HE EXAMINED the way his clothes hung off his frame, Meri frowned. "It's as if I've drunk that shrinking potion from *Alice's Adventures in Wonderland*. I could barely eat any lunch at all."

"You've lost weight, but your jacket will help mask the fact." Franklin helped him don the garment. "I'm sure your appetite will improve quickly now that you're back on your feet."

Meri fastened his buttons and then squinted at the mirror. Fresh from a haircut and shave, his reflection peered back at him. Although his face was thin and his complexion was overly pale, little else could be done to improve his appearance on such short notice. At least the cuts on his face were healing nicely.

"Your vanity is in fine form." Franklin produced a pair of spectacles. "Here you are."

The world came into focus as Meri did as he was told. "That's better." He straightened his cravat. "I wish I knew what Sterling and Dora meant by coming here."

"You'll know in short order. It's nearly four o'clock, and the Ladds have assembled in the drawing room."

"The new arrivals should arrive any moment, then. Are there bedrooms enough for everyone?"

"Of course."

"And has Cook been informed we've two more guests for meals?"

"Mrs. Gallagher is helping in the kitchen as needed." Franklin paused. "You seem anxious."

"It's just that I'm not used to having so many people under my roof."

"Does it bother you?"

"No." Meri's frown disappeared. "Quite the contrary, oddly enough. I've lived such a singular existence, I thought I'd grown used to it. Having guests—even the Yates—makes me feel like I'm part of a family again." He gave Franklin a sidelong glance. "And how are you getting along with Mrs. Gallagher?"

"I'm rather astonished she sees anything in me at all."

Meri chuckled. "I'm not, but I can understand your sentiment completely. Every day I wake up wondering when Miss Ladd will realize she's made a serious error in judgment."

Moments later, he was descending the stairs with one cautious hand on the bannister to compensate for the fact his muscles were weak from lack of use. Voices were emanating from with the drawing room, and when Meri recognized Sterling's distinctive laugh, he shot Franklin a startled glance.

"The Yates came early?"

The man looked sheepish. "They arrived at half past three, but Miss Ladd pressed me into silence."

Meri made a sound of exasperation. "I should have been downstairs to welcome them to my home!"

"Perhaps, but Miss Ladd assured me the delay was for a good cause." Franklin smiled. "Excuse me while I pop into the kitchen and check on the tea."

Mystified at the man's cryptic response, Meri crossed through the entrance hall and passed into the drawing room. Sterling and Sir Andrew were in the process of prying the lids off several crates while Lady Ladd, Nell, Dora, and Clare were lifting out the contents. In the middle of the room, Dinah was jumping in and out of a large pile of discarded brown paper wrappings.

Clare straightened. "Hello, Meri! As you see, Dora and Sterling have come."

"I'm sorry I wasn't able to welcome you to Phoenix Downs properly." Meri bowed. "Tea will be here shortly."

"Thank you for allowing us to visit, especially with such little warning." Dora's expression was contrite. "I'm sorry to hear you've been ill."

"I'm on the mend." He gestured toward the crates. "What's all this?"

Sterling's reply was free of his usual condescension. "It was mother's idea, actually. She thought you might enjoy having some art from the Fortescue side of the family. Most of it has been sitting in a warehouse for decades." He picked up a large portrait of a pretty young woman and angled it so Meri could have a proper look. "This is your mother, when she was Dora's age."

Meri crossed over to the portrait, itching to examine it more closely. "May I?"

"It's yours to do with what you please."

Meri carried the painting nearer a window, where the light was best. His fair-haired mother had posed for the portrait underneath a garden arbor, with a single white rose in her hand. Her golden tresses had been plaited into a single long braid, and allowed to fall over one shoulder, and her snowy white gown bespoke all the innocence of youth. His throat closed up as he gazed at the painting, and he found himself unable to speak.

Clare joined him, gazing at the portrait with undisguised pleasure. "How very beautiful, Meri. Is it a good representation?"

"Yes, except she's not wearing her spectacles." He frowned. "I'd nearly forgotten what she looked like." He leaned the portrait against the wall and glanced at Sterling. "Thank you."

"The entire Yates family would like to apologize for any mistreatment you've had to endure." Sterling hunched his shoulders. "No one expects a few paintings to assuage your resentment, of course."

"Yes, Mama asked me to say she realizes her actions toward you are unforgivable, but she's genuinely sorry nevertheless."

Dora gave him a sweet smile. "And as for Sterling and me, we hope you'll allow us to become better acquainted with you going forward."

Meri was wary, but all he could discern from his visitors was candor. "And Mrs. Yates?"

Sterling frowned. "Lottie would have liked to come, but she's been a trifle indisposed the last few days. Perhaps she may visit another time…if you'll have us."

Meri's glance flickered toward Clare. Despite her tiny nod of encouragement, he found it difficult to let his guard down. Yet Dora *was* legally his cousin and entitled to courtesy. As far as Sterling was concerned, if Clare harbored no lingering bitterness toward him, Meri had no call to be churlish.

"Let us see how things unfold," he managed.

Dora's lips curved upward with obvious relief. "Good." She reached into a crate and lifted out a framed charcoal study of a young man. "This might be of interest to you. According to the attached note, it's a sketch Aunt Primrose did of Uncle Barnabas when they were courting." She put it into his hands. "The two of you look a great deal alike, I must say."

Clare blinked. "I might have mistaken that picture for you, Meri."

He peered at the sketch with avid interest. The artistic technique demonstrated was somewhat rudimentary—obviously one of his mother's earlier efforts—but she'd captured his father's mischievous eyes well. Several pleasant recollections came flooding back, such as memories of his father stealing kisses from his adoring mother. He never missed the opportunity to surprise his wife with little gifts or trips to London, and he was always solicitous of her health. Often, he would urge her to wear her spectacles so she wouldn't get a headache.

"Primrose, you're so much more beautiful when you wear your spectacles," his father would say. "Wear them for me."

She would pat his face with a fond smile. "Perhaps it's you who needs spectacles, dearest."

Suddenly the more pleasant reminiscences were supplanted by the vision of their dead bodies. As the shocking scene crystallized in his mind, he was struck by certain details that had never registered with him before.

"You're shaking, Meri." Clare gave him a look of concern. "Has your fever returned?"

"No, but my memories have awakened." He swallowed hard. "I realize now my father didn't kill himself. He was murdered."

WHITE RABBIT

Silence greeted Meri's announcement, but he wasn't surprised. Why should anyone believe his recollections could exonerate his father after so many years? At best, his assertions would seem self-serving, and at worst he might be viewed as unhinged.

"Your father was murdered?" Clare peered at him. "What makes you say that?"

"Forgive me if I sound like a lunatic." He shook his head. "I'm sorry…I was just thinking out loud."

Sir Andrew spoke up. "I, for one, would like to hear more. I've always believed the lack of investigation into your parents' deaths to be a dereliction of duty."

A flicker of worry crossed Lady Ladd's countenance. "Dearest, perhaps you ought not pry. The last thing dear Meri needs after his illness is to be emotionally upset."

"Thank you for your concern, madame, but I'm feeling more lucid than I have in a long while." Meri glanced around the drawing room. "Still, I don't want to put a damper on the afternoon."

"As a member of the family, the case affects me too," Dora said. "I'd like to hear what you have to say."

"Since you're to marry Clare, it affects all of us, actually." Nell nodded. "I'm entitled to know the truth as much as anyone."

Franklin appeared in the doorway. "Excuse me, but tea is ready. Would you prefer it served in here or the dining room?"

Meri's glance rested on his mother's portrait. "In here, Franklin, and I'd like you to join us. I want to talk about that night."

"Oh?" The older man's eyebrows rose. "I'll be right back with a cart."

Clare poured the tea while Meri introduced Franklin to Dora and Sterling and detailed the history of their relationship.

"Even though I've known Franklin my whole life, he's never heard what I'm about to say…partly because I couldn't bear to discuss it, and partly because I seemed to have walled things off in my mind."

Meri took a deep breath and told everything he could remember the night of the fire, from waking up in bed to the terrible scene in his parents' bedchamber.

"I was so shocked at the time, I drew erroneous conclusions. Looking back, however, certain details aren't congruent at all. My father was sprawled on the carpet, on his back, with a bullet hole in his right temple. The exit wound on the other side of his head was…horrendous. Strangely enough, however, the pistol was in his left hand. It would have been exceedingly awkward for him to have shot himself in that fashion."

Franklin was pale. "Particularly since he was right-handed."

An audible gasp came from the people in the room.

Meri nodded. "Then there was the fire. I thought my father had knocked the lamp over when he fell, but that lamp always sat on the table near the door. I remembered that lamp in particular because the base was painted black and white, like a chessboard, and the chimney was shaped like a rook."

Sir Andrew stirred. "So you believe the murder suspect shot your father, put the gun in his hand, and then threw the lamp against the wall to start the fire?"

"That's the most logical explanation." Meri swallowed hard. "The only thing I can't account for is my mother's death. Her eyes were open when I found her and her skin was quite cold, but there was no blood on her nightclothes and no sign of a struggle."

"Laudanum overdose."

Everyone turned toward Franklin, but Meri could scarcely believe his ears. "What?"

The man frowned. "Lady Pallinger was addicted to laudanum, I'm afraid. At first she used the medicine to ease her headaches, but then she couldn't do without it. When His Lordship found out, he banned laudanum from the house. After that, Lady Pallinger paid your nanny to bring her laudanum on the sly."

"Miss Lapin?" Meri stared. "Why didn't you tell me?"

"A good valet keeps his master's secrets…and those of his wife." Franklin's shoulders moved up and down in a shrug. "Until now, I didn't think your mother's addiction had any bearing on the crime." His color rose. "Although I didn't approve of laudanum, my regard for Lady Pallinger was such that I would never have willingly besmirched her name."

Meri suddenly realized the man's regard for his mother must have been more tender than professional. Why else would he have risked life and limb to take care of her son?

"No, of course not." Meri's voice was soft. "I'm grateful for your discretion."

"Merciful heavens." Dora's hand went to her throat. "I shall never use laudanum again."

"Nor I." Sterling grimaced.

"The only thing remaining is to name the suspect," Sir Andrew said. "Was there anyone in the household with a motive to commit murder?"

"I believe so." Meri gestured toward his cousin's high button boots. "Dora, if you knew the house was on fire in the middle of the night, would you fasten your boots and take the time to put up your hair?"

Dora scoffed at the notion. "Of course not! I'd slide into a pair of slippers and flee for my life in my nightgown."

"Anybody would do the same." Meri glanced at Franklin. "The murderer was Miss Lapin."

His jaw dropped. "That mousy woman?"

Clare turned her wondering gaze on him. "Why would your nanny commit murder?"

"I don't think it was planned. After my mother overdosed on laudanum, however, Miss Lapin knew she'd be blamed. So she killed my father and set the fire to destroy any evidence."

"You may have a motive, but little else." Sir Andrew steepled his hands. "That's not enough to convict the woman in court."

Meri ticked off the points of evidence on his fingers. "Miss Lapin wasn't in her bed when I went to look for her that night, even though it was quite late." His eyes narrowed. "She might have been in my parents' room at the same time as I was, perhaps hiding behind the curtain or under the bed."

Dora shuddered. "How awful!"

"After Franklin rescued me from the fire, Mr. Holcroft took me to his carriage house apartment. When Miss Lapin found me, her hair was coiled up in the back and she wore high button boots underneath her wrapper. This at a time when every other woman evacuated from the house was in slippers with their hair down."

"She was fully dressed underneath her nightclothes, I

expect!" Lady Ladd was indignant. "The deceitful woman pretended she'd been asleep to make herself seem innocent."

"Exactly." Meri nodded. "I believe she wished to learn if I'd seen anything incriminating, and so came looking for me."

"What an evil, cold, calculating woman." Clare shook her head. "Once she satisfied herself there was nothing to fear, she fled."

"You've convinced me," Sterling said.

"Me as well." Lady Ladd stirred sugar into her tea. "And I'm not that easy to persuade."

"Nor am I. I certainly can't fault your logic." Sir Andrew met Meri's gaze. "You'd make a fine detective."

"Miss Lapin got away with murder, literally, and her victim was unfairly characterized as a monster." Clare reached out to touch Meri's arm. "I'm so sorry."

Dora piled a scone high with clotted cream. "Could the woman could be charged and convicted of murder? With the restoration of Uncle Barnabas's good name, our family would no longer be besmirched."

Nell sighed. "Even if she could, how is Miss Lapin to be found? She could be anywhere."

Franklin scratched the side of his head. "Meri, why don't you summon Bert Watson?"

He pondered the suggestion. "You know, I think that's a brilliant idea."

Lady Ladd frowned. "You don't mean that reporter, do you?"

"Bertie's not just any reporter, Lady Ladd. He was working for my father as a stable boy the night of the fire and wants to write articles about the murder. If he's done his research properly, he might know where Miss Lapin is."

"His business card is in your desk," Franklin said. "Perhaps you could send him a telegram?"

Sir Andrew cleared his throat. "If you jot down a message,

I'll ride to Stroud to send it—if I might have the use of your bicycle, that is."

Clare and Nell exchanged a surprised glance.

"Papa, you know how to ride a bicycle?" Clare asked. "I thought you couldn't abide the things."

He stuck his forefinger inside his collar as if to loosen it. "Er…my objection is for young ladies only. In fact, I learned how to ride a bicycle from the vicar himself."

As Sir Andrew's daughters rolled their eyes toward the ceiling, Meri suppressed a smile.

"Of course you may borrow my bicycle, my carriages, or any of my horses for that matter." He rose. "If you'll excuse me, I'll nip into my study to compose a message. Afterward, I'd like to show my guests around Phoenix Downs properly."

Dora smiled. "Sterling and I aren't exactly guests, are we? We're family."

"After Meri and Clare are wed, we'll all be family." Nell giggled. "Won't that be droll?"

A knot seemed to loosen in Meri's chest. "It *will* be droll."

Clare rose and reached for his hand. "It will be wonderful."

～

BERT, Meri, Franklin, and Sir Andrew rode in a hired carriage through the crowded streets of London, along with a plain-clothes detective inspector from Scotland Yard named Tiberius McNaughton.

Bert cleared his throat. "Finding Miss Lapin wasn't easy, I assure you. She's been married twice to men of some means, each of whom suffered an untimely end. The woman now lives in Soho and has retaken her maiden name—I imagine to avoid creditors."

"Two dead husbands?" The inspector pursed his lips. "We may have a serial murderess on our hands."

"I wouldn't be surprised," Sir Andrew said. "Leopards don't change their spots."

"No, they don't," McNaughton said.

Meri glanced at Bert. "Did you actually speak with her?"

"Only briefly. When I tracked her down for an interview several weeks ago, she refused to cooperate. I was a bit bewildered by her attitude, but now I realize she had something to hide."

"Miss Lapin won't have the luxury of refusing to cooperate with me." McNaughton's expression was grim. "I'm bringing her in for questioning whether she likes it or not."

"Since she'll be riding in that luxurious police wagon right behind us, she'll have no cause for complaint," Sir Andrew said.

"Not at first, anyway." McNaughton chuckled. "After a mile or two, I'm told the benches become rather hard."

"I don't know if it's important, Inspector, but when I rode off to fetch the doctor the night of the fire, I saw Miss Lapin leaving the Pallinger estate. She was walking at the side of the road carrying a carpet bag." Bert frowned. "I remembered thinking it remarkable that she'd managed to gather her possessions during the evacuation, but because I was intent on the business at hand, I didn't give it another thought."

"It's very important, I'll warrant," Meri said. "I wouldn't be surprised to learn Miss Lapin stole my mother's jewelry, even as her dead body was cooling nearby."

When Franklin flinched, Meri felt a pang of remorse for his tactlessness. "Sorry, old boy. I shouldn't have been so blunt."

Franklin shook his head. "I ought not be so squeamish after all these years."

"I suspect your conjecture about the theft is accurate, Your Lordship," McNaughton said. "If Barnabas Pallinger interrupted Miss Lapin in the midst of her crime, she would have had even more incentive to kill him."

"Did she recognize you, Bert?" Franklin asked.

"No, but she remembered my name once I told her who I was."

A muscle worked in Meri's jaw. "She'll recognize me."

~

AS THE FOUR gentlemen climbed out of their carriage in the early morning fog, a distant church bell rang seven times. Several ladies clad in low-cut gowns sauntered over to flash their ankles in a fashion that brought color to Franklin's face. One garishly painted woman sidled up to the detective inspector and batted her lashes.

"Hullo, guv'nor! Would ye fancy a private theatrical performance? I'm a singer, I am."

McNaughton's lips twitched up at the corners as he pointed his thumb at the approaching police wagon. "Would you fancy a lift to Newgate Prison?"

"Can't say that I would, exactly." She tossed her head as the wagon pulled up to the curb. "Yer loss."

The woman and her companions hastened away down the pavement, leaving Meri a direct view of the smoke shop. The small, run-down establishment was not yet open for business.

He looked at Bert askance. "Miss Lapin lives here?"

The reporter shook his head. "She's in one of the residences over the shop." He gestured to a side door. "In through there."

McNaughton glanced at Meri. "Are you sure you want to accompany us?"

"Absolutely." He spoke with more conviction than he felt. "My presence might cause the woman to blurt out something incriminating."

"That's the only reason I'm allowing it." The detective gave him a level glance. "Leave the police work to me and my men, right? If you attempt to harm Miss Lapin, I'll put you in handcuffs myself."

"Since my goal is to have her stand trial for murder, I wouldn't dream of harming her, Inspector." He paused. "You have my word as a gentleman."

The man nodded. "Good enough."

After the detective conferred with the policemen in the wagon, he and Bert led the way up the narrow dirt-encrusted stairs. As Franklin and Meri followed, the older man lowered his voice to whisper, "Do you know, I think those ladies were prostitutes."

The quip brought a bit of much-needed levity to the tense situation, and Meri chuckled. "Yes, I imagine you're right."

Bert pointed out Miss Lapin's door, but nobody answered McNaughton's knock. When he knocked again, a woman's shrill voice sounded from somewhere in the residence beyond.

"Go answer the door, you lazy lout! What do you think I pay you for?"

Running footsteps ensued, and the door was wrenched open by a barefooted young girl, perhaps nine years old. Her hair was covered by a soot-streaked mob cap, and the white apron over her thin cotton dress was stained and worn. Meri's mood darkened further when he saw the greenish yellow bruise on the child's cheek.

"We're here to see Miss Lapin, on a matter of some urgency," McNaughton said.

Her eyes widened, and she turned her head to call out, "Miss Lapin! You've gentlemen visitors!"

Meri crooked his finger and the girl edged forward.

"Do you have anywhere else to go, lass?" He spoke as quietly as possible.

A flicker of fear crossed her face. "Me mum's house in Spitalfields. Why?"

Meri gave her two five-pound notes. "Put that money in your pocket where you won't lose it and go home. You can find employment elsewhere."

"Thank ye, sir." The girl snatched the money from his fingertips. "I'll get me shoes."

She dashed off into the apartment, just as her employer appeared. "Where are you going with your hair on fire, stupid girl?"

The child disappeared through another door without a reply. Miss Lapin crossed the room, peering at her visitors with narrowed eyes. The years had not been kind to the former nanny, who was thin as a whip. The sparse hair on her head was completely white, and the lines on her hardened face had become grooves. Meri stayed behind Franklin for the moment.

"What's all this?" Her gaze fell on Bert. "Oh, it's you, back again? I told you, I've no time to talk to reporters."

McNaughton cleared his throat. "You'll talk to me, Miss Lapin. I'm Detective Inspector McNaughton, from Scotland Yard."

"Scotland Yard wants nothing to do with me!" The woman made a sound of disbelief. "You must have the wrong address."

Meri removed his hat and spectacles before stepping into view. "Hello, Miss Lapin."

Her lips parted and her complexion lost all color. "Lord Pallinger!" She drew back, staring at him as if he were an unholy specter. "Y-You're dead!"

"Not quite." He donned his spectacles. "No thanks to you."

"You're Meriweather." Her mouth turned down. "You look exactly like your father."

"And you're a murderess."

"How silly!" A mirthless chuckle escaped her thin lips. "You can't prove that."

Meri gestured toward the brooch pinned at her neck. "That's my mother's jewelry."

"So it is." Her chin lifted. "She gave it to me of my own free will."

Franklin took a step forward. "Lady Pallinger was in the habit of paying you for laudanum with money, not jewelry."

Miss Lapin's voice became mocking. "Says the poor, besotted valet who couldn't breathe until he'd had a glance or a kind word from the mistress of the house." Her gaze returned to Meri. "I'll wager you didn't know your mother was a flirt, did you?"

Franklin bristled. "How dare you!"

Meri rested a hand on the man's shoulder. "Never mind her bile. She's a cornered snake, spitting venom."

Despite the admonition, Franklin continued to scowl at the old woman. "Lady Pallinger was the finest woman who ever lived, and you're not fit to say her name."

The confrontation had devolved into an exchange of insults and Meri still didn't have his confession. He decided a slight bit of deceit was in order.

"Miss Lapin, I witnessed what you did to my father that night. I followed you down the hall and saw the entire thing from the door. It's over for you."

"Ha!" Her eyes darted to McNaughton. "I'm certain Lord Pallinger would say or do anything to prove his father wasn't a cold-blooded killer. I can't say that I blame him, but he has no right to accuse a perfectly innocent woman."

Meri shook his head. "You almost got away with it, but my memories finally came back. Tell me, Miss Lapin, when you close your eyes at night, do you see my father's bloody body?"

"You poor lad." She sighed. "The son of Barnabas the Butcher has apparently inherited his madness."

Unbidden, Meri felt his hands forming into fists at his side, but McNaughton gave him a quelling glance. "Let's sort it all out properly at Scotland Yard, shall we?"

"Of course." Miss Lapin called over her shoulder. "Elsie, bring me my pink straw bag."

"Yes, mum." The girl appeared in the doorway, clad in a pair of oversized boots and a threadbare coat. She lifted up a bag the color of raspberries. "Is this the one?"

"Yes." Her employer snapped her fingers impatiently. "Come along then!"

Else darted forward to give the bag to Miss Lapin and the woman clamped down on her by the shoulder.

"Why are you dressed for an outing? You're not coming with me to Scotland Yard."

"No, I..." The child gulped. "Me mum's sick."

"Then you'd best get along."

Miss Lapin shoved Elsie at McNaughton with such force as to push the detective backward. Time seemingly slowed as the woman pulled a pearl-handled palm pistol from her carryall and leveled it at Meri. He saw the weapon for only a split second before Franklin leaped in front of him with his left hand held out defensively. The report of the firearm in the small room made Meri's ears ring, but he sprang toward Miss Lapin and knocked the pistol to the ground before she could fire again. Moments later, McNaughton scrambled over to cuff her wrists behind her back.

The detective gave Meri a worried look. "Are you hurt, Lord Pallinger?"

"Mercifully not."

Bert was helping Elsie to her feet, just as policemen poured into the room. Meri turned toward Franklin, who was sitting on the floor looking shaken. As Meri approached, the man gave a feeble chuckle and waved his shattered wooden hand.

"This was awfully expensive, and now I've gone and broken it."

Meri laughed. "I'll buy you a new one."

Franklin gave a wheezing cough. "I don't think that will be necessary."

Meri's heart thudded. "Are you shot?"

"My chest is on fire, I'm afraid." He grimaced in pain and his eyelids fluttered. "It's all right. I've lived long enough to see you perfectly matched with Miss Ladd and to expect your father's good name will be restored. I'm ready to die." He slumped over.

After a brief moment of panic, Meri sprang into action. "You can't die. I won't let you."

With trembling fingers, he opened Franklin's jacket and unfastened the buttons on his shirt to see where the bullet had pierced his skin. As he peered at what lay underneath, he rocked back on his heels, utterly dumbfounded.

RIGHT SIDE UP

Three days later...

As the train rolled toward Stroud, Meri passed his thumb over the sterling silver locket in his hand. Although no tarnish discolored the gleaming metal, a deep depression now marred the front. When he opened the heavy round locket, the time piece enclosed in the left-hand side had stopped at ten past seven. On the right side of the locket was a small portrait of his mother—a self-portrait, if he was to be the judge. The back surface of the ornament featured the inscription and a date...*From Primrose to Barnabas. Our love is timeless.* Meri recognized the date as his father's birthday—a week after his death. Pensive, he closed the locket and stared out the window. More mysteries surrounded his parents' deaths than he'd ever suspected, obviously.

On the facing seat of the private compartment, Franklin stirred. Moments later, his eyes opened and he groaned in pain.

Meri gave him a sympathetic glance. "Would you like a drop or two of laudanum? The doctor gave me a small bottle." He made a sound of impatience when Franklin shook his head.

"Heavens, man, it's meant to relieve your pain, not send you to perdition. I comprehend your squeamishness, but don't be such a stubborn old goat!"

To Meri's surprise, Franklin accepted the drops without further protest.

"Now you have me worried, old boy." He frowned. "It's not like you to be so compliant."

Franklin chuckled. "I'm only compliant on the outside. Inside, I'm ever the rebel."

Meri lifted an eyebrow. "I never knew how rebellious until a few moments after Miss Lapin employed her pistol." He held up the ornament which had spared Franklin's life. "Can you tell me about this, and how it came to be in your possession?"

"Your mother commissioned the locket as a birthday gift for your father and asked my opinion on the design. It was perhaps a month after the fire when I felt fit enough to visit the jeweler's shop. The fellow had heard about the tragedy, of course, and had given up hope of being paid. He'd put the locket up for sale, but fortunately I arrived in time to redeem it." He averted his eyes. "I should have told you about it before now."

"Once Mr. Dandridge has repaired the locket, I'll return it to your possession."

"That's not necessary."

"Of course it is. Your property was damaged while you were once again busy saving my life, and you're entitled to have it returned in working order." Meri nodded at Franklin's gloved left hand. "I'm glad we were able to get that replaced before leaving London."

"Yes, and the wood sports a lovely polish. It was the surgeon's opinion that the impact with my former hand slowed the bullet and the locket stopped its progress altogether."

Meri chuckled. "You look as if a rotting eggplant took up residence on your chest."

"Since a large bruise on my chest and lungs is infinitely

preferable to a bullet hole, I shan't complain." Franklin grimaced as he shifted his position. "Not much, at any rate. By all means, have the locket repaired, but I'd like you to have it." A smile played on his lips. "Perhaps I'll have a locket made with Mrs. Gallagher's hair, if she'll indulge me."

"Your previous infatuation is over, then?"

"It's faded into a fond remembrance." His lips tightened. "What Miss Lapin said about your mother was a horrendous lie, you know. Although I admired Lady Pallinger very much, she never had eyes for anyone else but your father."

"I never doubted it." Meri gave the damaged ornament one final glance before sliding it into the pocket of his coat. As he did so, his fingertips encountered another bit of metal, which he produced with a grin. "Let me give you this in return."

Franklin chortled with laughter as he took the spent slug. "A fair trade." As he closed his fingers around the object, his smile slipped. "I wish I were certain Miss Lapin could be convicted of murdering your father. She didn't confess outright, and so much time has gone by, after all."

"She tried to kill me and nearly killed you in the process, so she'll at least be convicted of attempted murder."

Franklin tossed the slug into the air and caught it again. "Hear, hear."

"Furthermore, Inspector McNaughton believes her desperate actions show consciousness of guilt, which is akin to a confession in a court of law. In addition, the police recovered several stolen pieces of jewelry belonging to my mother, so she's been charged with theft."

"I'm sure she stole more than a few pieces, but probably sold the remainder over the years. Unfortunately, there's no way to recover them."

"No, and there are no guarantees Miss Lapin will ever be convicted of murdering my father. To my way of thinking, however, that doesn't matter."

"Doesn't matter?" Franklin gave him an incredulous glance. "The whole point of confronting Miss Lapin was to gain a confession to clear your father's name."

"I have every reason to believe the woman *will* be found guilty of the murder, but I can't count on it. Bert's first article about the case was published in the paper this morning, so now everyone in England will know about her involvement. Either way, my father's reputation has already been restored."

"Then you and Miss Ladd may marry at your leisure."

"Or as quickly as a special license may be procured." Meri smiled. "And suddenly it seems as if my life has turned right side up again."

"It's been a long time coming." Franklin sat back in his seat with a satisfied expression. "I couldn't be more pleased."

~

Mid-September

CLAD IN WEDDING FINERY, Clare and Meri stood arm and arm on the newly constructed footbridge between their two properties. Although the dam was gone, a narrow channel had been carved into the ground to shunt water to the pond. Wedding breakfast revelry was underway on both sides of the stream, with local townspeople, Nell, Sterling, and even Lottie in attendance. With the scandal regarding Lord Barnabas Pallinger assuaged, Lord and Lady Yates had relented on their banishment—for now.

As a group of children thundered past with Dinah at their heels, Clare laid her head on her husband's shoulder.

"I'm the happiest woman in England."

"And I'm the happiest man." He nodded toward Robbins Nest. "I notice your vegetable and rose gardens are coming along nicely. I think it rather generous of you to offer the cottage to Franklin and Mrs. Gallagher to live in after their wedding."

"I knew you'd like to have Mr. Franklin settled nearby. This is terribly confidential, but Mrs. Gallagher hopes she might bear him children."

Meri's expression reflected pleased surprise. "Wouldn't that be something? I'll tell you a confidence about Franklin in exchange, but you must promise not to say anything to anyone yet."

"You may count on my discretion." She gave him a sidelong glance. "I simply adore secrets."

"Bert's articles have made quite a splash, as you know, and many of my father's highly-placed friends have reached out to me. Through them, I'm trying to arrange for Franklin's elevation to the knighthood."

Clare's eyes widened. "Why, Mrs. Gallagher won't know what to do with herself. She'll be Lady Franklin!"

He frowned. "Yes, but that brings up a sticky point. Since your father and Franklin would then be the same rank, I'm trying to arrange a baronetcy for Sir Andrew. That must also remain a secret for now."

"You're exceedingly generous and thoughtful. If I hadn't just married you, I would marry you again."

He chuckled. "While I'm at it, I've an early birthday present for you."

"Not too early. My spinsterhood would have been official in three days."

"Sorry, Alice, but you'll never be a spinster now." He produced a gold heart-shaped locket and dangled it by its chain. "These things seem to have become a tradition in my family, so you should have one of your own."

She gasped with delight as she took the ornament in her hands. "You and Mr. Dandridge have outdone yourselves." When she opened the golden heart, she discovered a woven lock of dark hair on one side and Meri's name inscribed opposite. "It's beautiful." She raised up on her tiptoes to kiss her husband on the cheek. "Thank you."

His glance was heavy-lidded. "Is that all the gratitude I'm to expect?"

Her lips curved upward as she traced the lines of his lapels with her fingertips. "That's all you are entitled to in front of our guests, you *estimable* man. I can assure you, my outpouring of gratitude will be ample to satisfy you tonight."

"I suppose I must be patient, then, but I'll require a nightly demonstration of your esteem for many years to come before I'll truly be satisfied."

Their gentle kiss was interrupted by Franklin's arrival.

"Forgive me for intruding, but you've just had a wedding present delivered—from Mr. and Mrs. Fortescue."

MERI STOOD in the drawing room, staring at the large family portrait with astonishment. The painting, featuring his maternal grandparents, a very young Delphine, and her elder sister, Primrose, brought with it a sense of nostalgia.

"I never thought I'd see this again."

Franklin cocked his head. "It's a very good likeness to your mother, I think, although I was always partial to her when she wore her spectacles." He gave a little cough.

Meri rolled his eyes and donned the pair of spectacles he'd tucked in his breast pocket.

Clare knelt to have a closer look at the painting. "It's wonderful." She glanced up at her husband. "Your grandparents must have been loathe to part with it."

Franklin frowned. "No doubt they felt guilty once they learned the truth about their daughter's death."

Lottie popped up from the sheltering sides of a wing chair. "If it were me, I'd send it back forthwith!"

"Would you?" Meri shrugged. "One can grow awfully lonely, slamming doors in people's faces all the time."

"'To err is human, to forgive divine,'" Franklin quoted. "Alexander Pope."

Lottie scrunched up her nose. "Who?"

"What are you doing in here, Lottie?" Clare asked. "All the fun is outside."

"The smell of food makes my insides terribly unsettled just now, and I don't want to disgrace myself in front of people." The young woman pressed a handkerchief to her lips for a few moments before she could continue. "Since all the servants are busy, Sterling went to the kitchen to fetch me a cup of ginger tea." She glanced at the painting over Meri's mantle. "Are you quite sure you don't want to sell us *Alice*, since we're related? It's perfect for a nursery."

Meri exchanged a smile with his wife.

"Lottie, does Sterling know you're *enceinte?*" Clare asked.

"Well, I—"

Sterling bustled into the room carrying a tray laden with a teapot, china cup, and a sugar bowl. "Here we are, dearest." An expression of confusion crossed his face. "Did I just hear the word *enceinte?*"

Lottie giggled. "Indeed you did. I would have thought you had figured things out for yourself by now."

"Are you saying...?" Sterling's countenance lost color and he swayed on his feet. "Oh, my."

Franklin hastened to take the tray from the fellow before it fell to the ground, while Clare put a supporting arm around Sterling's waist and guided him to the sofa.

"Perhaps you need a cup of strong tea as well?"

He shook his head. "A glass of whiskey would be more bracing."

Meri roared with laughter as he poured the libation and pressed it into Sterling's hands. "You have my heartiest congratulations, but drink that down before you swoon."

The man knocked back the drink and then rushed to take Lottie into his arms. "You're my most darling girl."

The young woman rolled her eyes. "Don't go on so or I may be sick all over your suit!"

Clare nodded at Franklin and tugged on Meri's arm. "Let's give the parents-to-be some privacy."

The trio emerged into the entrance hall, where the older man sketched a bow.

"If you'll excuse me, I think I'll find Mrs. Gallagher and ask for a dance with my fiancée."

As he hurried down the hall, Meri gave Clare a fond smile. "That's not a bad idea, really. I'd love to dance with my wife."

She slid her arms around his neck and glanced at him through her lashes. "In a moment. First, I'd like to show my husband a little gratitude."

Clare's passionate kiss sent his soul soaring with blissful joy.

Tired of being unfavorably compared to her beautiful younger sister, Melanie travels to a distant city for a lengthy visit with her stylish aunt. She throws herself into volunteer work and settles into her new life—only to get caught trespassing on Lord Peyton's neighboring property. Lord Peyton is the most arrogant, aggravating, conceited, and condescending man she's ever met, but women seem to fall at his feet. As Melanie and Lord Peyton work together to help a local orphanage, will the cold enmity between them ever thaw?

The Prettier Sister is a standalone novel that shares a common world with the Mannequin Series. Read on for a sneak peek…

EXCERPT

THE PRETTIER SISTER

Mr. Starhope glanced through the morning post and gasped, "Merciful heavens."

Both Melanie and Blanche glanced up from eating breakfast.

Mrs. Starhope put down her fork. "What is it, James?"

"I've had a letter from *Genevieve*." He said the name as if it were a shocking event.

Mrs. Starhope grimaced. "Oh, dear."

As Mr. Starhope opened the letter and began reading the contents, Melanie felt a warm furry body brush up against her ankle. She cut a piece of kipper on her plate and surreptitiously lowered it toward the door. After she felt tiny teeth take the morsel of food from her fingertips, she wiped them on her napkin.

"You're not feeding that cat at the table again, are you?" Her mother's blue eyes met Melanie's. "You know I don't approve."

"I'm sorry, Mama."

Melanie pretended to be abashed, but when she heard the sound of her cat's purr, she couldn't suppress a smile. In short order, another piece of kipper found its way to Penguin's belly.

"I've never met Aunt Genevieve." Blanche wrinkled her nose. "Is she so very disagreeable?"

"I wouldn't say she's disagreeable." Mrs. Starhope stirred a teaspoon of sugar into her tea. "Genevieve can be quite pleasant — as long as she gets her way."

"I met Aunt Genevieve once when Grandpapa passed on and then again at her wedding to Mr. Hornsby." Melanie spooned a bit of fried apples onto her toast. "She was a beautiful bride." Penguin darted under her skirts and draped herself over her slipper-clad foot.

Blanche cocked her head. "I don't remember Grandpapa — or Grandmama, for that matter — and I don't recall attending Aunt Genevieve's wedding."

"You were an infant back then." Melanie focused her gaze on her father. "Is everything all right, Papa?"

"I'm not entirely certain." He tossed the letter to the table. "Your aunt has asked you to visit her over the summer."

Blanche groaned. "But I don't *want* to leave Bromley just now! All manner of entertaining things are planned for the summer and now that I'm of age, I'm finally old enough to attend. In fact, Mr. Jones offered to escort me to the Easter recital at church."

Had he, indeed? Annoyed, Melanie hid her pique behind her napkin.

"You needn't miss a thing." Her father chuckled. "Ginny has asked Melanie, not you."

ABOUT THE AUTHOR

Suzanne G. Rogers is a California native, but she changed coastlines and now lives in romantic Savannah, Georgia, on an island populated by deer, exotic birds, turtles, otters, and gators.

ALSO BY SUZANNE G. ROGERS

HISTORICAL ROMANCE

Graceling Hall Series

Larken (Book One)*

Lord Apollo & the Colleen (Book Two)

The Vanishing Beauty (Book Three)

The Beaucroft Girls Series

Ruse & Romance (Book One)*

Rake & Romance (Book Two)*

The Mannequin Series

The Mannequin (Book One)*

Grace Unmasked (Book Two)

The Star-Crossed Seamstress (Book Three)

A Chance of Rayne (Book Four)

The Substitute (Book Five)

The Gilded Age Series

Duke of a Gilded Age (Book One)

Lady of a Gilded Age (Book Two)

Standalone Titles

*Spinster**

A Gift for Fiona

Lady Fallows' Secrets

*My Fair Guardian**

*Jessamine's Folly**

*The Ice Captain's Daughter**

An American in Paris of the West

Rumer Has It

The Glass Heart

Courtship on Eaton Square

The Prettier Sister

One Little Kiss

*Audiobook available

ALSO BY SUZANNE G. ROGERS

FANTASY

<u>The Yden Series</u>

The Last Great Wizard of Yden (Book One)

Dragon Clan of Yden (Book Two)

Secrets of Yden (Book Three)

Kira (Prequel to the Yden Trilogy)

<u>Standalone Titles</u>

Dani & the Immortals

*The Dragon Rider's Daughter**

Clash of Wills

Tournament of Chance: Dragon Rebel

Magical Misperception

*Whimsical Tendencies**

Something Wicked in L.A.

Royal Promenade

**Audiobook Available*

www.ingramcontent.com/pod-product-compliance
Lightning Source LLC
Chambersburg PA
CBHW060907140726
47996CB00001B/145